SURVIVAL

OF

FIGHTS

Luke Bloyd

Green Ivy Publishing
One Lincoln Centre
18W140 Butterfield Road
Suite 1500
Oakbrook Terrace IL 60181-4843
www.greenivybooks.com

ISBN: 978-1-945379-29-1

A Dedication

When I first decided to write this book, I chose the name *Survival of Fights* because we all struggle through difficult times in our lives and have to fight through them. However, some of us have to flight more than we would like to. Jon Reeverts has fought the battle of cancer several times, and as I watched and prayed for him, I realized how strong man can truly become when he places his faith in the hands of God. He continued to fight even when the odds were against him, just as they can be for all of us.

I would like to dedicate my book, *Survival of Fights*, to Mr. Jon Reeverts. This extraordinary man has inspired me greatly the last three years of my high school career. I could not have asked for a better person to keep my inspiration flowing. His faith in God has moved me greatly as well.

Words can't explain how thankful I am to have you in my life, Mr. Reeverts. Thank you so much for all that you have done for me. God bless you, and keep inspiring people!

Luke Bloyd

Chapter 1 An Untold Story

Walking into the old rickety club on the corner of Center and Thirteenth Street for a strong alcoholic concoction that snowy New Year's Eve night, the young woman didn't expect to have her life threatened because of the misfortunate story of the Titans. The tavern was packed with partygoers. Men were grinding on other men, women were giving each other lap dances, and the straight couples were making out around the wooden chamber. The room echoed with the sound of blazing, upbeat music. The young woman's long brown fur coat glided across the wooden floor as she walked up to the dark-haired, handsome bartender, who wore a white, button up, long-sleeved shirt, and loose blue jeans. His muscles bulged from underneath his garments.

"Good evening. Give me a glass of tequila and vodka, please," she politely said, yelling over the music.

The Bartender looked at her for a few moments and then said, "Right away, madam."

The Bartender pulled out two large crystal clear wineglasses from underneath the bar and placed them in front of her. He went through a door behind him and entered a cluttered storage room filled with bottles of different kinds of alcohol. Upon returning, he held two large clear bottles in his hands. Each had its own label to help identify its acquired taste. He poured one bottle per cup. Once both glasses were filled to the brim, he placed a slice of lime on each glass, and handed them to her.

Looking at her with sharp eyes, the Bartender said, "The left one is the tequila, and the right one is the vodka."

With a small smile, the young woman grabbed the two glass cups in her gloved hands and said, "Thank you, just put it on my tab,

Sam."

She turned to go and find a seat within the crowded room. The doors to the old place blew open, and a young man with black spiked hair, a black leather jacket, and holey blue jeans walked in.

The woman smiled thinly as she looked away from the doors and sat at the table in the back. She took off her coat and draped it on the back of the chair, then removed her gloves and stuffed them into her coat pockets. Taking a sip of the tequila, she noticed that the man that had walked in just as she had got her drinks was now staring at her from the other side of the room. She stared back at him, but noticed that he broke eye contact. It was clear to her that he was interested in her, but was too shy to come over and strike up a conversation.

The young woman looked back down at her two drinks for a few moments before taking a sip of the vodka. As the burn of the drink made its way down her throat, the young woman looked up to a painting of a beautiful woman hung on the wall beside her. The woman had long curly black hair, and she wore a necklace with a sliver pendent attached to it. As the burn from the alcoholic drink faded, she glanced over to a young couple being intimate then back over to the doors to get another look at the mysterious man, but was startled to see that he was now standing in front of her table.

Clearing her throat, the young woman said, "Can I help you?"

"I'm sorry if I startled you, madam. My name is Thoi-Thagian. I couldn't help but admire your beauty," he said with a shy look as he stretched his hand out to her.

Grabbing his hand with hers, she said, "It's nice to meet you, Thoi-Thagian. You have a very interesting name, a name that reminds me a lot about my past. Speaking of which, while I have you here, have you ever heard of the great and misfortunate story of the Titans?"

With a look of confusion on his face, Thoi-Thagian said, "Titans? I don't believe that I have. Tell me, madam, these Titans, as you so called them, who were they?"

With a small chuckle, the young woman said, "Ah, such a wonderful, but tragic, tale. Sit down, I'll tell you their story."

Pulling out the chair opposite the young woman, Thoi-Thagian sat down and leaned onto the table. He smiled at her as he reached for one of her drinks and stole a sip. She looked at him in shock but dismissed it as nothing more than a gesture of interest.

"So, what is their story, love?"

"The Titans were a clan of immortals that ruled over this world long ago. Before their untimely deaths, they kept peace and prosperity throughout the realms. Their sole purpose in this world was to keep The Darkness from swallowing it up," she began. She took a sip of her vodka and then looked back into the dark eyes of the man listening to her enthralling tale. "Unfortunately, they were betrayed. In fact it was one of their very own."

"Sorry to interrupt, but judging by what you are telling me, is it safe to assume that you don't believe in the Heavenly Father?"

"Oh no, I believe in him. The Heavenly Father is but a small part in all of this. In times of great need the Titans would even look to Him for answers."

"Even though they were deities themselves?" he asked.

"Precisely."

"Okay, but if they were immortal, then how were the defeated? I was always under the impression that an immortal couldn't die."

"Don't be fooled by folklore. An immortal can be killed. They just can't die due to natural causes such as old age or illness. Why don't I start the story from the moment they faced their doom? The place I begin is with the events that led up to their betrayal."

Thoi-Thagian wasn't sure what to think of this strange woman, but she had an abnormal aura to her. He sensed a strange power that pulled at his very being. Leaning closer to her, he stared into her brown eyes, yearning for more.

Chapter 2 The Betrayal

In the glorious Titan Temple with a sum of five hundred rooms, located in the center of Rowmodea Isle, where the jagged mountains rose from the sacred earth and the peaceful seas surrounded the island, the Titans sat in their stone thrones and looked down at a massive pool filled with a glowing watery substance. Within the substance, the Titans watched the mortals do their day to day activities.

Upon the dismissal of the morning council meeting, Max, the Titan of War, made his way towards the temple library. It was located deep within the ancient structure. It was one of the largest chambers in the temple. Each of the four platforms that made up the chamber was filled with ancient novels of long lost knowledge. The fourth floor contained scrolls and spell books with enchantments protected by the strongest of magic to prevent mortals from getting their hands on them, along with a journal filled with vital information where the Titans kept their prized oracles' locations hidden. Temple guards were constantly patrolling that section, and the only two who had access to that area were the Titans of Death and Life.

The third floor contained tomes about powerful objects that were hidden across the planet. These powerful tools were hidden by the immortals in hopes that the foolish mortals would never be capable of wielding such power.

The second floor was full of knowledge about the whole of the world and its history. It had information on locations of great battles between the Titans and their parents, as well as selective entries made by all of the Titans concerning pressing thoughts about their creators, and the horrendous truth about The Darkness.

The main floor had the most common of knowledge gathered throughout the centuries. If one wanted to know a little information recorded about the mortals or exotic animals, they would find it on the first floor.

Max gracefully walked up the stone steps into the ancient library and stared up the center of the chamber, examining the four floors. He watched in amazement as temple servants carried stacks of books to their appropriate floor and section.

"Can I help you, Master?" came a soothing, young voice.

Max looked over to his right and saw the temple's head librarian. She wore beautiful, flowing white robes and allowed her wavy dark brown hair to flow freely down her back.

"Yes. I am searching for some information."

"What can I help you with, Master of War?"

"Madam Regina," came an adolescent male voice.

A young man no older than eighteen dressed in dark brown robes approached the two of them and said, "I can't seem to find where this belongs."

He handed Regina a spell book with a demonic face raised on its leather surface. It had a rusted chain dangling off the top of it. As she examined it, her eyes briefly grew wide. She handed it back to the young man and gave him a quick smile.

"That belongs on the fourth floor, section fifteen. Be sure to have one of the temple guards assist you," Regina said as she patted his back and pushed him along. Turning her gaze back to the Titan of War, she said, "Sorry about that. How can I assist you?"

"I am looking for information on…" he began, but stopped and placed his right hand against his head and squeezed his eyelids shut.

"*You want the locations of each of the other Titans' oracles,*" came a supernatural whisper.

Shaking his head, he said, "Uh, I was wondering if you could point me in the direction of the locations of each of the other Titans' oracles. I have reason to believe that one of them may have vital information about a conspiracy we discovered earlier this morning."

Looking at him in confusion Regina said, "Oh, I'm sorry, My Worship, but that information is locked away under restrictive access. I'm afraid unless you have permission from either Life or Death I can't grant you entrance."

"But they told me to come and retrieve the list."

"Do you have a note stating so?"

"No, but—"

"Then I'm sorry, but I can't give you access," Regina said, interrupting him. She quickly turned away from him and left.

"*You must get that information if you wish to become the leader of the Titan Council,*" came the mysterious voice again.

Max walked over to the stairwell and proceeded to climb it. Regina watched him and quietly followed after, afraid that he might attempt to enter the fourth floor even though she had denied him entrance. But as he climbed up to the third floor, he realized he was being followed and quickly turned onto the third platform, walking up to the first bookshelf.

Regina noticed he was examining the novels and smiled as she walked passed him. She disappeared within the sections of endless books, and Max darted back up towards the stairwell and snuck up to the fourth floor. At the top, two guards stood. They wore golden armor against their bulky tan bodies. He tried to enter the room, but they drew their weapons and crossed them across the archway.

"Stand down. I have direct orders from Death to be here," Max ordered.

The guards briefly looked at each other before retracting their weapons and allowing him to walk inside. Max examined the towering bookshelves filled with ancient secrets. At the back of the room rested a stone podium with a large, dusty, leather-bound book laying cracked open. He approached it and examined the pages. Hearing a noise, he quickly glanced behind him before returning his gaze to the yellow pages.

He flipped through the frail parchment and came across an ancient spell. Strange symbols were drawn onto the page along with the spell. "*Dinb rehtegot eht srewop fo efil, dna htaed, gnimorf eht etamitlu noitcetorp.*" Max knew this spell as one that had been banned. He quickly ripped the page free from the book and crammed it deep into his pocket. He flipped a couple more pages and came across a list of all the locations of the hidden oracles of the Titan Council. Ripping it from the ancient ledger, he folded it up and proceeded to place it in his other pocket.

A youthful hand grabbed his shoulder and whirled him around. As his eyes adjusted, he saw Regina standing before him. She was furious.

"I thought I had made myself clear that you weren't allowed up here," She said glancing over at the book. She saw the torn remains of a page. "If Death truly sent you here, you wouldn't have needed to rip the page out. Max…" she said as she reached to move his unkempt hair from his eyes. A vision manifested within her mind, forcing her to yank her hand back towards her. "The Gods? They are using you. Whatever they have told you, you must resist their temptations. If you go down that path, you will destroy us all."

"Oh, Regina…" Max said as he placed both his hands on her smooth face. He looked at her with saddened eyes.

"Kill her…"

"It's too late for that," he concluded, and he forcibly turned her head and snapped her neck. He watched her body fall to the ground and then pulled her out of the walkway into aisle.

Exiting the library, Max gracefully walked down the stone steps. He pulled the folded up piece of parchment out of his pocket and glanced at the names and locations of the many different oracles. He smiled evilly as he made his departure for the first of several locations.

While he ventured to each village and destroyed those who would defy him, Life stood alone in the throne room. She peered into the large Pool of Images and watched over the mortals. As she stalked a group of children running in a wheat field, a sharp pain erupted from deep within her chest, and she knew it as a pain of protection. She heard the cries of countless souls calling out to her for protection, but she could not pinpoint where the cries were coming from.

She knelt down next to the circular pool, waved her hand over it, and said, "Show me what all of the other Titans are doing."

The water swirled around violently and revealed Death sitting at his desk writing in his journal, Storm looking up into the cloudy sky from her balcony, Winter producing a shimmering snowflake in her hands from within her iced over room, Fire burning away corruption in the Dreadscar Valley, and Shadow creating revolting monsters to guard the Shadow Realms, but when she saw what Max was doing, her face went from a pleasant look to one of horror. She ran out of the throne room, up staircases, and through several hallways until she reached Death's chamber located on the southern end of the temple. She pounded on the splintery wooden doors to Death's room until he opened them.

Seeing Life outside his doors Death said, "Life? What are you doing here?"

With a worried face, and out of breath Life said, "Death, something terrible has happened. Max—"

In a harsh voice, Death said, "I am well aware of Max's deceit. The temple guards found Regina an hour ago. Her neck was broken. The temple guards also informed me that the list of all our oracles was missing. I have already contacted as many as I could to move to another location. However, the matter of Max betraying our trust like this is unsettling. I want you to go to his chamber immediately and confront him about this. Tell him that you and I both know what he has done and that if he does not change his ways, then I will take action personally."

Without a word of disagreement, Life ran out of his room and headed for Max's chamber, located on the far northern end of the temple. After a long run through the halls of the temple, Life finally reached Max's chamber. She lightly tapped on his wooden doors and waited for a few moments. After several minutes of no answer, she knocked on the doors harder.

"Max, will you open the doors? I need to talk to you!"

After a few more moments, the doors slowly opened and Max stood on the inside. With a confused look on his face Max said, "Life, can I help you?"

"Yes, may I come in?"

Max moved sideways and allowed her to enter.

As she entered the room, she let out a sigh and said, "Max, we know what you have done. The death of Regina and the missing pages from the tome are evidence enough for termination from the council. Know this. With every village you destroy, the wrath of the Titan

Council grows. Soon I will not be able to stop Death from destroying your immortal life, and possibly your mortal one as well."

With a displeased face Max said, "I'm not afraid of him! I am more powerful than he is, and I will continue to destroy as many villages as I please. I am the Titan of War after all."

With a hint of displeasure in her voice Life said, "Then you leave the Titans no choice...If you will not change your ways, then Death will come for you."

Life quickly left the room without another word and made her way back towards Death's chamber. Once she arrived, she vigorously knocked on the doors so that she could speak with him. In an instant, Death opened the doors as if he had been waiting for her and invited her in.

With a look of aggravation on her face Life said, "Death, after I confronted Max he told me that he would not change his ways. He told me that he will continue to destroy as many of our villages as he pleases. He is taking the great power we bestowed upon him for granted. I believe we need to take his titanic powers and strip him of his title as the Titan of War."

For a few moments, Death continued to look out his window. He slowly turned around to face her and said, "Max is a fool to betray us. You are right, Life. Payment must be made for his sins. His punishment will be his powers taken from him, and he will be removed from the Titan Council for the rest of his mortal days." He said grabbing his titanic great sword and walking out of the room.

Max knew Life would tell Death about the sins he had committed and knew that Death would come for him. Thinking quickly, he came up with an insidious plot to strike back. He figured that if he were to be kicked off of the Titan Council, then all of the Titans would die by his hand for their treason. He knew he didn't have much time before Death would break through his weak threshold, so he quickly contacted his secret apprentice.

He used his powers to summon forth his apprentice. He leaned into his ear and whispered, "Herladrick, listen closely. The Titans have betrayed me, and Death will be here shortly to take my powers and remove me from the council."

"Master, did they learn of me? Is that why?"

"No, it's because I went against their rules and learned a terrible truth that I must expose. They plan on destroying all of the mortals. It would appear they are the evil ones. I must release the Fallen Gods and aid them in destroying the Titan Council."

"To do that you will need an army, one that knew the Titans before they were known to the world under such a title. Master, I implore you…If this is the right course of action; seek out those who are made up of the mortal government under the banner of the Covenant."

"The Covenant? I'm not familiar with them. Where are they located?"

"Last I knew they still resided in the fallen city of Melagas."

"Very well. I shall seek them out. One final thing. If any of the Titans survive this assault, they will likely strike back. If such a fate arises, join their ranks."

With a confused look on his face Herladrick said, "Master, with me on their side how will you be able to kill them? I can't just let you through my line of defense. They would know the truth."

"Herladrick, you are extremely special. You possess great power. They will undoubtedly make you a member of the Titan Council to ensure the balance remains intact. You can distract them long enough for me to reveal my true intentions. When they defeat me, you must ensure that the process of rebuilding is at hand. During that time, the son of Death will help bring me back to the world of the living."

"The son of Death? I didn't know Death had a son."

"No one does. He has covered his tracks well throughout the years. When I went to kill his oracle, she, like many of the others, had already been warned and had escaped to somewhere else. However, she left behind a letter from Death himself. It stated that she must keep his son hidden for all time. None could know the truth."

"And what of your draconic pet that looms within the Ancestreyalwood Forest? Shall I send it to attack?"

"No. I have other plans for it. If I know Death, and trust me, I do, he will see it as a possible threat. He might just see it as enough of a threat that he will send some of the temple guards to kill it. The beast will make quick work of them, and there will be that many less enemies that will have to be slaughtered."

"I understand. I will follow you to my dying breath, Master. But are you sure this plan will work?"

"Though I am the Titan of War, I was once a powerful magic wielder. As one who can wield such a gift, we are often blessed with foresight. Though much of my magical ability has faded over the years, I can still see into the future when I use complete focus. I have foreseen victory. Now, be gone with you. Death will be here shortly."

With a quiet voice Herladrick said, "As you wish, Master. Your plans will be done in your name."

Max used his powers to teleport his apprentice out of the temple and then walked over to the table in the center of the room and pushed it out of the way. He quickly removed the stone tile in the center of the floor and knelt down. He pulled a silver chain with a vial of swirling red sand from his neck and stuck it inside, and then put everything back in its original place before Death would arrive.

The doors flew open and hit the stone walls in Max's chamber as Death stormed in. Turning to face him, Max grabbed a sword that hung on the wall next to the window.

"You want my powers?! Fine then, come and get them…"

He charged at Death with his uplifted sword, but Death simply raised his hand and chanted a spell. "Emoceb latrom ecno erom!"

A ghostly hand shot from Death's armored palm and flew across the room into Max's chest. Escaping from his back, it circled around the chamber clutching a small red, misty orb. As it circled the room one final time, the ghostly hand retreated back into Death's hand with the misty orb. Falling to the ground weakened from the ghostly hand stealing his power, Max coughed, raised his head defiantly, and looked at Death with evil in his eyes.

In a harsh voice Max said, "You have just started a war that you can't possibly win! I have already foreseen my victory!"

He crawled over to his private balcony and reached up to the latch to open it. As soon as the glass doors swung open, it revealed a balcony with a white armored Pegasus. Max rose to his feet long enough to climb on to the majestic animal and flicked the reins. It rose onto its hind legs and flew away from the temple.

Death walked out onto the balcony and watched as the winged steed flew from the structure. He watched it shrink in the distance allowing Max to flee.

"Goodbye, Max…May your fate be close at hand."

Upon returning to his room, Death saw Life sitting on his bed. She quickly stood up and ran over to him. "Are you hurt?" she asked as she grabbed on to him and hugged him.

"No, Max put up very little resistance compared to my titanic powers. We must be cautious, though. Max pronounced a threat to the Titan Council that we can't take lightly."

"Death, you did what had to be done; however, the role of War can't stand empty. Someone must fill it. The throne mustn't be allowed to sit empty like the throne of Time."

"Yes, I believe Alashani would make a perfect figure for a role such as this. He is strong, wise, and brave."

"I agree…"

The two of them slowly left his chamber and headed for the throne room, where they would gather the other Titans and announce the change of events. As they walked towards the throne room, Life grabbed his hand and intertwined her fingers with his.

"Death, might I discuss something with you? Preferably without the other Titans or our apprentices around?" Death glanced towards her and nodded. "Your apprentice will become the new Titan of War. That is, if he accepts it. However, my apprentice has been amongst us far longer. I fear she might become jealous if we give Alashani such a great title and not her. Why not have her fill the role of Time?"

"You're right. However, I disagree with making her the Titan of Time. How about we make her the Guardian of the Titans? She can possess a small amount of the Titan Council's powers within her very body and protect us by going on quests that we can't make time for but still need our attention."

"Such as?" she asked.

"Such as the quest concerning that dragon that threatens the lands of the Ancestreyalwood Forest. Nethemious will pose a great threat now that Max is no longer our ally. He will surely send it to attack us."

"You think he would really do such a thing?"

"You saw what he did to Regina. And he raised it from an egg. It is bound to him."

"I see your concern…Very well, she will take on this new responsibility and defeat this beast before it can be used to destroy us," Life concluded as they closed in on the throne room.

Entering the throne room, Life and Death examined the stone thrones that sat in a semi-circle around the chamber. Mythdariz, the Titan of Death, approached the middle throne. He was the leader of the Titan Council, the most powerful out of the seven of them. He had a deep voice that echoed with power every time he spoke. The throne to his left belonged to Selineane, the Titan of Life. When Death was away from the temple on a quest, Life was looked at as the leader, for she was the second most powerful Titan. She, unlike Death, had a soothing voice that seeped into the souls of all with the power of prosperity. To the further left of Death sat Serenity, the Titan of Storms, and her daughter, Nyads, the Titan of Winter. To his right sat an empty throne that was once owned by the Titan of Time. The throne of War rested next to the hallowed throne, and further to the right sat Telareous, the Titan of Fire, and Temhota, the Titan of Shadows.

Death had beautifully crafted armor that was dark gray, and it had been raised in places to make it look like there were skulls emerging from it. His helmet covered his face and spiked backwards. His breastplate had a demonic skull on the center of it, and his pauldrons carried a design of skulls with three horns as well. Finally, guarding his kneecaps, his armor took the shape of another skull design. He had hair that was white as snow that draped down his back from underneath his helmet onto his tattered black cloak, and his eyes glowed icy blue with coldness.

Life wore green robes and a small breastplate over her chest. The breastplate was emerald green while her long flowing robes had many different shades of green. There were emerald hues mixed with lime greens down the front of her elegant robes, and towards the back of her garments the color was more of a dark green. She always kept her lime green hair down, and her glowing emerald eyes always revealed peace. She wore a silver chain, and dangling from it was an emerald crystal that radiated pure power.

Death and Life were considered to be the structure of the Titan Council which gave them their titles as leaders. They were also the only two that were allowed to have apprentices. Death's apprentice was Alashani, and he hardly ever left Death's side unless told to. Alashani was a master in fighting and had gruesome gladiator armor given to him by Death himself. What made his armor different from all other gladiators was that his armor had been touched by the dark shadows of the Shadow Realms.

Life's apprentice was Sellithia, and like Alashani she never left Life's side unless told to. Sellithia was a quiet person, but loved to accessorize her wardrobe. She wore brown leather boots, tight brown leather pants, and a gold-trimmed white blazer over her white shirt. She allowed her long brown hair to flow freely down her back, and around her neck was a silver chain with three turquoise stones that held a small portion of the entire Titan Councils' powers.

Though everyone who was part of the Titan Council agreed in Death's decision of them being the only two capable of having apprentices, Max had secretly despised him for it. As the Titan of War, he felt that he was the structure of the Titan Council. Without him, warfare would be unorthodox and a bloodbath that would wipe out the mortal race. Envy took root inside him and began to poison his mind, allowing the remnants of the evil Gods, who were locked away within the Hourglass Dome on the other side of the temple, to spread their darkened whispers.

With the betrayal of Max, Death had no choice but to inform the other Titans of the horrible things Max had committed. Death would do all in his power to ensure Max wouldn't get away with his treason.

Chapter 3 Traitor's Revenge

Max approached the ruins of an ancient city that was cloaked in the darkness of night. As his steed glided down to the sandy beach below, Max stiffened and braced for impact. The armored Pegasus's hooves dug deep into the damp sand as it came to a sudden stop. Max slid off its back and took in a deep breath.

"Ah, Melagas…How fitting it will be to reap my revenge on those who have wronged me just as they wronged your people."

Max walked through the darkened streets of the forgotten city of Melagas and knew that he could recruit men to fight for him if he went into the slums of the city. He examined the desolation wrought on the forsaken city that once homed millions. Those who had stayed had been all but forgotten. Once in the slums he walked up to the large groups of poverty-stricken men that were gambling on what little they had.

In a rude voice Max said, "By your unpleasant looks and smells, I can assume that you are also outcasts of the Titans. Your lives are meaningless because of them. I can sense in your tortured souls that you want revenge. Rise up and follow me and you will have what you desire."

After hearing that they could overthrow the Titans, all of the men in the groups rose to their feet and began to follow Max into an old, run down blacksmith shop. All sorts of unfinished armor and different types of metal littered the floor.

"Begin building your armor and weapons, for at dawn we march on the Titans," Max bellowed.

While his recruits forged their weapons and armor, the followers of the Titans gathered in the beautiful valley outside the temple's main entrances. The Titans slowly glided out of the temple dressed in robes to cover their original garments and armor. They wore hoods as they entered the moonlit valley. Behind them came two temple guards carrying a gurney with the body of Regina on it.

The guards took her body to the center of the crowd and gently placed her cot on the ground. The Titans circled her body and began to swirl their arms in the air in a unified ritual. As they did so, their powers swirled around them and flowed towards Regina's motionless body.

Slowly, Regina's body was dissolved by the Titan Council's powers as she became one with them and floated off towards Life's large garden. The many different auras of the Titans' powers acted like a cyclone as they swirled towards the ground and produced a magnificent flourishing tree.

"Though Regina has passed from this realm of existence, may her new form be a sign that she will always be amongst us. Her spirit has passed on, but we can still look upon the beauty of her soul through this tree," Life said, and they all returned to the confidences of the temple.

***

As Max watched his newly formed army build their armor and weapons, he came to realize that the Titans were masters in defense and offence. There was no plausible way that he could defeat the Titans, and their handfuls of soldiers that helped guard the temple, with these kinds of supplies. He was determined to kill all of the Titans though, and so he remembered back to his early training in wizardry, back before he became a Titan, and switched from magic to melee.

He remembered a spell that his former master had shown him that would allow him to strengthen his and his followers', armor and weapons. He grabbed his sword from his side and raised it high into the air. He closed his eyes and concentrated on the spell that would work.

"Ekam eseht snopaew regnorts!" he yelled.

His sword began to glow with a dim orange aura of magic and sent out small beams of orange light as if it were alive. The beams swirled around the entire room and settled over all the armor and weapons that Max's men had finished.

As the magic faded into the armor Max said, "The time to act is nigh! Follow me and together we will destroy the Titans and all their followers!"

Everyone let out a loud roar of pleasure and began following Max out of the blacksmith shop. Max got on his armored Pegasus and began to ride off towards the beach. As he rode closer and closer to the shore, his men formed up in to small squads and marched proudly behind him through the darkened streets of Melagas.

Once they were all on the sandy beach, all of Max's men saw three large wooden ships. Max dismounted his winged steed, climbed up the rope ladder onto the ship closest to him, and headed up towards the deck above the Captain's Cabin. Soon after he was on board, his men began boarding the ships and took their positions on the decks of the vessels. Max looked at all the men on the three ships, noticing that he had fifty men on each of them, but there were still five more men on the beach awaiting their turn to board. He knew that five more men would not be able to fit on any of the ships, but he didn't want to exclude them and risk them contacting the Titans and warning them of the insidious plot to destroy them. He couldn't take that risk, so he walked through the crowded decks of his men and headed below to the room where the cannons were stored. He loaded the cannon nearest to the door, pointed it at the crowd still standing on the beach, and lit the fuse. It went off with a loud bang as Max covered his ears. It sailed over the men's heads who still stood on the damp, sandy shore. The cannonball hit a large dead tree and caused it to fall over on top of the five men with a loud thud. As the tree lay resting on the beach, blood began to seep from underneath it, staining the grains of sand.

With a bit of a shocked face Max said, "Well…That went well…"

He walked back up to the deck and looked at all his men as they stared in awe at him.   With an evil smile on his face Max said, "Set sail for Rowmodea Isle. We're going to pay the Titans a little visit."

The ships' white sails dropped and caught a gust of wind as the three ships turned towards open water. They smoothly glided through the black sea as Max walked to the back of his vessel and opened a door that led to the Captain's Cabin. He shut the door behind him as he walked into the room, then walked up to the grime filled windows and watched as Melagas faded into the darkness of the night.

After Melagas was no longer visible by the naked eye, Max reached into his pocket and pulled out the crumpled up piece of parchment that had strange symbols on it. He closed his eyes as the memory of what he had done back in the library came rushing back. Pushing the thought out of his head, he focused on the spell he was trying to cast.

On the ground, symbols similar to the ones on the piece of paper began to form around Max as if they were being etched into the wooden floor. The symbols appeared on the wooden floor, blazing to life with lime green fire, producing an eerie green light that rose like a weak fog while the floor in the center turned black. The gravity slipped away in the surrounding area, and Max slowly rose into the air, beginning to levitate over the moving symbols on the ground. He opened his eyes and began to speak in the language of demonology. He muttered a curse that he knew was banned by the Titans ten thousand years before he had become the Titan of War.

"Dinb rehtegot eht srewop fo efil, dna htaed, gnimorf eht etamitlu noitcetorp," Max bellowed.

The symbols on the ground began to move faster and the lime green light that had been seeping off of the symbols became more intense looking. With a paralyzing flash and a loud crack, the symbols, the black hole, and the green light vanished as though they had never been there. Gravity became present once more and Max fell to the ground. He slowly rose to his feet and saw that his sword and tarnished silver armor had a faint dark green glow to it. He grabbed a mace that was lying on the table and brought it down on the blade of his sword. Instead of breaking the steel, the mace bounced off of it, not even leaving a mark. He dropped the mace and gripped his sword tighter in his hand. To test out the spell further, he took his sword and shoved it deep into his stomach. He felt no pain, nor did he bleed. Pulling the sword out of his abdomen, he saw that there was no hole from where it had been either. It was as if he had never been stabbed.

A knock came from the other side of the door, causing Max to lose his concentration. He quickly walked over to the door and pulled it open just as his armor and sword stopped glowing. He found that one of the men that he had recruited was standing on the other side.

In a rude voice Max said, "What do you want?"

"Sir, I came to inform you that we are coming up behind the ship known as The Dawnalow."

"The Dawnalow? That's my Father's ship. The Titans must have requested his presence. Go have the rest of the men load the cannons," he shouted.

"Yes sir!"

As the soldier and several others of the men went below the decks and loaded the cannons, Max went to the main deck and watched as his ship pulled up alongside The Dawnalow. One quick look and Max saw the anchor in the water, and he knew that the men aboard his Father's ship had retired for the night. He looked towards the back of the ship and saw the windows that led to the Captain's Cabin were yellow with the reflection of candlelight.

Looking back at his men Max said, "Hold your fire. I'm going aboard to visit my dear old Father."

He grabbed a rope that hung from the main mast and swung over to the other ship. Once on board, he stomped across the wooden deck, grabbed the iron handle on the door to the Captain's Cabin, and pushed it.

Inside the cluttered cabin, an old man with long curly, gray hair and wrinkles all over his face sat at a rectangular table with maps on its surface. He wore a comfortable sailing outfit that seemed relatively new. Hearing the door creek open, Max's Father looked up from the map he was studying to see his oldest son standing before him.

With a confused look on his face Max's Father said, "Max? What are you doing here? I was just on my way to visit you and the other Titans."

Without a word, Max pulled his sword from his side and walked over to the table. As soon as he got in striking range of his Father, he swung his sword in an upward motion, slicing his throat open. In an instant his Father brought up his left hand to his throat in an attempt to stop the bleeding, but that moment ended. He dropped his head onto the table and his hand fell to his side. More blood gushed out of his throat onto the table, staining maps as it dripped onto the floor.

Looking at his Father's corpse Max said, "Sorry Father, but you will not stand in my way of destroying the Titans. Not after all I have done to ensure that I become the leading member of the godly council I intend on creating."

He turned back towards the door and slowly walked out of the cabin back onto the deck. He grabbed the rope and swung back over to his ship just as his men began firing a few of the cannons.

Yelling over the cannon fire Max said, "Fire all cannons! Leave no evidence of us being here!"

One by one the cannons from all three vessels went off with a loud bang, and each one left its fatal mark on the doomed ship. One of the cannonballs hit the bow of the ship just below the waterline, causing gallons of water to slip inside the ship and pull it down beneath the crushing dark waves. Within minutes The Dawnalow was completely submerged beneath the dark water. Feeling satisfied with the destruction of his Father's vessel, Max let out an evil laugh.

"I shall retire for the night. Wake me when we arrive at Rowmodea," he said as he turned to leave.

The next morning came with rain, thunder, and lightning. The storm woke Max up from his dreams and was so loud that he couldn't fall back asleep. He walked out onto the deck, saw land far to the north, and knew that it was Rowmodea Isle. As the ship slowly inched its way towards the island far to the north, Max gathered all his men on the main decks of each of the three ships.

In an attempt to give a speech Max said, "My brave soldiers, today marks the first rebellion against the Titans. None of you will die because while you were asleep I placed a spell on us that will keep even death at bay. The only thing that could kill you is the plague, but Death would never release it. Our time has finally come, the Titans were entrusted to lead the mortals through wisdom, but they assumed nothing could ever challenge them. The time of the Titans is coming to an end! We shall show them no mercy!"

With a loud cheer, all of Max's men raised their swords, axes, and bows and swung them around in the air as their ships crept even closer to Rowmodea Isle.

The ships creaked and cracked, their wooden frames dragging against the rocky sea floor as they came up onto the beach. When all three of the ships came to a halt, Max and his followers climbed from the vessels and spread out across the beach. As soon as everyone was off of the transports, Max noticed that the storm had lifted. He ordered the ships to be demolished and the pieces made into catapults.

Hours of grueling labor stole time from the mortals as the ships slowly transformed into catapults. The remains of the wooden vessels were scavenged and placed in piles to be used in the construction of the weapons.

"Sir, the men are hard at work in building the catapults, but what will we use for ammo? We didn't bring anything with us," one of Max's men asked.

"The remains of the ships shall be used, along with the rocks from the mountains," Max began as he picked up a pickaxe. "Here," he said, shoving the tool into the soldier's chest. "Make yourself useful and start chiseling away the wall of rocks."

As Max watched half of his men chisel away at the mountain, he saw an elderly man with long gray hair and a long, gray, wiry beard. He wore purple and blue robes and stood near the edge of the entrance to the mountain paths. The old man seemed to be trying to hide from him. Max took a few steps forward, but suddenly stopped as the mysterious man disappeared.

"Master?" Max mumbled in confusion.

As the catapults neared completion and large clumps of rocks were gathered, Max used some of the spare boards from the ships to create pallets to carry their ammunition. Once the catapults were finished, he ordered his men into two rows. They began to march down the beach with the catapults and other supplies towards the Crystalrock

Mountains, knowing that the Titan Temple was being protected within. The jagged pathways within the mountains were too narrow to bring the catapults through, however, so Max had to use what little control over magic he had to levitate them above the paths while they walked through. As they went through the winding rocky paths of the mountains, Max began to walk more slowly and allowed his men to get ahead of him. For a moment he began to feel grief for what he was doing, but he couldn't stop now. An unseen force was pushing him forward. It wouldn't allow him to retreat.

They walked into the valley that surrounded the temple.

"Stop here," Max yelled.

All of his recruits stopped walking and turned to face him as he came back to the front of his army. As he made his way towards the frontlines, he allowed the catapults to float down and gently rest behind his army. He turned towards the Titan Temple, stretched his arms forward, and closed his eyes. Though his connection to magic had been severed for many years, he knew that it would still aid him. Through his willpower, he influenced the magic that surrounded the temple to be pulled into a single space suitable for destruction. Through his complete focus a massive explosion of molten fire and debris filled the air. The men looked around and saw that one of the rooms close to the throne room had exploded and black smoke was rolling out of the destroyed structure. Several of the temple guards that were stationed on the outside perimeters began running around in a frenzied state of panic preparing for an attack that would soon come.

Chapter 4 Fall of the Immortals

Minutes before the explosion, Death and the other Titans sat in the throne room and discussed future events.

"I have asked everyone to gather upon these ancient grounds for two reasons. We all know about Max's betrayal and that I took his powers from him. We have another empty seat amongst us now, though. The role of War must be filled. Therefore, I recommend that we make my apprentice, Alashani, the new Titan of War," Death announced.

Alashani looked up at his master with shock in his face and said, "Master, are you sure?"

"Yes my young apprentice. You have been trained by one of the greatest Titans to ever live and I have no doubt that you will make a great Titan of War," he replied with amusement in his deep voice.

"I would be honored to be the new Titan of War; that is if the others would like me to be the one that fills this role."

Life slowly rose from her throne and looked at each of the other Titans. In a calm voice, she said, "I agree with Death on this matter. What say you, Winter?"

Winter looked down on Alashani with cold eyes, then back at Life. "He has the stamina for this role. I say let him be the Titan of War."

Storm smiled at her daughter and said, "A wise evaluation, my daughter. I too vote to have him become the new Titan of War."

Fire rose from his throne with outstretched arms and said, "It's settled then, Alashani will be the new Titan of War."

Death raised his left armored hand and faced his palm upwards. A mass of red, swirling magic materialized and hovered above his hand as he rose from his throne.

"This power once lived inside the veins of Max, but now they are yours. Treat them carefully. If you go down the path that Max took, the council will have no choice but to end you."

The power sank back into his palm as he faced it towards his apprentice. A few moments went by, but nothing happened. Alashani looked to the ground in disappointment and began to walk away, when a ghostly hand with long, boney fingers leaped out of Death's palm and lunged at Alashani. It went through his chest then back into Death's hand. He began to move forward, but the boney hand shot out of Death's chest holding the red aura of power. It swirled around Alashani three times before entering his body through his chest. He felt his body change as the power entered him and began to course through his very veins. The boney hand left his body from his back and retreated back into Death's body as he sat back down in his throne.

With great excitement in his voice Alashani said, "Thank you, fellow Titans! Today marks a—"

A loud explosion rang through the stone halls of the temple causing all of the other Titans to rise from their thrones and run out onto the rectangular balcony overlooking the valley below the temple. Death placed both his armored hands on the stone railing and looked down to the valley.

Down on the grassy plains, he saw hundreds of mortals yelling and screaming as catapults launched boulders in the direction of the temple. Turning away from the balcony, Death furiously walked back into the throne room and shouted at the temple guard standing at the doorway.

"Order all the guards to report down to the valley. We are under attack!"

"Right away, Master!" the guard yelled back, bowing and leaving the chamber.

Death walked over to the circular pool and knelt down beside it. He looked into it as the other Titans formed in behind him.

In an outraged voice Death said, "Show me all the mortals who dare attack our beloved temple." The watery substance within the circular pool began to glow as it produced a large image of all the mortals down in the valley. "Show me their leader!" The image shifted and began to take on a new form. As it changed from many mortals to one, Death rose to his feet in outrage. "Max, you will pay for this treachery! Brothers and Sisters, draw your weapons and prepare for war!"

The Titans ran to their rooms and grabbed their weapons as Death grabbed his titanic great sword. It had four gems socketed into it. Two of which were at the end of the blade, and the other two were near the hilt. The four gems were two dark gray opals and two blood red rubies. The dark gray opals represented the power of Shadow and the blood red rubies represented the power of War. His blade had these gems because Shadow was his closest friend and War had been the first mortal he had ever taken on as an apprentice.

Life grabbed her wooden staff that was crafted from an old oak tree that grew around the valley of the temple. At the top of her staff was an emerald stone that was cut into a diamond shape. It was protected by small branches that stretched around it. Wrapped around the base of the staff was a light green ribbon with a pattern of leaves on it.

Alashani, the new Titan of War grabbed a scythe that Death had given him when he was still his apprentice. The scythe was made entirely out of rare metal and had dents in it from many years of use. At the tip of the scythe was a ring of shadows.

Fire went into his room, but didn't grab a weapon. He didn't rely on weapons to serve him. Instead, he grabbed a book that lay by his bedside table. The book had a leather cover and a symbol of fire on it. He waved his hand across the tome and the symbol on the cover flashed bright orange then popped open from its lock. As he began to open it, the pages began to glow and radiate heat with the powers of the Titan of Fire.

Shadow entered his room and grabbed his staff which looked like it had been mistreated since the day it was made. It was cracked and the wood was black in several spots. He also grabbed a book that lay on a table in the center of the room. The cover of the book was leather with several ware and tare spots all over it. As he opened the book, yellow and torn pages were revealed from age. The writing in the book was also smudged, making it hard to read. He examined a page with a picture of a zombie dressed in tattered and torn black robes. On the beast's robes, directly in the center of the chest, was a symbol of a scythe.

The zombie had one regular-looking rotting hand while the other had been replaced by a metal scythe with shadows swirling around the blade. As he waved his hand over the illustration, a portal to the Shadow Realms opened and beasts of the same characteristics on the page began to crawl out of the portal. Shadowscythes were their names, a creation of Shadow to guard the Shadow Realms and to stop souls from escaping their final judgment.

Running into her room covered with ice and snow, Winter grabbed her staff that was made entirely out of ice. It was smooth on the bottom for walking with and came to a sharp jagged point at the top. As she held it in her right hand, small streams of mist fell from the sides of the staff and fell to the ground.

Storm raised her right hand towards the ceiling and a staff fell from the dark, stormy clouds. Landing in her hands, the staff was made out of shiny metal. The top branched out limbs that twisted around each other, the center had a blue sapphire crystal resting within the twisting branches, and the base had a blue ribbon with a lightning bolt spiraling down it.

Death stood at the main entrance to the temple and waited for all of the Titans to arrive.

After several minutes of waiting, all of the Titans came running to the front of the room, gathering at the doors to the valley. As they prepared for a fight that would start the war, boulders continued to smash against the walls of the temple, each leaving a fatal mark. One boulder smashed into the wall that led to Shadow's chamber, allowing the Shadowscythes to begin pouring out of the hole, crawling down the walls to the ground.

The doors to the temple swung open, and all of the Titans began running out to the valley to meet their enemies. Death began to follow his friends to the battlefield, but noticed Sellithia charging for the open threshold. He threw out his hand and grabbed her arm, pulling her close to him.

"I feel as though you may think that it's unfair that Alashani became a Titan and you didn't, for you have been amongst us far longer than he, but Life and I had planned to make you the Guardian of the Titans. Being the guardian means that you wield a bit of power from each of the Titans," Death said as he held up a small vial filled with a glowing liquid.

Placing the vial in her hands Death said, "Drink it and you will have part of each of the Titans' powers running in your veins. You will become the Guardian of the Titans."

She placed her hand over her necklace and said, "Don't I already have some of each of the Titans' powers?"

"Yes, but this vial I have given you will allow the powers to run through your veins, not just the necklace."

Sellithia placed the small vial to her lips and chocked the liquid down. As the powers ran down her throat, she felt something happening to her, something amazing.

With a small smile on her face Sellithia said, "Thank you, Master."

"I have one final power to give you, Sellithia, a power that was not in the vial. A power that will allow you to see all of the Titans and what they are doing at any time."

He raised both of his hands and the ghostly hand leaped out of his left palm. It flew over Sellithia and went through the ceiling to the throne room. When it returned, it shimmered with a coating of the watery substance from the Pool of Images. It circled around her and entered her body through her nose. As it made its way up her nostrils, she grunted, attempting to catch her breath.

"Now that you have your last power, you are a true Guardian of the Titans. Your first task is to go into the far reaches of the Ancestreyalwood Forest. Even further beyond the watchful eyes of the Titans. There is a dragon named Nethemious there and he has terrorized those lands for far too long. I task you in finding this beast and destroying it, lest it destroy us all."

"This dragon…Where did it come from?"

"Max raised it from an egg. He wanted to use it as a weapon to destroy any who got in his way. It is constructed for evil. It must be hunted down and defeated."

"I will kill this dragon in your name, Master. Or die trying..."

"I'm sure with all of the powers of the Titans you will not fail. The powers I have given you will continue to live on within your vessel as long as we live. Protect them, for you will need their strength to kill Nethemious. He is a very powerful dragon, so don't take him lightly. Good luck, Sellithia."

He raised his left hand and began to cast a spell. His hand flashed bright blue as the area surrounding Sellithia began to glow. The glowing area shot up into the air and covered Sellithia from sight. When the glowing light faded, Sellithia was gone and where she had stood were small streams of smoke that rose from the ground.

Death began to run out of the temple, but when he got to the frame of the doorway, he stopped and placed his left hand on his chest. Another explosion went off next to him, and the force of the explosion caused him to be launched out into the valley far from the temple as the entrance to the structure fell to ruin.

Sellithia's vision blurred as she was ripped through a swirling rift of magic. Falling to the ground, she slowly raised her head to see that she lay on the floor of the Ancestreyalwood Forest. Rising to her feet, she brushed the dirt from her hands and began to take a step forward.

A quaking stomp stopped her from moving, and the rumble of a draconic roar deep within the belly of a beast echoed throughout the silent forest. Slowly turning with a fearful face to see the monstrosity that had landed behind her, Sellithia shook in fear. A large, scaly golden-brown lizard with large, twisting horns and sharp teeth that poked out of its thin lips stared at Sellithia. The dragon's tongue glided across its toothy lips as it licked its chomps, eager to make her its next meal.

Sellithia slowly took a step backwards, but quickly dove away as the dragon lurched forward and took a ferocious bit towards her. She ran towards two large trees that stood close to each other, slipping in between them. Darting after her, all the while roaring with rage, the dragon produced a fountain of flames that set the two towering trees ablaze.

As they burned, they grew weaker. Sellithia ran back around the trees and stared into the yellow eyes of the beast one final time. It leaned in closer to her and exhaled a cloud of hot, snotty breath. Two loud cracks filled the air as the twin trees broke from their bases and fell forward. Sellithia jumped out of the way just as the dragon dove forward and was crushed by the weight of the two trees collapsing on it.

Sellithia watched as the beast lay squashed under the burned trees and knew that she had been successful. She didn't know where she was, but she could hear the yelling from the battle at the temple. She knew she could find her way back.

She was surprised, however, that the beast had fallen so easily. It was then that she realized that the powers of the Titan Council were keeping her safe the whole time and had given her the ability to outwit the dragon. She knew that by the time Max learned of its death, it would be late. Though she knew the Titans were struggling to keep the battle in their favor, she also knew that by killing this monstrosity they had struck a devastating blow to the enemy.

Chapter 5 Immortals Downfall

Death lay on his back stunned from the blast, but as his body readjusted from it, he turned over on his right side to see his former apprentice laying on the ground with his left leg laying over his right and his left arm bent above his head. He turned over, getting on his hands and knees, and looked at his former apprentice. With half opened, foggy eyes and a half opened mouth, the apprentice laid still on the ground. Death examined the large hole in his chest and knew that he had met his end in a deadly sword fight. He grabbed a small vial that was on a silver chain around Alashani's neck, the same necklace that he had found hidden underneath the stone floor of Max's old room.

He rose to his feet and looked down at the corpse. Cracks began to appear all over Alashani's face and armor and, as the cracks spread out across his body, the magic Death had given him began to pour out faster and faster into the sky until it became impossible to see Alashani's body. The dark red power violently swirled up into the air like a cyclone, blinding Death as it escaped into the sky. When his vision returned to him, he noticed that Alashani's body had vanished and all that was left behind was his weapon and pieces of his armor.

Looking back out to the horizon of the valley, Death saw another body cloaked in tattered robes five hundred feet from him. Sprinting to the body, he knew it was one of the other Titans. He passed several other bodies on the way, which he knew were temple guards. Once he reached the body, he fell to his knees and pulled the body closer to him to reveal Shadow. Looking closely at his best friend's face, Death saw a small hint of life. It wasn't strong, but there was enough to communicate. He leaned closer to Shadow's face.

"Shadow, can you hear me?"

In a weak and confused voice Shadow said, "Death? Is that you?"

"Yes, it's me!"

In a weak attempt, Shadow looked at Death and said, "Death, listen closely. Max is too powerful...He has used the forbidden curse. There...There isn't much time...Get Life and get out of here!*cough* S-save the Titans, Death...They need...you."

"The forbidden curse? How did he even get a hold of it? You were tasked with keeping it protected."

"We were deceived…The spell was hidden within the tome of secrets within the library…Max ripped the page from it. His deceit goes back further than once thought…Save us, Death," Shadow cried as he exhaled his last breath.

Feeling the life leave Shadow, Death rose to his feet and watched cracks begin to appear on Shadow's face and tattered robes. The cracks widened and pitch black shadows flew out of the cracks escaping into the atmosphere. Within minutes, Shadow's body had completely evaporated into thin air leaving nothing but his tattered robes behind.

Death looked around the valley and saw Max and his men far off to the north. He began to run towards the fighting, but was delayed by a loud cracking sound that penetrated the air. The wind picked up, blowing his hair around, and a bolt of lightning spiraled up into the sky. The air became cold as ice and the sky grew dark with pitch black storm clouds that covered every inch of the valley. As it spread like an evil hand across the island, it blotted out the sun, causing the valley to become dark and visibility to be impossible. Rain and hail began to fall from the sky, and the fighting became impossible to hear over the loud rumbles of thunder. Lightning began to flash through and across the black blanket of clouds, causing the valley to briefly light up.

A massive bolt of lightning shot across the valley, lighting it all up for a few moments. During that time, Death looked around the ancient vale and saw Storm standing on a large clump of stone holding her staff high into the sky. He watched as she released the harsh elements of all possible storms combined.

He ran up to aid her and, when he was in range of her, he shouted, "Storm! Where are the others?"

Still concentrating on the sky Storm said, "Life is in the temple trying to mend what Max has destroyed. I'm not sure where Winter is, and unfortunately Fire was killed by one of the boulders."

In a confused voice Death asked, "How did he die from a boulder?"

"One of the boulders flew in and was in line with Life. She didn't see it coming, but Fire did. Life was standing on a pedestal she made out of the earth, and Fire had to use his fire abilities to fly up to the platform. Once he was up there, he pushed her down to the ground right as the boulder smashed into it. The force of the impact threw Fire into the wall above us. After a few minutes we noticed smoke was rising out of the hole. Then a massive explosion occurred. Life ran into the temple and headed to the room above us, but when she got there she only found Fire's chard robes."

"This is an unfortunate day. Keep pressing the attack, I'll go and find Life."

As he walked away, he heard Storm scream in pain. Quickly turning around on his heels, he saw her with an arrow sticking out of her chest. She dropped her staff and fell off of the boulder on to her side.

Running up to her, Death fell to his knees and placed one hand on her cheek and the other on the ground. He looked around the area for the one who shot her, but it was still too dark to see anyone far off in the distance. He looked back down at Storm and saw that her eyes were now closed and lightning was jumping out of her wound. He rose to his feet and backed away from her so that he wouldn't get electrocuted. The lightning jumped all around her body then began to shoot into the sky. As the bolts of lightning zigzagged upwards into the sky, the rain and hail stopped falling and the storm clouds began to break apart and turn white as the sun broke through. He looked into the cloudy sky and took in the view for a few moments. He looked back down towards Storm to see that her body had vanished and the bloody arrow was lying on the muddy ground through her leather robes.

Chapter 6 The Exile

Death ran into the temple through the eastside's entrance due to the main entrance being destroyed and ran through the stone hallways. He went through doors and up several staircases until he finally reached the throne room. He walked into the magnificent chamber and noticed Life standing on the balcony casting spells at the invading enemies. Between her magic and the few handfuls of guards surviving, they were the only ones that were keeping Max and his men out of the temple. Death walked up to her and saw she was commanding the wild animals to attack the intruders as well.

"Life, save your strength. Max is too powerful for us to defeat now. None of his men are dying, and even with my powers of death, they won't die. He is using the spell to cheat death, the very spell that uses the powers of life to keep death at bay. If we stay here we will surely be killed. We need to leave while we still have a chance."

Life interrupted the spell she was casting and turned around to face Death.

In a sad voice, she said, "I have lived in this sacred temple for all of my immortal life, and in a single day I'm just expected to leave?"

"I know it's difficult to accept, but look around you. All of the other Titans have fallen by Max's hand, but if we leave while we still have a chance, we can plot our return. We shall be the reapers of what he has sown."

Looking out to the valley, Life let out a sigh of sadness. "I regret the day we brought Max into the temple. The day you brought Alashani into the temple, Max thought it an act of treason. I fear from that day forward, he was conspiring against us."

"It would seem that way. Come on, we must get out of here before it's too late."

The two of them ran out of the throne room and went into another corridor that led them to a large staircase. They climbed to the top of the marble stairs and opened a door at the top that led to a spiral staircase. They reached the top and opened the hatchway that led them on to the Spire of Wisdom. As they walked onto the platform more towers and bridges collapsed from boulders and twisted magic. Two guards walked around the platform and spoke in a language only the Titans understood.

In a harsh voice Death said, "Guards, bring us a transport, we're leaving."

The guard closest to him turned around. "Leaving?!B-but, Master, the temple is under attack!"

"Yes I know! Just go get us a transport!"

"Y-yes, Master."

The guard slowly walked off to a panel on the platform, pressed a few buttons, and entered a few commands. He returned to Life and Death a few moments later.

"Your transport will be here shortly."

As the guard went on with his business, a large airship, made out of rare metal only found deep within the caves of Rowmodea, pulled alongside the platform. The gate opened to let the two Titans aboard. Several guards that were onboard lined up in respect as Death walked across the platform and boarded the airship. He turned around and stretched out his hand to help Life aboard then looked at the guards on the platform and nodded for them to get aboard as well. Once they were all on the airship, Death turned his attention towards the pilot.

"I have never underestimated the technology that engineers can build, even with knowledge pulled from different timelines. I'm sure we will be fine."

"Death, do you really think it wise that we have taken mortals from the future to aid us now? Perhaps this is one of the reasons why we face extinction. We have put the creation of weapons of mass destruction in the hands of mortals," Life said as she examined the twisting propellers towards the back of the vessel.

"Time is irreverent, Life. We are the Titans. Everything we do is not for the better of the mortals who share this world with us, but for our benefit. Tell me, if we hadn't taken this knowledge for our own, how do you think we would escape this carnage?"

"Death, you are one of the most selfish immortals I know. You care more about your small clan of family than anything else. You could care less of the consequences of some of our actions."

"Family is everything, my dear. Nevertheless, I will not have this discussion with you, Life. All I do is for the best interest of the Titan Council," he replied as he looked over to the pilot of the aircraft. "Can we get underway?" he asked in annoyance.

The airship glided forward and began to fly away from the temple, but as it flew higher to pass over the larger towers of the structure, Death looked over the edge of the ship and saw that boulders were still hitting the temple. He wondered how much longer the temple could last before it would collapse. It wasn't looking very good, and he assumed that it would soon come crashing down. He watched as the last few remaining guards and Shadowscythes were maliciously slaughtered.

Max saw the airship pass over the temple and instantly knew that some of the Titans were trying to escape. He ran back to his men using the catapults and ordered them to launch the boulders higher into the sky. As they did so, the boulders began to miss the aircraft by just a hair and fell into the roof of the temple, weakening it even further. One boulder sailed by and managed to destroy the back right propeller, causing it to explode in a fiery rage. Due to the destruction of the propeller, the airship made a hard left towards the mountains.

Yelling at the top of his lungs Death yelled, "Life, shape shift into a bird and go!"

Yelling back at him, she yelled, "What about you?!"

"I'll be fine, just go!"

Life turned into a beautiful hawk and flew away from the airship. She turned around just as the large vessel collided with the mountain and exploded into a pool of molten debris. The explosion shook the whole valley as pieces of the smoldering wreckage fell to the ground. Before Max could see her, Life flew down to the burning rubble and examined a cave twenty feet from the crash site. She also noticed footprints in the mud leading to the dark indention of the mountain. She quickly flew across the footprints and entered the cave to see who had survived.

Dropping her bird form and landing on the floor of the dark cave, Life walked deeper into it and could hear Max's voice echoing through the stone walls. She could tell that he and his men were cheering which made her feel disgusted.

As she watched in horror at what Max had done, a hand dropped onto her shoulder. She quickly turned around to face who had touched her and found that it was Death.

"Death, I thought you were dead!"

"No, I jumped off of the airship seconds before it collided with the mountain."

"You jumped from two hundred feet? That would be roughly twenty stories! No one could survive something like that."

"Well I did, and I—"

Looking back at the wreckage of the airship, Death noticed that Max and his men were quickly approaching it. Grabbing Life's arm, he pulled her away from the entrance of the cave. As he and Life stood in the dark, damp cave and quietly breathed, they could hear Max yelling at his men. Straining to hear what Max was saying, Death moved closer to the entrance. He could hear Max say, "Search for their bodies!"

As Max watched his men tear through the smoldering rubble of the airship, he noticed the cave. He slowly approached it, but one of his commanding officers ran up and placed their hand on his shoulder.

"There is no sign of their bodies, Sir."

In hearing those words, Max's lips formed a snarl and he became enraged. He whirled around with his sword and sliced off the officer's head. As the officer's head and body fell to the ground, Max looked up from the ground and saw all of the other soldiers looking at him in shock.

In bitter anger Max said, "Well, what are you all looking at? Get back to work!"

Fearing their Master's rage, all of the soldiers ran around in a frenzied state of panic in search of the two remaining Titans.

Back in the cave, Death and Life stood in the shadows, hidden from the evil eyes of Max.

With pure hatred in his voice Death said, "Pathetic little maggots! You will suffer for your treason."

Throwing his hands up into the air, he began to chant a spell. He knew if his normal powers of death couldn't kill the traitors, then there was only one spell that no mortal could survive.

"Ylf ssorca eht tenalp, dna rettacs eht eugalp!"

Over and over, he chanted the spell, and as he did so, the clouds in the sky turned pitch black and began to swirl around like a forming cyclone. The clouds opened in the center and thousands of insects flew out of the eerie opening. Sweeping across the valley like a devastating plague, the insects destroyed everything in their path. They flew into the area where Max and his men were and began to feast on their flesh.

Hearing the screams of the mortals out in the valley, Life ran to the entrance of the cave and saw the horror she was afraid that Death would release one day.

"Death, no, you mustn't release the plague!"

Seeing that she could not break his trance, she positioned herself in front of him and placed both her soft hands on each side of his metal helmet.

"Death, look at me! Don't release the plague yet!"

Her hands glowed with ominous green power. The auras of green energy sunk into Death's helmet, and then moments later, he came back to reality. He broke out of his trance and stopped the plague with a wave of his left hand. The screams from the mortals out in the valley died shortly after, and Death walked to the entrance of his hideout. He saw several piles of bones and rotting flesh scattered across the muddy vale. He realized that if he would have let the plague last for just a few more minutes, it would have destroyed all of the mortals in the cleft. He looked around for a bit longer and saw Max ordering the remainder of his men to secure the rest of the sacred land.

In a quiet voice Life said, "Death, you can't fuel your anger by releasing the plague. If you do, then you're no better than the Gods."

Steaming with anger Death said, "They deserve to die!"

Trying to calm him down, she took hold of his hands. "Maybe so, but if you release it now it will sweep across the whole world and kill the innocent. Promise me that you won't release the plague unless such a time arise that it is our only solution."

Taking a deep breath, he said, "I promise that I won't release the plague."

"Thank you. Now, if you don't mind, I'll head out to the Ancestreyalwood Forest to find a place to hide."

Turning his back on her, he said, "Go ahead. If I need you I will write you a letter or talk to you through your mind."

Seeing that the conversation was over, Life turned herself into a small white bird to keep Max from detecting her and flew off to the south.

When Life reached the Ancestreyalwood Forest, she began to search for a perfect place to hide. She searched for hours until finally she came upon a hollowed out tree that would allow her to live in. While she used her magic to grow flowers, grass, and furniture out of the earth, Death stood in his dark, damp cave, beaming out at Max's men.

In a cruel voice Death said to himself, "I *promised that I wouldn't release the plague on your command, Life, but, you didn't make me promise not to release the Curse of the Immortals. The foolish mortals that scurry around the valley must pay for their sins...*" He closed his eyes, folded his arms across his chest, and began to chant a spell.

"Srewop dia em, dia em ni gnisaeler eht esruc fo eht slatrommi." As he chanted the spell, the white clouds began to turn black with a tint of green in them and began to come together as one massive shroud. The air became ice cold and began to freeze the land, covering it with a thin layer of ice. It began to snow on the isle, covering the layer of ice with a thick blanket of fluffy snow. Snow even fell into the ocean as the clouds stretched across the world. As it drifted above the water like an eerie fog, the water began to churn and swirl around in a massive circle until it formed a titanic maelstrom.

The current of the maelstrom was so powerful that it pulled ships that got within fifty miles from it into its stomach. The swirling water was so intense that it even created massive waves that would travel for thousands upon thousands of miles across the ocean, and when it hit a small port it would create a tsunami.

The Curse of the Immortals did not stop at the Maelstrom, however. It continued to spread like a horrific plague across the whole world. It blocked out the sun and settled over all the villages, farms, and cities like a cloud of smog. As it settled over the whole world, it released the elements of Hell itself. Acid rain fell in the farmlands destroying everything it touched, leaving families hungry, hail and rain fell in the villages and cities, smashing through windows and roofs as it fell. Villages had to evacuate and try to make it to the cities while the cities ordered all to take shelter within the catacombs.

As the clouds blotted out the sun in the Ancestreyalwood Forest, Life thought it was due to the death of Storm. She thought the power was too much for the world to take. She feared the electrical currents of magic chaotically spreading throughout the atmosphere were beginning to destroy the planet. If there was any hope in saving the world, she would have to use every ounce of her powers to restore order. She prepared to cast a calming spell towards the sky, but stopped when she noticed the clouds briefly flash green from the reflection of tainted magic then back to black.

In a horrified voice Life said to herself, "*Death, what have you done?*"

Knowing that Death had released the Curse of the Immortals, Life turned back towards her hollowed out tree and quickly ran back inside. She sat down in the center of her tree and began to meditate.

She set all her focus on the curse that was surrounding the whole world and knew if she meditated long enough she could counteract the spell.

As she tried to mentally destroy Death's enchantment, Death's voice rang in her head, causing her to disrupt her meditation.

"Why would you attempt to cast your counter spells against me, Life? What you attempt is hubris. Every moment you spend attempting to disrupt this curse only makes it stronger."

As his voice faded in her mind, Life began to realize that Death was too powerful to be stopped. Only he could disrupt this enchantment now. She slowly rose to her feet, walked over to the entrance of her tree, and looked up to notice that the pitch black clouds were beginning to break apart. As the massive clouds shattered into several little clouds, they began to turn white and fluffy. Having a small smile form on her face, Life turned around to go back inside her tree to see Death standing behind her.

"Death, what are you doing here?" Life said, startled.

"I have come to tell you that I have destroyed part of the cruse in your favor. However, the maelstrom and the horrific storms in the farmlands, villages, and cities will stay. The mortals will see and learn how cruel I can truly be."

"I don't agree with your decision, but I can see there is no changing your mind."

"I hate to sound like this evil monster, but as you and I both know, I am a necessary evil; a gateway to a greater cause."

"I know this, Death. Sometimes, it's hard to agree with you though. Our roles are complete opposites. Your role is based solely on death and the afterlife. Whereas mine is focused on birth and preparing those so they can meet you."

"Though this is true, it has never stopped us from being extremely close allies. You must have faith that everything I do is for the greater good." As he finished his sentence, he faded into the shadows as if he had only been a dream.

Chapter 7 The Plot

Max stood in the destroyed throne room and examined the aftermath of the battle. He stared blankly at the eight empty thrones. As he glared at them, one of his men came up beside him.

"Remarkable isn't it? You challenged the great Titans and survived whilst destroying them."

Still staring at the thrones Max said, "Yes...It feels good to be the ender of the Titans."

In a whisper the soldier said, "You didn't do it alone."

Turning to face the soldier, Max unsheathed his sword and placed it across the man's throat.

In a harsh voice Max said, "I destroyed the Titan Council, and I am the reason they are no more! Now, go make yourself useful and start rebuilding the temple."

"Y-yes Sir," the soldier said, clearly afraid.

As the soldier ran out of the room, Max turned to the large pool in the center of the chamber. He slowly walked up to it and knelt down.

He placed his face closer to its watery surface and in a quiet voice, he said, "Show me the bodies of Life and Death."

As the pool's images changed to show Max what he demanded, a massive chunk of the ceiling fell into the pool, causing the floor to give way from the impact.

With a hole in the center of the pool, the watery substance began to drain out onto the floor below the throne room.

Max rose to his feet and shouted, "No! How will I know if they survived or not now?!"

He thought for several minutes then remembered the plot that he had told to his secret apprentice. He walked out of the throne room and made his way down the stairs to the east entrance of the temple. He walked out into the valley and visited the locations where each Titan had fallen. He walked up to the robes of Storm and knelt down to reach inside the hole where her head would have been. As he pulled his hand out of the leather garments, he held a small chain that was firmly wrapped around a small glass vial that contained swirling purplish-blue sand.

Placing the chain and vial around his neck, Max walked a few hundred feet and reached the tattered robes of Shadow. He reached down to the top of his robes and picked up a similar chain and vial with dark gray sand contained inside. He placed it around his neck with the other vial and then began his search for Winter's body.

Though Max searched for Winter for many hours, he found no sign of her. While this angered him, he knew he didn't need to have her necklace. He knew that he only needed three out of the seven necklaces for his plan to work. He didn't bother with going over to Alashani's armor to retrieve the chain and vial of War because he assumed that it was still safely hidden beneath the floor of his former chamber.

Max returned to the temple and made his way up towards his former bed chamber to grab the chain and vial that he had hid under the middle stone in the floor. As he passed a room with a giant hole in the wall, Max noticed the charred remains of the Titan of Fire's robes and armor. He ran to the remains of Fire's garments and noticed that a chain and vial similar to the other two he had was resting on top of the charred remains of the gown. With an insidious smile, Max placed the chain around his neck and walked out of the room back out into the cold empty hallway.

As he walked into the Chamber of War, Max saw the beautifully crafted swords, maces, and axes that had been mounted on the walls when he owned the room. Part of him missed being a Titan, but the other part told him what he had done today was better than being one. He walked up to a table that rested in the middle of the room and pushed it out of the center of the room with all of his might. Once he got it up next to the wall, he returned to the center of the room and knelt down on one knee. He lifted the middle stone tile to retrieve the vial, but when he peered inside the hole, the flask was gone.

In an outraged voice Max said, "Death, you dare steal from me, the fallen Titan of War?! You will pay with your life if you are not already dead!"

He placed the stone title back in its place, walked out of the room, and headed for the throne room. From the throne room, he walked out onto the balcony and placed both his hands on the stone railing. He looked down to the valley and saw all of his men cleaning up the rubble of the destroyed areas of the temple and the bloody weapons and armor from his fallen troops. They were also picking up the bodies of the temple guards and servants and placing them in a pile to be burned.

In a loud voice to get his soldiers attention Max yelled, "Men, your attention please! Today marks the first victory against the Titans! I have learned that they were going to release the Fallen Gods upon our world to cleanse it of what they considered mortal scum! We acted just in time to save our lives! From this day forward...I call for a union! The Gods and all of us will come together as one, and we will worship the very powers that their creator, The Aikanadenbaria, gave them! I will bring the Gods back from the judgment the Titans gave them almost three millennia ago and return them to their former glory! Together we will become, The Ancient Destroyers!"

As he finished his speech, all of the men down in the valley broke out in cheer. It was at that moment Max realized that no matter how stupid or horrible his speech sounded; he could get those down in the valley to follow him blindly.

Max walked back into the throne room and looked around at the destruction he had caused. With a small smile, he left the grand chamber and went into the south side of the temple. He opened an old splintery wooden door on the left side of the south corridor. He walked through the door and noticed that it was nothing but a stone spiral staircase. He walked down the stone steps and, once he reached the bottom, he realized that the steps had led him down to the dungeons. With one look around the place, he saw cobwebs covering chunks of the walls and doorways and he knew that no one had been down in this place of confinement for centuries. Then he realized that this was where the Titans rooms were when their parents still ruled the world.

He walked through the corridors and as he did so, he could hear water dripping from somewhere else within the dungeons. He assumed that the dripping water was from the Pool of Images that had drained from the throne room. He continued to walk through the halls of the dungeons until he came to a dead end. He placed both of his hands on the wall and felt each brick. He felt that it was odd that there was a random dead end. He pushed on the center brick and it fell out of its place within the wall. Max looked through the hole and saw a small cobweb-infested chamber with a swirling portal in the center of it.

The portal ominously swirled around, producing different hues as it rotated clockwise. From the blackness of night it slowly twirled into green. From that aura the foreboding portal portrayed the essence of a glowing yellow light. As the yellowish power faded, the magical threshold expelled a shade of silver that quickly morphed into a frosty blue tint. As the chilling color darkened into a dark blue, Max began to understand what this portal truly was. He continued to watch as it changed colors. The swirling mass briefly took on a fiery orange tone before becoming blood red. As the bloody doorway that led somewhere far away faded into black again, Max realized that this portal was created by the Titans and if one were to enter the magical doorway, it would lead them to the lost fortress of the Titans. He began to hit each brick with the hilt of his sword until they were loose enough to push or grab. Once enough bricks had been removed from the wall, Max crawled through the opening.

He stood in front of the portal for a few moments to take in its power. He slowly emerged into the portal and was blinded by a bright light. When his vision cleared, he noticed that the magical threshold had teleported him inside the Fortress of the Titans.

With an evil smile Max said, "Perfect...This is the perfect place to begin freeing the Fallen Gods."

Max walked through the empty stone halls until he came upon a large room with a glass roof. In the center of the chamber rested the six statues of the Fallen Gods. The left statue looked like a normal human, but his armor had images of skulls all over it. Max knew that this Fallen God was Plentodeos, the father of Mythdariz the Titan of Death. Knowing the past history on the Gods and the Titans, he knew that the Titans truly didn't exist until *after* the fall of the Gods. He remembered reading a book in the temple's library about it.

Five of the six Gods had attempted to murder their children in fear that one day they would take their thrones from them. The children of the Gods were forsaken and they wanted revenge. It was a bloodbath and at the end of the war the six children had imprisoned all of the Gods except for the Goddess of Life. She was the only one to fall in the last battle. As Max examined the other five statues, he began to notice similarities between them and the Titans. Each one almost looked like an identical twin to the Titan counterpart. There were just slight facial differences. What struck Max as odd was only the left statue had a plaque with its name on it. However, knowing the history of the Gods, Max knew that they were lined up as the Gods of Death, Fire, Storm, Shadow, War, and Life. He examined the statues a bit longer and noticed a hole large enough for the glass vials he had around his neck to fit in their chests.

Removing the glass vials from the chains around his neck, Max began to shove the three flasks into the holes. He knew that he didn't possess the vial of the God of Death but hoped in placing the vial of Shadow in his chest it would still release him. As he placed the final vial into the third statue, a loud siren penetrated the air. As it became louder, Max clapped his hands over his ears and buried his head deeper into his shoulders. After a few moments of going off, the siren faded and a voice recording filled the air.

In what sounded like a robotic woman's voice the voice recording said, "Threat detected. Any attempt to free the Fallen Gods will result in planetary cleansing. Permission from the two must be entered to allow this release."

Max examined the room to see if he could spot any machines the Titans might have installed to keep better security. However, there was no sign of such devices. He could only conclude that the Titans were trying to trick him.

In a confused voice Max said, "The two? What the hell does that mean?"

"Permission from Mythdariz, the Titan of Death, and Selineane, the Titan of Life, must approve of this order."

"What if they are dead?" Max asked.

As if asked a sarcastic question the voice recording replied, "Impossible. The only thing that can defeat Life and Death is each other. Without Life, Death couldn't exist, and without Death, Life couldn't exist. For every mortal that dies, one must take its place in birth to keep the balance in the world. Therefore, the powers of Life and Death cannot die."

Taking in all of this information Max asked, "I see…and how do I get their permission?"

"That is prohibited."

"Look, you stupid…whatever you are, I know you are the creation of one of the Titans, and I know I am speaking to the real one right now. You are merely disguising your voice to throw me off your whereabouts. I command you to give me permission or I will destroy you."

The voice recording was silent for a moment.

"Threat detected! Threat has issued primary defense mechanisms. Prepare to die!"

The voice faded and, as the room fell silent, the light coming through the sunroof mysteriously intensified and began to heat up the ancient stone chamber. The floor became hotter and hotter until it was too hot to stand on. Max jumped up on to the Statue of Plentodeos and positioned himself behind it to stay cool.

After minutes of standing behind the statue, Max saw a small orb of yellow light with particles of sand swirling around it appear. It danced around the room and left a trail of sand as it went. Max knew who he was dealing with now. The forgotten Titan of Time was playing him.

When the glowing orb had circled the room a few times, the voice recording came back on and said, "Threat resolved. All primary functions reset to bzzzzzt."

The connection was lost due to unknown reasons as it made a horrific noise and faded. Max wasn't sure if this was another trick orchestrated by the Titan of Time, or if something had really happened that caused her to break her connection.

Max jumped down from the statue and noticed that the statues that had the vials placed in their chests were now glowing. After a few minutes of staring at the three glowing statues, he noticed that they had slid backwards; revealing three large holes that were pitch black.

Deep down in the holes, the three Gods that had been trapped within knew that their prisons had been unlocked. Each of them weakly walked up to their hole and looked up.

In a weak attempt to speak Plentodeos said, "You have broken the locks on our prisons, but we are still banished from the realm of the living. In order to free us, you must sacrifice three things. Sacrificing three items will allow us to return to your world in a state so that we can stay, but to complete our arrival we must give you a gift as well."

"Before I sacrifice anything, I want to know why you three are here instead of in the Hourglass Dome with the other Gods and their oracles," Max said.

Plentodeos let out a sigh and said, "Our children judged us all and we three were looked at as the most dangerous, so they put us here under tighter security. Finally the connection that the Titans had over this place has been broken. With you stepping foot in this sacred place as an enemy of the Titans, their ancient spell was undone."

With an evil smile spreading across his face Max said, "The power of the Gods knows no bounds. It is time that you retook what was rightfully yours. The Titans will finally be no more, and from the ashes of their demise the Gods shall rise again."

"Excellent…I knew that one day our children would fail. Now it seems only fitting that we return to rebuild what they destroyed. With your help we can return to the old days and shape this world into what it was destined to be. What will you sacrifice to allow us entrance into your world?"

Without a moment of thought Max said, "I sacrifice my mother, Taylor Dawnalow, my sister, Jessi Dawnalow, and my brother, Jack Dawnalow."

As those words left his lips, three beams of a purplish black color shot out of the three holes and shattered the glass roof. They stretched across the world in search of the sacrifices Max had offered up. In no time at all the beams retracted back into the holes and screams began to fill the air. Once the beams had retracted back far enough into the room, Max saw each beam had wrapped itself firmly around his Sister, Brother, and Mother. As the beams sucked them into the holes, their screams went from panic to a mixture of panic and fear. Just before his Mother's head disappeared into the hole, she screamed, "Max, help us! Please!"

As the three screams fell silent, the Gods had just enough strength to climb out of their prisons. They stood before Max and smiled evilly at him.

"Max...The Ancient Destroyer...We are forever indebted to you. We can never repay you enough, but here is a small gift that we think you will enjoy. The effects will take some time to complete," Plentodeos said.

"Wait, how did you know of the union I created?"

"The Titans aren't the only ones who are gifted with foresight. Max, we can show you things that the Titans could not. We can share secrets that the Titans wished to keep buried. All this can be yours if you let us help you," the God of Fire announced.

"However, if it weren't for my whispers, you would have never discovered the spell that allowed you to conquer Death and survive the assault on the sacred Titan Temple," the God of Storms replied.

"That was your voice I heard?" Max asked in shock.

"It was indeed."

Plentodeos and the other two Gods raised their right hands into the air and began to chant a spell as their hands began to glow with dark magic.

In a deep, dark voice Plentodeos said, "Max, the Destroyer of the Titans, is hereby blessed with the powers of the Death God, Fire God, and Storm God!"

Dark magic exploded from within Max and, when the roar of the explosion died, he fell backwards, unconscious.

Max awoke an hour later and his brown eyes had changed to pure black with no white showing, his teeth had become sharp points, and his peach colored skin had turned gray with sadness. He was a demon in human form.

This transformation created a rift in Death's design for Max and set off an alarm in his mind. He knew what Max had done and what he had become. He also knew that he would attempt to bring back the other Gods still trapped within the Hourglass Dome. He knew that he had to warn Life of this mishap, so he created a small baby bird made entirely out of bones. He grabbed a small piece of parchment from one of the books that had been thrown out of the temple by the blasts. The paper was burned in several places, but was still suitable enough to write on. He used an extra bone and his own blood to write the letter. Once he had the letter written, Death plucked a strand of his white hair, tied the letter to the small bird's leg, and sent it on its way to Life's hiding place within the Ancestreyalwood Forest.

Chapter 8 The Letter

Life was standing at the opening of her hollowed out tree, staring out at the forest around her, and watched the animals wander around. She was about to return to the confines of her evergreen when the small bone bird appeared and landed on the ground in front of her. As she examined the small creature, she noticed the letter tied to the animal's leg. She quickly untied it, released the bird as she walked into her tree, and unfolded the missive. The letter read:

Life, this is urgent. You need to come back to the Crystalrock Peaks. It's about Max. If you haven't felt the atrocities he has committed yet, you soon will.

Death

Life immediately dropped the letter and ran out of her temporary home. As she reached the peak of her run, she jumped into the air, and transformed into a small white bird with a shade of lime green on its wings. She flew high into the sky; above the clouds and, as she flew towards the Crystalrock Peaks, she began to wonder what was so urgent that would cause Death to risk her life by making her come out of hiding.

Death had his back turned towards his dark, damp cave and waited for Life to arrive.

As she flew in from the south and landed in front of him, he said, "Life...It's good to see you're still alive. I'm sure you are wondering why I have asked you to come out of hiding, am I correct?"

"What's this about, Death? You know it's extremely risky to be coming out of hiding during this time. What is it you need me to know?"

"I know this is risky, but it's of high importance. You see...it's Max..."

"What about him?"

Looking at Life with his emotionless, glowing eyes Death said, "It's nothing on his betrayal...Its' just that..." he turned away from her to face the inside of his underground chamber." Max is adding to his army."

"Of course he is getting more men to join his army. He's scared, Death. He knows that the two most powerful Titans are still out there plotting their return."

"You don't understand..."

"What do you mean? Of course I understand. Max is being a fool as always."

Death whirled around and said, "Gods, Life. Gods..."

With a puzzled look on her face, she said, "I, I don't understand. Why would he usher the Fallen Gods back into the world? They can't be trusted. As soon as they get what they want, they will toss him aside."

"Only a God has a chance at being successful in killing the last two Titans. If he manages to bring back the Gods that we imprisoned millions of years ago, the events that will take place will become an apocalypse for immortals and mortals alike."

"But, Death, how could Max even begin to bring back the Gods? He's mortal now, and he has very little power."

"When he killed the other Titans, he took something from each corpse after they were destroyed. The items he took were the very items we confiscated from the Gods when we imprisoned them."

Gasping in shock Life said, "The vials of essences? No, he can't!"

"He can, and he is. Have you not felt the unsettling disturbance that settles all around us ever since I released the Curse of the Immortals? The Ancient Gods are being awakened."

"But how did he even get the vials, and how many did he get?"

"I was a fool. I remembered to take the one I found in Max's room from Alashani, but I never even thought about it with the other Titans. He obtained three."

"Well then, we have quite the dilemma. How do you propose we stop him?"

In a low voice Death said, "I don't know, but we must move quickly if we want to destroy this conspiracy against us. If he manages to bring the Gods back and return their nefarious powers to them, it will be a catastrophic event with our end."

"How will it be our end? We have endured where others have failed. Eventually we will destroy the Gods once again."

"Unfortunately not, my dear friend. The Gods aren't the only ones we should worry about. The Darkness has been alerted to the atrocities Max has committed. Its dark master has begun his search for us once again." Death looked into the sky and noticed the sun was beginning to set behind the mountain wall. "It's getting late and Max's patrols will be coming around soon. Come into my cave for the night."

They entered the cave and Death made a small campfire.

Looking into the fire Life said, "Won't this attract the attention of Max's patrols?"

"No because I have placed an illusion on the cave so that it looks like its pitch black inside."

"So...When do you think he will begin bringing back the Gods?"

"He already has. If we still had control of the temple, I could use the Pool of Images to spy on him."

Tears began to stream down Life's face and weeping came soon after. Death placed his armored hand on her shoulder to try and calm her.

"Life, I know why you're crying. I miss the other Titans too, but we must stay strong. We can't spend our time mourning over the fallen."

"I know, it's just...I can't believe Max did this."

"His betrayal caught all of us off guard. We weren't prepared for his deception. However, we both need to rest. Try and get some rest. You'll need to leave at first light."

While they slept, Life had a vision. She stood within the Titan Fortress. As she walked around the area, she found herself in the chamber that the three Gods had been imprisoned in. She saw Max enter and shove the vials of essences into the first three statues. She could hear the muffled robotic voice that she knew was truly the Titan of Time.

As the vision played out in her mind, she thrashed around on the rocky floor. Though she tried to get a better visual of the situation at hand, Life couldn't control this vision like most. Suddenly, the three Gods stood before her. Though they were looking at her, she knew that they were truly staring at Max.

The vision slowly faded away as the Gods and Max conversed. Life knew that though the Gods had been freed, it would take some time for them to regain their strength. Max would have to leave them behind so that they could absorb the magic within the fortress.

The next morning came with even more bitter weather than the day before. When Life awoke, she noticed that it was extremely cold outside and that Death was standing at the opening of his cave.

Without even turning around to face her Death said, "Good morning, Life...You had a vision, didn't you?"

With a puzzled look on her face Life said, "Yes...How did you know?"

"You were muttering in your sleep. What was your vision about?"

Closing her eyes, Life tried to remember what the vision had been. "I saw...our Fortress. Max has released the three Gods there."

"We shared this vision, Life...What you just told me, I envisioned as well."

"What should we do to stop him?"

"We must recruit the men that are still loyal to the Titans."

"Should we recruit the mortals in the Nygensa Nation?"

Thinking for a moment, Death pondered the situation. Pacing back and forth, he was silent for what seemed like an hour. "Yes, but watch who you tell in the Nygensa Nation. Max has many spies. Don't even ask those who are in league with the Covenant, they are already on his side."

"Okay, but why must I watch who I tell in the Nygensa Nation? The Covenant isn't welcome within their territory."

"Some of them are disguised as Nygenians. They were sent to spy on the denizens of Golmasik, the capital of the Nygensa Nation. Now Life, I hate to rush you off, but now is the best time to head back to your shelter. Max's patrols are not in the area, and they won't be again until noon."

With a small sigh Life said, "Very well...We will meet again another day perhaps."

She transformed into a hawk and took to the sky.

"Remember, Life, do not go to the mortal lands just yet, it is still too dangerous. I couldn't bear to lose you as well."

Instead of flying back to her shelter like Death had told her to, Life flew off to the capital city of Golmasik to seek help from the leader of the Nygensa Nation. She passed over thousands of acres of farmland, several small villages, and a few neighboring cities that were all part of the Nygensa Nation. When she arrived at the capital, she flew over the other sections of the city and went straight to the palace that lay in the center. She knew the head leader of the Nygensa Nation would be there and it was vital that she spoke with him. With cunning speed, she flew through the palace doors as a soldier walked out and flew through the outstanding halls of the palace until she reached the center room where the stone throne rested. She circled the room once then landed in the center of the chamber in front of the throne. Still in her hawk form, Life bowed her head before the King.

"Your majesty, it is a great honor to finally meet you."

Terrified at the fact that a hawk was talking to him, the King grabbed his sword that was attached to his side and pointed it at her.

Seeing that the King was frightened by her, Life morphed back into her true form. "Great King of Golmasik, allow me to introduce myself. I am Selineane, the Titan of Life. I come to you on a dire importance."

"A Titan? I thought you only watched over us."

With a bit of a chuckle in her voice Life said, "Well, we do watch over all of our children, but we also are involved with your day to day actions."

"I see...why then, have you come to me?"

"I come to you to ask for your help. "The King remained silent to see what else she would say. "You see, recently we fell victim to a horrid betrayal, and because of the deceit several of the Titans have fallen. Have you not noticed the change in weather?" she continued.

In shock the King said, "What?! I have noticed the changes, but I thought the Titans were angry about something. I assumed that they were taking their wrath out on us. That's why I have had the whole city on lockdown. I didn't want anyone getting hurt by this horrible weather. Who is the one that betrayed you?"

With a grim face Life said, "His name is Max, Max Dawnalow." Thunder could be heard from inside the palace as Life uttered his name. "He murdered all of the Titans except for Death and me."

With a surprised look on his face the King said, "Did you say, Max? He was part of my army for several years, but he tried to kill me in my sleep. He wanted the throne so he could rule the Nygensa Nation. I kicked him out of the city and he swore that he would get his revenge on me. Oh, Great Titan of Life, why did he betray the Titans?"

"It started out when he came to us for help. He showed a great potential for the role of War. The stamina he mustered, the will of force. For many years he was a great asset to us. We gave him the powers of War, but soon he started to take his powers for granted. He would attack the smaller villages that were the main worshipers of any of us except him and kill everyone. Death saw this as an act of treason and took the powers from him, but Max saw that as an act of betrayal and he then led an army to our temple and killed all but Death and me."

With anger filling his veins the King said, "What can I do to help?"

"You can start by putting your army under the Titan Council's control."

"Consider it done."

"Great. I must go now. I've come against the Titan of Death's wishes. He surely knows about me coming here by now. Though this is most likely the case, Death will still want to hear about the newly formed army. As soon as I tell Death, we will return to lead your men into battle."

"I'll have the army ready for when you return."

As she left the throne room the King yelled out to her. "Do you think you could do something about this storm?"

Life smiled and said, "I'm sure Death will make the storm stop when he finds out about the new army."

Once again, Life took on the form of a hawk and flew off to the Crystalrock Mountains to tell Death the great news. She arrived at his cave at one o'clock knowing that Max's patrols would not be in the area. When she arrived at the cave, she dropped to her knees in disbelief. Looking into the darkness of Death's hideout, seeing the pools of blood, she assumed that Death had been murdered. However, she saw a message written on the ground constructed out of the pools of crimson color. She stood up and looked at the dark puddles closer to see what they said. After a few seconds of looking at the blood, she made out the words *Dreadscar Valley*. She started to walk away from the cave, but quickly began to run. She ran faster and faster away from the dark indention of the mountain until she reached the peak of her run. She jumped up into the air and transformed into a brown and white hawk with armor on her head and chest. She turned to her left and headed for the Dreadscar Valley.

Chapter 9 The Trip

The trip was dangerous and Life knew that even if she made it to the Dreadscar Valley alive, she was not guaranteed to find her friend, Death. As she flew past the volcano in the Dreadscar Valley, she saw that several small farmsteads were on fire. She flew down to the ground and, as she landed, she saw several farmers fleeing as their pathetic excuses for crops burned. Why anyone would try to grow anything here was beyond her. She began to take back to the air when she saw a message written in the dirt next to a burning crop. She hopped over to it and looked at it through the small eyes of her bird form. Examining the scribbles, she made out the word *Netherfeild.* As she spread out her wings to fly back up into the air, she noticed a blackened rose that let off streams of black mist. She knew this plant as the Rose of Death. She took on her true form, knelt down next to the flower, and plucked one of the blackened thorns from its black stem. Placing the thorn in the lining of her green robes, Life took on her bird form and flew back up into the air. As she made her journey deeper into the Dreadscar Valley, knowing that Death was hiding in the deeper parts of corrupted, dark vale, she came up with a plan to use the poisonous thorn on Max if she ever got close enough to jab it into his tan flesh.

After hours of searching, Life was just about to give up when she saw a well armored man wielding a sword that only one life form owned.

Screaming at the top of her lungs Life said, "Death, is that you?!"

The man turned around to face his visitor. "Life, I see you got my messages."

"Yes, when I first saw your cave, I thought of the worst," she replied as she landed on the ground in front of him.

With a small chuckle Death said, "Max's men attacked me, but were no match for the Titan of Death. I assume you're back with news?"

"How did you know I didn't go back to my hiding place?"

"I'm the Titan of Death, Life. I see everything and besides, it would be beyond my judgment if you would have actually listened to me in going back to the Ancestreyalwood Forest. I knew that you would go to Golmasik instead."

"I guess I should tell you what I have obtained. The King of Golmasik has pledged his men to our service. He wants to see Max dead just as much as we do. He told me that Max used to serve him as a bodyguard, but he tried to kill him in his sleep so he could have the throne," Life said.

Death nodded in agreement. "It would appear that Max's corruption runs deeper than we once thought. This isn't Max's first betrayal. For all we know, when he was a young man practicing in the arts of magic, he got mad at his master and killed him."

"It seems that way, doesn't it? However, we can't worry about his past. Now that we have our army, should we make our return?" Life asked.

Shaking his head Death replied, "Not yet, Life. Max is still too strong. Once he finishes freeing the other Gods, he will become weaker."

With a puzzled look on her face Life asked, "What do you mean? Wouldn't he become stronger with the aid of the Gods?"

"No, the Gods will want their..."He trailed off into thought.

"What is it?" she said, grabbing his arm.

"He is going to have the few Gods that he has freed make him a God. He is freeing them in a state where they aren't fully in this world. I know this because I just had a vision of them making him a God. It's quite clever, really. After spending so much time in the library he had to have known how deceitful the Gods truly are. In making him one of them, they can't get rid of him."

"If they make him a God, then..."

"He will have a higher chance at killing us," he said, finishing her sentence. "Our time to come out of hiding and take our revenge is soon at hand."

"One thing before we discuss events any further. Will you make the storm that surrounds the world stop?" she curiously asked.

"Of course I will. Now that we have an army, I have no reason to keep this horrific storm alive. You should know, however, that the maelstrom won't fade away. Its power will dwindle, but it now has a life of its own. It is now part of our very existence." He looked out across the darkened vale and saw some of Max's men snooping around. "It would appear that Max has men scouting out here for us as well."

Life looked out towards the direction Death was examining and saw the small group of mortals searching for them. "He must be really desperate if he has to conduct a search clear across the world."

"Apparently. How we ever saw a potential in him is beyond me. He is naive, just like most mortals."

"After everything that has occurred, we will come out of this stronger. We must move forward…What is the first step?"

"We are going to do what needs to be done. We will use our combined powers to create a grand city for our army to show our thanks. However, we will need to come up with a name, a name that will symbolize strength and freedom." He paced back and forth in front of Life a few times then stopped suddenly and looked at her. "How about Forza Liberta? It can float close to our temple, which will allow us to travel to and from there easily."

Life excitedly nodded in agreement.

"It can float in the Ancestreyalwood Forest just south of the Crystalrock Peaks. However, the power needed to keep a city made entirely out of stone afloat is beyond what we can muster right now. We will need very powerful magic to hold up the structure. The materials we will need to accomplish such a feat will be the metals found deep within the world," he finished.

"Yes, it could work. We can harness the raw energy from the ore and use it to create a large magical sphere."

"Precisely. We will use what this world has to offer to gain victory."

Overexcited at Death's plan Life said, "That is a splendid idea. Let's get going so we can start building the city."

Life began to take on her hawk form, but Death laid his hand on her shoulder. "You have flown enough for one day. I'll fly us back to Rowmodea Isle. After all, being Death has its advantages. I don't only have power over death, I have also learned how to shape shift into a dragon."

While saying that, Death fell to his knees and let out a ferocious roar so fierce that it startled several inhabitants. With a loud crack and a flash of light, Death transformed into a large, black dragon that had armor on its chest, head, and tail. He also had large black crystal-like spikes on his tale and snout, and his pupils became slivers instead of ovals.

"When did you learn to do that?" she asked in shock.

"That doesn't matter right now. Ask me again if and when we have won the war. Now, get on. We have a long ways to fly if we want to begin constructing our grand city."

As Life crawled onto his scaly, black back and adjusted herself, Death flew into the dark sky and began to fly back to Rowmodea Isle.

Back in the beautiful lands of Rowmodea, Death flew into the Ancestreyalwood Forest. He glided into an open circular area surrounded by trees and the mountain wall that separated the forest from the valley the Titan Temple was in. He settled down on a stone slap that stretched from the stone wall and allowed Life to climb down and get a footing on it. He then took on his true form and walked up next to her.

"Life, this is a good spot for our city. We have plenty of stone to use from the mountains, and look at those four large caves surrounding this open area. They would work perfectly to store the magical spheres."

They both worked hard for several hours teleporting to the planet's core to salvage the rare metal ore. Once they had enough to make the four powerful spheres, Death used his powers to harvest the raw energy from the ore fragments.

The spheres were large, rippling ovals that shined with the power of the sun and had electrical currents surging through them. With a little bit of sacrificed magic, they would be able to use and recycle Life's and Death's powers. Once they were all formed and in their appropriate locations, Death used his powers to activate them. Four large blue beams shot out of the caves, connecting in the middle. With the four beams all meeting in the middle with the energy, it began to create a small sphere of magic. Death was insured that it wasn't harmful and walked over to Life who was sitting on the stone slab, meditating.

Both Life and Death walked to the edge of the rocky platform and stretched out both of their hands. In unison, they chanted a spell that not one mortal had heard or been witness to.

"Etaerc eht tsetaerg ytic nwonk ot nam."

Hundreds of tiny different colored beams shot out of both their hands and began to carve away the mountains that surrounded them. In time, the beams took the carved pieces of the mountains and began placing them to create the city. There was a large stone platform that would allow for building the houses, towers, and buildings so that they wouldn't crumble. There was a large tower that rose in the center of the city and there was a stone wall placed around the platform so that no one would fall off to their death. With the city completely constructed, all of the small beams that were still pouring from the two Titans' hands gradually picked up the large city and lifted it into the air.

Rising into the sky and sliding into place within the four beams, gravity slipped away and it remained afloat. Life slowly looked at Death with fearful eyes as they concluded their spell.

"What happens now?"

Looking at her, Death patted her on her back and said, "We have the King send his men over to this island so we can place them in their new home."

Life flew back to Golmasik and told the King of the new city that his men would be stationed in. To help out, he gave as many ships as needed to shuttle his men over to Rowmodea as he bid the Titan of Life farewell. After hours of endless waiting, Death finally saw several ships on the horizon. It only took them a few minutes to get them in the city; however. Once they were all under the structure, Life waved her hand into the air and teleported everyone up to the city above. Death wasn't very pleased due to the fact that several of the soldiers had brought their wives and children with them.

Later that night, after Death had vented to Life about the women and children coming along, they both sat in the large central tower and discussed important events that were coming to pass.

"This is it, isn't it? The coming battles will determine who the victor will be."

"It will indeed, unfortunately I will not be fighting beside you," Death said as he looked over to the balcony.

"What? You're leaving?" Life asked.

"Yes. I must go on a journey."

"I'll go with you. When do we leave?"

"There isn't a *we* in this. I'm going alone. Please don't ask questions, but listen. You can't go because I need you here to help the men in the coming battles. I had another vision shortly after you teleported us up here. Max will attack the city from the forest floor. He is going to attempt to destroy us here and now to end this. He also believes that by destroying us he can summon our fallen foe that fled this world almost four millenniums ago."

"But, Death..."

Looking at her harshly Death continued, "No, let me finish. I want you to take every soldier down to the forest floor and fight. I will be back before the final battle with Max comes to a close. I just need to figure something out, something that requires me to enter the Shadow Realms."

With tear filled eyes Life hugged him and said, "We are at war, Death. Promise me you will stay safe."

He hugged her back to assure that he would and then turned towards the balcony. As he walked onto its platform, he opened the portal to the Shadow Realms and left, leaving Life alone in the circular candlelit chamber of the tower.

As the portal closed Life quietly said, "I love you...Stay safe, please."

She knew if something happened to him, she wouldn't be able to live with herself.

Chapter 10 Fall of Forza Liberta

The next morning came without a hint of hatred, for it was a very peaceful morning down on the forest floor. Birds were chirping, deer were prancing around, and even the venomous snakes were minding their own business while they hung from the branches of the trees. Life knew deep down inside her gut, however, that something bad was brewing. She stood on the balcony of the central tower within Forza Liberta and waited for something to happen. Finally, as the forest grew silent, deep within the dense fog that covered the forest floor Life saw Max and his gruesome army moving through the fog to the center of the opening right below the city. She quickly gathered all her men and teleported down to the forest floor.

Screaming at the top of her lungs Life said, "Men, Max's army will be in range at any moment. They will stop at nothing to destroy our army in one swift, brutal strike. It's our job to protect the magic within this forest. If Max destroys the magical spheres that are being contained within the four caves a lot of lives will be lost, and Max will be that much closer in his quest for victory. Go now, and protect this area for your wives and children up in the city."

"How is it he has more men following him? Wasn't most of his army destroyed at the Titan Temple?" one soldier asked.

"There were other followers from the mortal government of the Covenant thinly spread across the world. He rallied them together and now uses them to fight in his war," Life replied.

The soldiers who had brought their families with them were all nervous about their wives and children being so close to the battle and, to make things worse, they were watching from the city wall. The soldiers moved into small groups and readied themselves for a battle that would not be easily won.

Out of the fog, Max and his army came into view. The first thing Life noticed was that Max was leading his army this fight. Looking at Max caused memories of his betrayal to rush back into her mind. She remembered the day he had assaulted the temple clearly enough to know that Max had hidden behind his men for most of the fight, then took credit for all the kills.

A loud explosion rang in Life's ears causing her to come back to reality. Looking around franticly, she spotted the captain of her army.

Screaming as loud as possible, so she could be heard over the fighting Life yelled, "Captain, status report."

The Captain turned to face Life and yelled, "Max is ordering his men to attack us with heavy explosives while he destroys the magical spheres holding up the city. I was about to send some of the men to stop him."

"No, Captain, I shall deal with him personally. Keep pressing the attack."

As the Captain ran off to join his men on the battlefield, Life saw something move from the corner of her eye. She quickly turned her head in the direction of the movement and saw Max heading for the first power source.

With a bitter taste in her mouth Life said, "Max, you are a damn fool, and you will pay for what you have done."

Life ran after him at full speed and leaped into the air. Landing on the ground, she transformed into a ferocious white tiger. She dug her claws into the damp ground as she darted after him. The chase seemed to take longer than expected and Life felt that Max was moving more quickly than a mortal should have been able too. She finally caught up to him just as he entered the first cave out of the four that protected the magical spheres.

Life took on her true form and shouted, "Max, stop, you don't know what you're doing!"

Not knowing that he had been followed, Max turned around in surprise. "Life...How wonderful it is to see my old friend," he said in a sarcastic, demonic tone.

With an evil glare Life said, "Look at yourself! You have become a monster! You have become the very thing you swore to protect this world from and for that we cannot be friends, Max, we must be enemies."

With a puzzled look Max said, "Why are we enemies, Life?"

Outraged by a sarcastic question Life screamed, "You betrayed us, Max! You killed several of the Titans. Not only that, but you have joined The Darkness. How could you even consider doing a thing like that?"

"The Titans who perished deserved what they got and, as for my new transformation, it has allowed me to do things that only you pathetic Titans could dream of. You used me. I took the power of the Titan Council to a new level. I made the mortals fear us and how did you repay me? You took my powers and made me mortal! The Gods, on the other hand, witnessed the power I mustered and saw great potential to use it. They made me one of them because of my abilities."

"We took your gifts because you were using them for evil and the Titans only use their powers for good. I truly am sorry for what we have to do, Max, but it is for your own good. If you cannot withdrawal your hatred, then you leave me no choice but to end you."

She twisted her wrist above her head and produced a swirling aura of emerald green power. From the pureness she conjured came forth her staff. She darted towards him as she produced a spell from the emerald stone that rested at the top of the legendary weapon.

Dodging the incantation with incredible agility, Max knew he was at equal with her. Then, without warning, Max raised his hand and shot a bolt of dark energy out of his fingertips, sending it towards Life, causing her to be thrown backwards and land on her back.

Everything went dark for a short time. When she regained consciousness, the first magical sphere was contracting in and out as its contained fury was released. Devastating ripples coarsely moved throughout its structure as it weakened. Suddenly it exploded in an electrical rage, sending out uncontained power in all directions. Max was running out of the cave in pursuit for the second sphere as Life crawled away from the electrical threads of power zipping across the ground.

Life leaped up off the ground and chased after him. She had to stop his insidious plot to destroy all the good, otherwise the world would be suffocated with a cloak of darkness. Upon reaching the second cave, she noticed that Max was already preparing to destroy it.

Running up behind him, she said, "Max, stop this madness, you have no clue what you are doing!"

Turning to face her once again, he said, "When are you going to give up? You know you can't win. Without your other half, without your secret love, Death, you are weak and pathetic."

"You're a damned fool, Max! You should have never betrayed the Titans."

With an evil laugh, Max gripped the hilt of his sword. "It doesn't matter. Even if Death were to return, it would be too late! Your precious city will fall and everyone will die with it!"

He swung his sword with incredible force against the sphere of raw magic and allowed his sword to disrupt the stability contained inside. The result of his rage caused it to explode with such fury that it threw Life backwards, and she hit the cave wall behind her. While she was unresponsive, Max ran out of the cave and headed for the third. When she awoke, she was surrounded by black smoke and flames. Rising to her feet, but staying low, Life ran as fast as she could out of the smoldering cave. She looked up into the sky as she coughed and laid her emerald green eyes on *Forza Liberta*.

With two out of the four magical spheres destroyed, the city was beginning to lean forward from her position.

Looking back to the ground, Life closed her eyes and said to herself, "*Death, where are you? The city will fall soon and Max is unstoppable.*"

As she complained, she remembered what Death had told her many years before. Wishing for things wasn't going to get her anywhere. Keeping her head high and proud, she turned back into her tiger form and dashed for the third source of power, when another explosion rang through the air and the beam that held the city up from the third cave winked out.

With the third sphere obliterated, Forza Liberta leaned closer to the ground than before. It was only a matter of time before the city would fall out of the sky. Life knew if she had her men stay there any longer they all would parish. She had to make a choice, though. Would she save the soldiers that were fighting on the forest floor, or would she save the women and children that were clinging for their lives up in the city? She took in a deep breath and closed her eyes for a brief time. She knew she couldn't save them all; it would take way too much time to do that. When she made her decision, she darted for the frontlines of the battlefield. Running up to the Captain, Life took on her true form.

"Captain, order the retreat! The city is about to fall!"

Looking up into the sky, the Captain saw only one beam struggling to hold up the city. He looked back to the battlefield and yelled, "Fallback! Retreat! Head for the Crystalrock Peaks!"

All of the soldiers took off running full speed into the mountains with Max's men right behind them. They all thought of their wives and children up in the city, but knew that there was nothing they could do to save them. As the last few dozen were running under the city to get to the mountains, the last power beam winked out as the magical sphere exploded.

Forza Liberta plummeted towards the ground, and the women and children screamed and cried as it did. Faster and faster it fell out of the sky. Forza Liberta hit the ground with a massive quake, exploding into millions of pieces and tearing apart that part of the forest.

Max had taken shelter in the last cave while the city fell to the ground and, when it was all over, he walked out of the fourth and final cave and looked around. As the dust settled, he made out hundreds of bodies. All five hundred of Max's men fell due to the city falling, and because of his reckless tactics, he had killed them all. He had been so focused on destroying the Titan Council and their army that he had not thought about the harm it would bring to his army. Although he lost his entire army, he was not moved by it even the slightest bit. Forza Liberta was in ruin and, with that, his goal was almost complete. He looked around the ruins of the area for a while and saw a young woman's body buried underneath the rubble of the city. All that could be seen was her pale, white arm and that of a smaller child's hand in hers. Their hands were clenched together and Max assumed that this had been a mother and her only child. With an evil smile spread across his face, Max turned away from the destroyed city and headed for the Titan Temple.

Chapter 11 The Warning

As Life and her army pressed forward and deeper into the mountains, Max made his way up the large stone steps of the Titan Temple. Max stood on the Spire of Wisdom in wait for his Godly companions. After nearly an hour of standing in wait for them, Max was about to turn around and give up on them when they emerged from the cliffs. He turned towards the stairs that would lead down to the ground floor so he could greet his friends, when a small, glowing blue ball appeared. It floated in the center of the room and began to glow brighter and brighter until it hurt to look at it. It began to grow in size and took the shape of a human. The brightness began to dim and Max could finally make out what the little blue ball had become. He realized that the blue orb was in fact a wisp. The little manifestation had taken on the form of his deceased Father. Even as a ghost, his Father continued to watch over him and judge his decisions.

Staring in shock, Max looked at his Father and said, "F-father, what are you doing here?"

In a chilling, unforgiving voice, his Father said, "*Max, I am so disappointed in you. You have done the unforgivable. You have destroyed everything the Titans fought to protect! You have doomed this planet. The decisions you have made are just the beginning of a terrible plague that will swallow this world whole.*"

"You know nothing of the truth behind me actions, Father! I did what was best for the mortal people of this world. I freed them from the tyrannical reign of the Titan Council."

"*I know exactly why you did all of this…You felt betrayed, but I tell you that you will be punished for your sins, Max. I may have been the first to fall by your hand of evil, but you have thrown everything out of balance. You feel the Titans were Tyrants? The reign of The Darkness will be much…worse.*"

"The Titans got what was coming for them. I am not afraid of them like you were, Father! I am a God now, a true enemy to the Titans. Now, be gone, and never return!"

Slowly Max's Father faded away, leaving him alone on the tower once more.

Far across the grassy plains, Life led her men up the large grassy hills overlooking the Ancestreyalwood Forest. As they walked through the rocks and dirt, Life could feel the emotions that all her men were experiencing. She could sense the anger of losing the battle, the sadness from those who had lost their wives and children, and the doubts from those who felt that they were fighting a lost cause. It brought tears to her eyes, but she quickly blinked them away. She began to wonder what Death would think of her letting Forza Liberta fall. She knew he already knew about the loss because every one of the people that died in that battle would be flooding the Shadow Realms in wait for their final judgment. It would take quite some time to usher all of them into their final resting places.

She saw an opening in the mountains that was surrounded on three sides. She led all the soldiers into the enclosed area and then turned around to face them. "Alright, men, we shall rest here for the night. I also want to say I am very sorry for what happened to your families, but know this—I will do all in my power to help all of you get through this, but for now we must rest," she said in a quiet voice.

As the men set up campfires and tents, Life slowly walked a few feet and used her titanic powers to create a small hut. It was made entirely out of earth, roots, and leaves, with tulips, roses, and daisies scattered around it. As soon as the camp was set up, Life sat down with all of her men and had a small meal. She took hold of the two soldiers' hands that sat on each side of her and motioned everyone to grab each other's hands.

"Oh, Father, I beseech you. In these trying times, we ask for your guidance. Please guide us with your love and comfort. Amen."

"Forgive me, Mistress, but you are a Titan. Why would you be praying to another deity?" the soldier to her right asked.

"My dearest, Leopold," she began, and the soldier was surprised she knew his name. "The history of the Titans is very jumbled. In all reality, the Titans didn't exist for quite some time. First came the two brothers, who were created by the magic the world offered. From them came the six Gods. The Gods requested the gift of having children of their own. The demigods, also known as us Titans, rose from that request. In praying to the one that helped in the decision of our very existence, I give my ultimate loyalty to him."

"Again, I ask for you to forgive my inquiries."

"There is no need to apologize for something that you didn't fully understand," she concluded with a smile, and returned her attention to her meal.

After she had finished eating, she retired to her small earth hut earlier than any of the men. She walked into the hut and placed her staff up against the wall close to her bed. Growing tired, she climbed onto her earth bed and closed her eyes for some much needed rest to regain her energy after all of the day's events.

Chapter 12 Fights Between Immortals

As she fell into complete darkness, everything around her became hazy. Life awoke thinking it was already morning, only to find she was very sweaty and laying on lava rock. She rose to her feet and slowly looked around, frightened. She began to walk around the area as fire began to consume everything. She cautiously continued to walk around the mysterious place until she finally came upon a large stone altar surrounded by a pool of lava. As she moved closer to the altar, a creature consumed by flames emerged from it. She inched herself even closer to the altar to get a better look at the creature and, as she did, she knew by the details of the facial structure that the creature was male and that she had known him from somewhere before. Then it dawned on her, for how could she forget her friend, the Titan of Fire?

"Do not be afraid, Life."

"I'm not afraid. I've missed you, Fire," she replied in a voice of sadness.

"I've missed you too, my dear friend. There is so much to talk about in so little time."

With a confused look on her face Life said, "What do you mean by little time?"

With a small smile on his face Fire said, "The final battle draws near, Life..."

"How can I kill Max and the other Gods? Without Death it seems impossible," she said as tears began to stream down her face.

"Have faith, Life. When needed the most, Death will return..."

Things began to become blurry and the Titan of Fire began to fade as the fire and lava that surrounded the altar consumed the rest of the area. Everything went dark then back to light as Life awoke breathing very heavily. She stood up from her bed and walked out of the hut to find the men packing up all their camping supplies. Since the men were packing up, Life thought she should do the same. She turned around and used her powers to make the hut retract back into the earth. As the roots wiggled back into the ground, Life gave a peaceful smile as the presence of the Captain was felt.

She turned around to him and said, "Good morning, Captain. Are the men ready to move on?"

"Yes, Mistress, but before we move on, I should inform you that after you retired last night, a strange man appeared. He wore peculiar tattered and torn robes. At first glance he came off as one who practiced in the darker arts of magic."

With a surprised look on her face Life asked, "Darker as in... Blood magic?"

"No. More like demonic energies. Blood magic was destroyed long ago wasn't it?"

"Captain, magic can't be destroyed. It simply changes form. However, users of blood magic were hunted to extinction long ago. Besides that point, what is this man's name and is he still around?"

"He went by the name of Herladrick and, yes, he is over by the opening of this place. He told me that Max killed his family, and he wants revenge."

"Unfortunately we have very little time for small talk. I will chat with him briefly as we make our way towards the Titan Fortress."

She led her men out of the area and began their search for the forgotten Fortress of the Titans. As they walked through the mountains, Life could not wrap her mind around the reason she had that dream. She knew obsessing over it wasn't going to help any, so she tried her best to brush it off her mind and focus on getting to the fortress. She walked over towards the man who had appeared overnight and patted him on his shoulder.

"Tell me a little bit about yourself, soldier." Life began.

"Mistress, there isn't much to know. I am a wielder of magic… Only I prefer the darker aspects of it."

"There is no need to fear me, Herladrick. I will not judge you. I find it admirable that you wish to help us bring Max to an end."

"Do you think we will win?"

"Only time will tell." Life concluded as she returned her focus to finding the fortress.

Back at the Titan Temple, Max and the other Gods knew Life and her army were almost to the Titan Fortress.

"Fellow Gods, the time has finally come to take your revenge on the Titans. Selineane, the Titan of Life has an army headed for the lost fortress that I freed you from. Although my men have been killed in the destruction of Forza Liberta, we will not lose because we are the

Gods! So what do you say? Shall we go and destroy the last of the Titans once and for all?" Max asked in a ferocious, demonic voice.

"What of our brothers still trapped within the Hourglass Dome?" the God of Death asked.

"When we have defeated the last of the Titans, we shall free them. They have been imprisoned for far too long. They aren't strong enough to aid us in this fight. No, we go alone. Let us go and defeat the last of the Titans and rebuild the world on their bones."

As the other Gods let out a loud roar of cheers and levitated into the air, Max used his demonic powers to form a shell of demonic red flames around his body to lift himself off the ground and followed his Godly friends towards the fortress.

Life continued to push her men up the grassy slopes to the fortress as it came into view. Once they reached the stone doors, Life used her powers to open them. The moment she stepped inside the fortress walls, the memories of the past began flooding back into her mind. A tear fell down her cheek, and she knew more would follow. She didn't want to cry, so she kept her mind busy by ordering her men to begin building barriers around the fortress to protect it better.

As her men fulfilled their duties, Life noticed strange objects flying straight for the fortress. She immediately realized it was Max and the other Gods. She ran to warn her men of the arrival of their enemies, but as she screamed, "Everyone, prepare for..."An explosion caused the entrance to the fortress to crumble, cutting her short. Out of the rising smoke, Max and the other Gods came into view. When she looked at the three Gods' faces, she noticed that Max had freed Death's Father, Fire's Father, and Storm's Father. They were three of the most dangerous Gods to ever walk the planet.

"Ah, Selineane, the Demigoddess of Life. Do you still remember when I killed your mother, the Goddess of Life, for betraying her family?" the God of Death asked.

The name 'Demigoddess' angered Life. After all, she wasn't half mortal. The Gods only called their children Demigods because they didn't want them to fall into the same category as they did. She closed her eyes as the battle with their parents came rushing back.

The land of Rowmodea Isle had become a battlefield in the war between the Gods and their children. Even the Gods' oracles were there trying to kill the Demigods. Each child fought their own parent, except for Time. Since she had been created by all of the Demigods' powers, she didn't have a parent to fight, so to help, she used her divine powers to slow the attacks of the Gods as much as she could. Back during that battle, Mythdariz's hair was coal black like his Father's. It was at this battle, though, that it turned white as snow. The God of Death and his son clashed their swords together, each trying to defeat the other, but his son was quicker than he was. Mythdariz swung his sword, and sliced through his Father's breastplate, and cut his stomach. He let out a painful cry, and turned into black vapor, and fled from the battlefield.

The faithful oracle to the God of Death had seen what had happened and swore that Mythdariz would not get away with it. She raised her youthful hand into the air and used her wicked magic to try and drain the Demigod of Death's life. However, the spell did not go as planned. It didn't have the same effect on him as it did on mortals. Instead of killing him, the spell turned his long black hair white as snow. His tan skin turned pale white, and his muscles grew bigger and broader. The oracle's magic had turned against her. Instead of the spell making her live even longer like it was intended to, it drained her life and placed it inside the body of Mythdariz. She turned extremely old and began to die.

Mythdariz walked up to her and said, "You should know that spells have different effects on immortals, you stupid mortal. You are a waste of life and I will take great pleasure in killing you..."

He raised the sword he took from his Father, as a token of his victory over him, high into the air, then violently brought it down like an axe and beheaded the oracle.

One after another, the Gods began to fall to their children, but none of them wanted to kill their parents. They simply wanted to imprison them for all eternity and take their weapons as trophies of their victory. As the God to the child fell, Time walked up to each of them and handed them a small crystal hourglass to place their parent in. Finally, only the Goddess of Life was left standing, but she refused to fight anyone, even her own daughter.

All of the children surrounded her with their weapons drawn, but she simply raised her hands in defeat and handed her staff over to Selineane.

"The time of the Gods has come to an end and it is now time for you to have the power. I want each and every one of you to know that I was against this whole war with you and I never agreed with calling you Demigods. You have proven to be even stronger than the Gods. Therefore, you must create a new name for yourselves. I will take my place amongst the other Gods in their eternal prisons, but I want all of you to act in wisdom and strength and work together, for that was the Gods' damnation."

Mythdariz opened his mouth to speak, but he felt an invisible hand grab his arm and shove his sword forwards into the Goddess of Life's chest. She let out a painful gasp and all of the other children looked at Mythdariz in shock.

"I swear I didn't," he said as he pulled the sword out of the Goddess of Life and laid her on the ground.

She placed her soft hand on his face and said, "I know you didn't child. It was your Father."

She raised her right hand and cast a spell right beside Mythdariz. Roots from the earth shot up out of the ground and wrapped themselves tightly around an invisible man. The man let his invisible cloak fade, revealing himself to be the God of Death. All of the other children backed away, but Mythdariz swung his sword, sliced at the same wound again, and made his Father fall to the ground in pain. Time threw a small crystal hourglass to him and he used it to imprison his Father.

As the Goddess of Life died on the ground, she used the last of her power to repair the broken land and then looked at her daughter. "I love you so much, Selineane. You will do extraordinary things with Mythdariz."

She took one final breath, then closed her eyes and died as her body joined the earth.

Time knelt down beside Mythdariz and said, "Mythdariz, you know as well as I that your Father will eventually break out of a prison such as this. We should create a full scale defense mechanism to guard him for eternity."

"You're right, Velyndral, but there are two others that are just as strong as him. The Gods of Fire and Storm should be placed in high security as well."

Time raised her hands and used her powers to create a large fortress out of the stone in the area. They walked inside and she, Mythdariz, and Selineane used their powers to create magical locks on the three Gods' prisons, and they created a magical field that would allow Time to forever see the fortress and protect it. They threw the three Gods down into the dark holes, then sealed them with statues of them and placed very strong magic that could never be broken unless Mythdariz and Selineane gave permission.

Life was brought back to reality by the sound of Max's demonic voice.

"My fellow Gods, take your revenge!"

With that order, the three Gods burst into full speed and began attacking everyone who dared to oppose them. Life's men ran around franticly trying to defend the fortress, but walls crumbled and fell even with their best efforts. She ran deeper into the fortress and prepared for Max to confront her, but expected him to follow her through the doorway. Instead, the wall she stood in front of crumbled and fell. Max walked through it and looked at Life as the dark magic he had used to destroy the wall faded from his hands. Enraged at what Max was doing, Life summoned forth her sacred staff and charged at him with as much strength as she could muster.

With amazing agility, Max dodged her attacks and grabbed her by her neck. Looking into her eyes, Max could see pure horror. He rose her higher into the air and, with incredible strength, threw her across the room. She hit her head on the stone floor as she made the hard impact. Max slowly walked away, assuming that she was dead.

Chapter 13 The Confrontation

Darkness faded as light filled the areas where it had never touched. Life awoke surrounded by flames and engulfed in black smoke. Coughing the smoke out of her lungs, she slowly rose to her feet and looked around her in all directions. Surrounded by flames on all sides, she began to think that the fortress was burning and she would die either by the flames, or suffocate to death from the smoke.

As the flames grew bigger, Life began to see something emerge from them. It was a bulky young man with flickering robes of fire.

With a confused look on her face Life said, "Is that you, Telareous, the Titan that controls fire?"

With a small smile Fire said, "Don't worry, Life. I have visited Death within the Shadow Realms and told him it is now time to come back and help our friends. He is on his way to aid you in bringing Max to justice. However, he believes that the Gods that escaped should be put down for escaping their prisons, and I agree."

"Thank you, my friend, but..."

With an outstretched hand, Fire covered Life's mouth to stop her from talking.

"I need you to wake up, Life. Wake up, and fight another day."

Slowly, the fire surrounding her began to die as if the oxygen in the air was being sucked away. She began to sway back and forth as she blacked out and fell to the ground with a thud.

As she came too, she found herself back at the fortress, but saw a great change in it. She rose to her feet and saw several of her men scattered around the room slaughtered like animals. Looking at the bloody, beaten bodies and the pools of the crimson blood made Life sick to her stomach.

"Max, what have you become?" she said as she clinched her stomach with her hand.

Down one of the hallways that was still intact, Life could hear the clash of steel and armor and the hiss of spells being cast. She slowly began to walk down the hallway the noises were coming from. She began to walk faster as hope of winning the war filled her veins. She reached the courtyard where the sound of fighting was coming from and, looking out to the courtyard, she could see two out of the three Gods were lying in massive pools of blood. She saw that the last God still alive was Plentodeos, the God of Death. She began to walk out onto the courtyard when she saw something move out of the corner of her right eye. She saw Max, now the demon he had changed into, standing close to one of the exits to the fortress. She also saw three of her soldiers fighting the last God and recognized right away that two of the soldiers were the Captain of her soldiers and Herladrick, but the other one she didn't recognize.

She slowly walked onto the stone-paved floor of the courtyard and watched all the heads turn towards her.

Pointing with a strong finger Max said, "You were dead! I killed you!"

"No you didn't, Max, you only knocked me out," she replied with a disappointed look on her face.

Pulling his sword from his side Max said, "A mistake that I will not make again."

The three soldiers ran up to Life to aid her in stopping Max.

Looking at the three able bodies Life said, "Take care of the other God, Max is mine."

The three soldiers turned towards the final God and charged. They attacked him until he finally fell weak enough and made a fatal mistake that would cost him his life. The Captain brought up his sword and slit his throat, causing him to drown in his own crimson fluid. He fell with a thud in front of the three soldiers, staining the stone bricks of the courtyard around him with the red fluid that continued to flow from the wound in his neck.

Victorious in their accomplishment the three stood in a defensive stance by the fallen God of Death, just in case Max had a final trick.

The Captain turned towards Herladrick and said, "Should we help her?"

"No, this is her fight."

Life and Max fought with great strengths; no falters, or weaknesses to be seen. While they fought, Life remembered the thorn she had hidden in her robes. She knew she could use it if she had the right opening.

With bitter hatred in his face and pointed teeth showing Max said, "Why do you fight, Life?"

With a strained face, Life looked into Max's black eyes and said, "That is what Death would expect of me."

"I have drove Death into hiding just by the strength of my might! He has abandoned you, Life."

The earth began to shake as Max finished his sentence. More fortress walls collapsed.

With an insidious look upon her face Life said, "Are you sure he was hiding from you?"

Loud noises filled the air as the earth continued to shake. The shadows that were painted on the ground from where the light could not reach began to squirm and move around like snakes. It was as if they had been given a life of their own. The shadows grew darker, leaped into the air, and began to fly around in a circle. They chased one another for some time. The wind picked up and the shadows morphed together into one massive dark cloak. Faster and faster it moved in a circle until it became a black blur. The shadow broke its path, flew up into the air, and then came back down even faster than when it went up, slamming itself onto the ground. The ground cracked due to the pressure, and with a loud crack of thunder and a blinding flash, the portal to the Shadow Realms opened like a doorway to the mortal world. Purple and blue mist slowly swirled around the portal as Death emerged from it. As Life laid her eyes on him, she noticed that his armor looked different than the last time she saw him. She noticed that now it was more silver than gray and the mouths of the skulls that were scattered across him gave off an eerie chilling mist. She realized that by staying within the Shadow Realms for so long it enchanted his armor to make it stronger and give it a magical ability.

Frozen in fear at Deaths' return, Max found himself unable to move. Death looked around the courtyard and saw the three soldiers kneeling before him. As he turned back towards Life and Max, he saw Max shaking in fear as if he had seen a ghost.

"W-w-what caused you to come out of hiding?" Max asked with a stutter in his voice.

"I wasn't hiding, Max. I was only becoming more powerful. For you see, the longer I stay within the Shadow Realms the stronger I become. I found that by staying so long within the tortured lands, they began to enchant my armor with their darkness. You will find that it is now resistant to most magic and steel. While Life has fought you and the pathetic Gods valiantly, I have been binding my time within the Shadow Realms. I was preparing to return and use a spell beyond anything you have ever known."

"Does it truly matter if you have learned a new spell or not? I will still be the one that wins this war."

"I'll tell you what, Max. I'll make a deal with you. If you are able to strike me down even with my new spell, you may fight Life to the death," he replied sarcastically.

Life was shocked that Death was bargaining with her life. She had always thought he had cared more about her than that.

With a chuckle Max replied, "That's fine by me. I'll enjoy killing you either way."

With that act, Death pulled out his magnificent sword that glowed with cold power. He and Max charged at each other. While Max ran full speed at him, Death stopped to cast his new spell.

He waved his hand in a circle over his head several times while he said, "Soldiers of the dead...rise to meet your Master's calling."

As his hand moved over his head, a beam of black power shot out of his hand and landed in several different areas. As they hit the ground all around him, half rotted and decaying creatures began to crawl out of the stone paved floor of the fortress and gathered around their master waiting for his command. They moaned in agony, for they didn't belong in this world. With a long armored finger, Death pointed at Max, ordering his minions to attack.

Max brought up his silver sword and began swinging and hacking at the disturbing creatures for several minutes, all the while thinking that they were so weak that he could waste very little strength on them. As he chopped the zombies into pieces limb by limb, they began to screech in pain. Ones that Max hadn't even touched even began to fall apart. He stood still and in awe as he looked at all of the decaying pieces of the corpses for a moment, trying to comprehend what had happened.

In a deep and commanding voice Death said, "My minions can only last in the realm of the living for a short time. When their time has come to its end, they lose the will to live, and die."

"Why then, would you waste a pitiful spell like that on me?"

"If I truly wanted to, I could have stayed in the Shadow Realms just an hour or so longer, and made it to where they would never die. All I would have to do is simply command them to return to the earth until I needed them again. Harming you was not my overall goal with that though, Max. I simply used it to drain your strength. You may not feel it yet, but as we fight, you will soon begin to realize."

With uncanny speed he darted at Max, his white hair and black tattered cloak flowing behind him. As he approached Max, he felt an uneasiness about him. At first he assumed it was because of the darkness that had gripped his soul, but this was something else. He knew if he didn't end Max's tyranny of darkness, more people would fall.

As Life watched the two of them clash their sword together, she noticed that Max's blade was beginning to glow. She knew that it was a deadly spell that he was preparing to cast. She could sense the chaos that it would bring. She knew she had to warn Death of this because she knew that if he wasn't aware of the destruction that was yet to come, it could cost him his life.

Yelling at the top of her lungs, she said, "Look at Max's blade, Death!"

When he heard what Life had said, he couldn't help but look. He saw that the blade was now shimmering with blue power and realized what Max was attempting. He glanced back into the blackened eyes of Max and peered into his wretched soul. He foresaw all the things Max was planning on accomplishing. He saw the carnage spread across the world and all the darkness he would cause. Death knew that now his objective wasn't only to defeat Max, but to kill him as well.

Pushing Max's blade upwards, Death jumped high into the air and allowed gravity to take hold of him. As it pulled him back to the ground, he swung his sword like an axe downwards onto Max's sword. The pressure of the two swords colliding with one another was too much for Max's blade to handle. The blade shattered into several pieces, sending ripples of magic outwards to fade into the atmosphere.

"No! Everything I had planned…gone!" Max shouted as he fell to the ground in defeat.

Death turned away from the shattered sword and opened the portal to the Shadow Realms with an outstretched hand. As the twisting fog from the Shadow Realms flowed onto the stone-paved courtyard, Death watched as all the Titans who fell back at the temple emerged.

Though they had entered the realm of the living through the portal of a desolate, forgotten world of shadow and death, they had come from a beautiful city made out of white marble and diamonds that floated on a large puffy white cloud. This place was also known as Heaven.

Death turned back towards Max and saw that the spirits of the fallen Titans began to surround him. Max had fallen to his knees and was pleading with them to spare him their wrath. Life and Death walked up next to the spirits of the fallen and saw just how frightened Max truly was. As Death, Life, and all of the other Titans closed in on him, Death realized that yet another soul was among them.

The spirit of Max's Father kneeled down beside his son and said, "*I warned you Max; I warned you that your payment was soon at hand. Your judgment day has finally come.*"

"Father, please, help me. Don't leave me here to suffer."

"*Suffer? You ask to be spared after causing so much pain to others? No, Max, what's done is done. Your actions had consequences and now must be paid.*"

As he finished his sentence, he rose to his feet and walked into the portal, having no sympathy for his son who had been lost to The Darkness.

Chapter 14 Final Judgment

As the spirits of the fallen Titans judged Max, Life stretched up on her toes and whispered into Death's ear. "His soul has been corrupted, Death. We should cleanse it and give him another chance."

Death turned his head slightly, still looking at Max, and whispered, "No, his sins against us are unforgivable."

The fallen Titans turned to face Death and Life and, in unison, they said, "*We find the sinner, Max the fallen Titan of War, guilty of treason against the Titan Council. His punishment is death and to be tossed into the fiery pits of Hell.*"

Death raised his sword to end Max's life but, as he brought his sword down, Life grabbed his arm and stopped him. "If we strike him down like this, then we are no better than he is. Death, give him one more chance to change his ways, and if he turns on us again you can strike him down," Life pleaded.

"Life, what has come over you? Just an hour ago you wanted him dead as much as anyone else."

"Now that we have him surrounded, I realize just how wrong I was to judge him in such a crude manor. I just don't want to be a murderer."

Death looked into her glowing emerald green eyes and caught a glimpse of someone using magic on her. He knew it was Max trying to trick them into letting him go. "I'm sorry, Life, but the others have spoken," he concluded, acting like he hadn't caught on to what Max was doing.

Unable to change his mind, Life let go of his arm and moved out of his way. He raised his sword again, ready to strike.

With fear in his eyes Max pleaded, "Please don't kill me, I was only mad about you taking my powers, and the Gods told me to do this to get my revenge."

With a bitter taste in his mouth Death replied, "Your betrayal began long ago. You chose your side...You should have ignored the Gods' whispers."

"I'm begging you! Please don't do this!"

Terror consumed the whole of him as the invisible fingers of death wrapped around his soul. Without any sympathy for him, Death brought down his sword and shoved it into Max's chest.

Gasping in shock and struggling for breath as the sword penetrated his chest, Max looked into the cold eyes of Death. Tears streamed out of his black eyes. Death ripped his blade from Max's chest and watched as he fell backwards and slowly died. He could feel his life slipping away as blood poured out of the wound in his chest. As he closed his eyes, he coughed up a small pool of blood. With one final, painful breath, Max fell limp and died. Blood continued to pour out of his wound and mouth, drenching him in its crimson color.

Turning to face Life, Death noticed she was talking to an oracle that taught mortals about Life and how she worked. He slowly approached her and the oracle, but was stopped when he saw the other Titans entering the portal to the Shadow Realms. As he watched them, a hand grabbed his armored palm. Looking at his visitor, Death greeted Life with a masculine hug. He lifted her up into the air and twirled her around.

"I haven't seen that oracle since Lyranda's betrayal. How is she?"

"Lyranda? I haven't heard you talk about her in almost two hundred years, but Jennifer is doing great. She stopped by because she had a vision about this battle. She wanted to make sure we were alright."

"Is that so? Well, that was kind of her, unlike her wicked sister. Has she heard from the other sister, Vellintina?" he asked.

"Vellintina still resides somewhere in Golmasik. She fears that The Darkness is returning with a powerful vengeance."

"We will turn our attention to that soon, then. The Darkness mustn't be allowed to return. I am going to travel back to the Shadow Realms and attend to a few loose ends, and then I'll return to the temple."

"Very well, I shall head there now and begin repairing the damage that Max has wrought. Oh, and Death, what should we do with Max's body?"

"I'll send my last oracle to fetch him. She will know what to do with his wretched body."

She nodded at him in agreement and turned into her bird form. She flew into the air and headed for the temple. Death was about to enter the portal to the Shadow Realms, but was stopped as Herladrick, the Captain, and another soldier ran up to him.

"Sorry to intrude, Master, but we were wondering what you want us to do now?" Herladrick asked.

"All of you are to report to the Titan Temple just south of here. It is there you will be rewarded for your loyalty to the Titans. It is there where your futures will begin. Before you leave though, what are your names?"

"I'm Herladrick, Sir, and these two are Captain Blizmar and Brenda."

"It's good to meet all of you. Go to the temple now. Your destinies await you."

The three soldiers ran off and headed for the temple while Death turned to the portal and walked into it leaving the ruins of the fortress behind.

Once inside, he shut the portal behind him with a wave of his hand. He saw the spirit of Max curled up in a ball, crying. Just being back in the Shadow Realms, he could already feel himself becoming stronger. He walked up to Max and grabbed him by his neck. He raised him high into the air, so that he could look up to him. Max began panicking and screaming bloody murder trying to get free from Death's grasp. With the other hand, Death opened two portals. One led to a beautiful city that floated on a big, puffy, white cloud which was known as Heaven, and the other led to a land consumed by fire and molten lava. This place was known as Hell and it was the domain of the fallen Titan of Fire. He looked back at Max and noticed that he was still crying and breathing heavily.

In a cruel voice Death said, "You could have had great power, but you betrayed the Titans and committed sins of the highest degree that are punishable by death."

He removed his helmet and let it fall to the shadowy ground. With an evil snarl, he tightened his grip around Max's throat and said, "Telareous, the Titan of Fire, was the owner of Hell. Imagine what it will be like without his presence. It will probably be ten times worse now. Without him keeping the other souls chained up, I'm sure they will all want a piece of you. Welcome to Hell..."

He hurled Max into the land consumed by fire and watched him scream in pain as he burned and got dragged away in searing hot chains. He picked up his helmet and placed it back on his head. With a wave of his hand, he shut the two portals so that no soul would try to get out. He looked over at several of the Shadowscythes who were patrolling the area and bowed to them as he began to take his leave.

Life stood on the balcony at the temple and looked down at the valley below. She turned to go take a seat in her throne, but when she turned around, she noticed that the three brave soldiers that fought beside her were now standing in the room looking at her.

With a small smile on her face Life said, "Good evening. What brings you here on a fine summer evening such as this?"

"Death told us to come here. He said we would find our destinies here," Brenda nervously replied.

With a peaceful smile on her face Life said, "Death is many things. Wise, clever, cunning, and powerful. He is no fool. If he has truly sent you here, then he has something big planned for each of you."

Turning back towards the valley, Life thought about the plans Death had in store for the three mortal warriors. She took in a deep breath and felt a sharp pain. She grabbed her chest right where her perfect, purified heart was located and turned back to the three mortals. She sensed something inside them, something she had never felt before. Tears began to flow down her face as she came to the conclusion that these three mortals had a hint of titanic power locked within them. It was very rare for a mortal to be born and just end up obtaining some titanic power. It could only happen if the baby was born in a spot where a great battle between the Titans and their parents had broken out. She continued to stare at the three of them until she noticed that hers and the three others' shadows had grown very dark and were now squirming around on the floor like snakes that could not escape a trap.

The shadows leaped off of the ground and swirled around in a circle around Life and the three mortals, causing their hair to blow around in a tangled mess. As the shadows swirled around them, they slowly morphed into one big shadow. It went higher into the air and then plummeted towards the ground. With a fierce slam to the ground, the mysterious portal to the Shadow Realms opened, and Death walked out of it.

"Good evening, mortals. By now you are probably curious as to why I have asked you to come to the glorious temple of the Titans. You see, after defeating Max, I felt a hint of power in your souls and that kind of power only a Titan can hold. Each of you holds a different power, a power that was passed on to you by the earth. Blizmar, I see a burning rage in you and, with Life's and my help, you will become the new Titan of Fire."

With a shocked face Blizmar said, "Thank you, Master!"

Turning to Brenda Death said, "Brenda, you have the power the create love. From the time you were just an adolescent girl, both men and women have been attracted to your beauty. This power is used to create new generations of mortals. It is very unusual to see this power actually have a physical form. It used to be the responsibility of Life to do this. This power may not be one of the main powers to help keep the world in balance, but it is very important because never has there been a Titan of Love. Your power is a very rare one at that."

With a bit of a stutter in her voice Brenda said, "T-thank you, Master."

Turning to the last of the mortals Death said, "Herladrick, I see you commanding curses. The Titan of Curses is another powerful Titan, but not a main one to keep the Titans thriving. Don't think that if you don't have one of the main powers that it makes you less important because a Titan is a Titan, no matter how powerful. That is the reason why Max fell from the Titan Council. He was a mortal we took in and gave the power of War. He thought that he should have been the most powerful Titan to ever live, but it wasn't meant to be that way. War comes under Life and Death, and he committed an act of treason, which led to his downfall. He never understood that without Life and Death, there could be no wars or balance. He was clearly not ready, either. Max was—"

Cutting him off in mid-sentence Life said, "I think they get the point, Death," she turned her attention to the mortals. "Now that you know your powers and what your responsibilities will be, I believe it's time to unlock them so you can help us keep the world in balance. When your powers are released your mortal bodies will die and you will become one of the Titans. Also, you will notice that your physical attributes will change slightly."

Grinning at Death, Life raised her hand at the same time as him. In unison, they said a spell to unlock the three mortals' powers.

Chapter 15 The Rebirth

In unison, Death and Life chanted, "Kcolnu rieht srewop!"

Over and over they repeated the spell and, as they said the words, a piercing noise rang in the three mortals' ears. Soon it became so high pitched that they could no longer stand the sound. They placed their hands over their ears in an attempt to drown out the unbearable screeches, but to no avail. The noises were so loud and high pitched that it brought them to their hands and knees. They begged the two Titans to stop, but they pushed forward allowing the eerie humming to muffle their voices. A beam of white light broke through the cloudy sky and hit the three mortals still cringing in pain. Gravity slipped away within the area where the light hit and the three of them began to slowly rise into the air. The light seeped into their bodies and caused an outburst of pure golden auras to leave their eyes, mouths, and noses. The light faded into thin air and gravity returned causing the three mortals to fall to the ground unconscious.

They awoke hours later. It was completely dark out and the moon was high in the sky. It was the only source of light that lit up the valley. They slowly stood up, still dizzy from the incantation. They noticed the changes that had occurred to each of them. Blizmar's hair had become long and was completely made of fire. Brenda had become even more irresistible than she had been before. Her skin glistened in the moonlight and her blue eyes had changed to magenta. Herladrick's skin was now an ashy pale and his eyes glowed red. Fire had been born anew, but the other two had just now begun their birth. Being the new Titan of Fire, Blizmar wanted to test his newly founded powers. He raised his hand, thought about a ball of fire and how it looked, along with the temperatures a ball of fire could fluctuate between. Then, a fireball shot out of his hand and flew off the balcony.

With extreme excitement, he said, "Amazing!"

"The magic you possess is there to aid you, not to play with. They are there to aid you as long as you don't abuse them. In time you will become more powerful and will learn your roles in your immortal lives," Death said.

"Go explore the temple and look for your rooms," Life said in a calm, but commanding, voice.

"Before you depart, there is one rule a Titan must always obey. There will be no using your powers on other Titans to harm them and, for the mortals, you are not allowed to use your powers to hurt them unless they have plans to hurt one of the Titans in any way, shape, or form."

As the three new Titans left the chamber, Death turned towards Life and carried on a private conversation.

"Do you think it is wise to make them this powerful so soon? They are only in their mid- twenties. Maybe even their early thirties," Life said with worry in her voice.

She looked around to see if they were still anywhere nearby.

"No, which is why I said, 'In time you will become more powerful.' That was our mistake with Max. We allowed him to ascend into power too fast. It ended up leading to his downfall, and we can't have that happening again." He took in a deep breath. "I think I'll retire to my chamber for the night, Life. I'll see you in the morning."

As he walked off, Life shouted back at him and said, "Goodnight, I think I'll stay up for a bit longer and attend to more things."

He nodded his armored head, bowed to her, and then walked out of the throne room. He made his way towards his chamber, knowing that his oracle would know of his return to the temple and would want to speak with him.

He walked into his depressing chamber and locked the doors behind him. He took in another deep breath as he examined his room. Everything looked the same. The bed was still neatly made and the black curtains were still fastened to their posts on the bed. The glass doors that led to his private balcony were still shut and the black curtains there were still drawn. The table in the center of his chamber was still cluttered with books and parchment, along with a wooden box. This box had some of the most demented, insidious, malevolent souls locked within it because Death felt that Hell itself couldn't hold those demons. He sat down in the chair at the table and moved some papers around to tidy things up. Once done, a small dish of sparkling water was revealed to be resting right in front of him. He swirled his armored finger in it and waited. The water glowed brightly and came to life as a faint image of an elderly woman appeared through the crystal clear fluid.

"Sorry to contact you at this late hour, Master, but your *prisoner*, as you so delicately put it, is starting to awaken after these past twenty years," the oracle said in a faint, raspy, old voice. "I fear in you having me move his body to avoid Max has steered him."

"Keep him restrained…Do not let him wake. If he breaks free I want you to cast a containment spell on him. He mustn't be allowed to escape and become known to the world."

With a bit of a stutter in her voice, the old oracle said, "W-w-why is it so bad if he breaks free?"

"It is bad because if he breaks free, I will have to accelerate all the plans I have put in motion. He will destroy all of the plots I have set forth for the next several generations."

"But Master, he is your—"

Cutting her off in mid-sentence Death harshly said, "Don't you dare call him my son. He is not, and never will be! Immortals and mortals are forbidden to mate. If they do, the child becomes a demigod. He is from my flesh and blood so I can't simply kill him, but you can. This is why I am ordering you to kill him. Put a curse on him, and the moment he wakes up, contact me. I'm sorry, but anyone in the village that gets in my way when he awakens will die. I will not let a stupid decision I made twenty years ago be the downfall of the Titans!"

"Yes, Master. I will do as you command. Master, can I ask you something?"

"What is it?"

"How is my daughter, Lyranda, doing in her studies of the ways of death?"

Death didn't dare tell her that she had betrayed the Titans and now lived somewhere deep within the Dreadscar Valley

"She…she is doing fine. Why do you ask?"

"I grow weak in my old age. I can't live forever. I wish for her to take my place when you have finished with her training."

"I will take that into consideration."

The oracle's image smiled and shimmered. She bowed her head in respect to show that she was done with the conversation. What would happen next would put the Titans in terrible danger.

*****

"Sorry to interrupt your story madam, but I am a little confused. From what I am gathering, the Titan Council was this extremely powerful force. How were they defeated so easily by this mortal?" Thoi-Thagian asked still sitting at the table in the old bar.

"Weren't you listening?" she asked.

"Well, yes, but this Max fellow seemed very stupid. If the Titans were in fact immortal, they shouldn't have been defeated so easily."

"The Titans had grown comfortable in their seat of power. They truly never believed anyone could challenge them. They grew relaxed in their rule, and when the invasion began, they weren't prepared for it."

"Okay, but when the time came for the three mortals to join their ranks, why not seek out ones who could replace the Titans who had previously served?"

"The mortals who joined the Titan Council were just a small part in a sliver of hope the Titans saw. One of those mortals destroyed everything though."

"The one who became the Titan of Curses, huh?"

The woman drank the last of her vodka and said, "Let me continue, and you will find out." She took in a deep breath. "Now where was I? Oh yes," she said, remembering where she had been in the story before she was interrupted by Thoi-Thagian.

***

The dish of water lost its intense glow as the oracle cut the link between her and Death. When she knew he could no longer see her, she turned towards an old wooden chair where Death's son sat. He wore rags for clothing. Draped over him was a dark gray sheet. He sipped on a small cup of water.

With pity in her voice the oracle said, "I can't kill you. You may be a demigod, but you aren't evil. I can't let you run free though, either. The Titans would sense your power and come kill you. I will be breaking many rules of the Titans, but I know one way to save you, Phoenix."

The old oracle still couldn't figure out why his mother named him that.

In a curious voice Phoenix said, "How, Jade? I'm a demigod and a weak one at that. I haven't learned to transform into other things yet."

"No, but before I became Death's oracle, I was a witch. I had just learned how to put a soul from one body into another when Death came to me and asked me to be his oracle. I can take your soul and place it into another's body. It just so happens that I have a fresh corpse that your soul can take."

She walked over to a table where a white sheet lay over a body. She grabbed the sheet with her two boney hands and pulled it off of the body, letting the sheet fall to the ground.

"Do you recognize this person, Phoenix?" Jade asked, pointing at the body.

"No, who is he?"

With a small smile, Jade took Phoenix's hand and said, "This is what's left of Max, the Betrayer of the Titans. He died by your Fathers' hand. This is the body your soul will be placed in, but, be warned, once your soul is put in this vessel, if you die by one of the Titans hands, the former person that lived in this body will come back to life. If you were to die, your soul would travel back to your current vessel. So, please, try not to get yourself killed by a Titan. We don't need Max returning to this world."

A toothy grin spread across his face, and Phoenix said, "I'm ready for the switch."

Jade let go of his hand and said, "Lous fo Phoenix, refsnart ot eht ydob fo Max."

Finishing the spell, she pointed at Phoenix, then at the body of Max. A loud crack and a flash of light filled the small room. Phoenix dropped to the ground like a dead fly and passed out.

He awoke three hours later and noticed that he was lying on the table where Max had been. He looked around and saw his body lying on the ground. For a moment he thought he was dead and that he was looking at his body. Then, he saw Jade smiling down at him.

"Couldn't have done a better job if I tried, if I do say so myself."

"I can't believe it worked," Phoenix said in disbelief.

"Well of course it worked, silly boy. Now the Titans will be deceived. At least long enough for you to go into hiding. You need to go now, though. Your Father visits frequently and if he decides to come see me right now, he would kill us both, along with all the villagers."

She went into the other room and didn't come back. Phoenix was beginning to think that she was done with him, so he turned to leave.

As he got to the door, Jade shouted, "Wait! I have something for you."

She walked up to him and handed him a beautifully crafted sword. It was titanium and had a skull etched into the hilt of it. It faintly glowed with black power and had a black diamond at the very end of the hilt. A dark brown leather strap was wrapped tightly around the handle, which also dangled down from it a bit.

"Take this sword. It is the Blessed Sword of Death. Your Father left it with me to keep it hidden, but you need it more than I do and I know you will keep it safe."

Phoenix examined the blade for a moment, then looked at the oracle and said, "I…I'm sorry, Jade…"

"Sorry?"

Without saying another word, he took the Blessed Sword of Death and ran it through her stomach. Gasping for breath as it penetrated her body, the old oracle collapsed onto the ground.

He bent down, pulled the sword from her body, and said, "Sorry Jade, but I have to go visit the Titans and I can't have one of their oracles in my way. It seems that I have inherited Max's lust for revenge. I plan on fulfilling what he failed to do."

He walked over to his former body and dragged it into the other room to hide it from sight, and then looked at Jade for a moment longer before leaving her to bleed out. As he left the small hut, she weakly stared out at him. She stretched her arm forward to try and stop him from leaving, but the Blessed Sword of Death was quickly draining her life.

She glanced over to the table where Max's body once lay and said, "What have I done?"

As she laid on the ground near death, she realized the deception that had been played upon her. She realized that Phoenix had been influenced by Max long before he had ever awakened. Max had somehow used his powerful magic to whisper to Phoenix in his sleep and turned him against everyone.

Chapter 16 The Beginning of the End

Death gazed out his window the next morning and watched Life tend to her garden when a knock came from the other side of the doors.

Without turning around, he said, "Enter."

The door slowly creaked open and Brenda, the Titan of Love, walked into the room. He was still facing the window as she walked up behind him.

"I know I shouldn't be here, but I can't resist you. I want your body pressed up against mine. I want to feel your touch."

She slowly placed her hands on his armored shoulders and

turned him around. She moved upward towards his helmet and slowly removed it. No living soul, not even Life, had seen his face in over three millenniums. He slowly breathed, waiting for her to make a move.

Love stretched up on her toes and slowly pressed her rosy red lips against his. She was shocked at how cold they were. At some point during the contact between the two of them, Death found himself slowly undressing her. He quickly pulled his head away and walked over to the doors. Love thought that he had had enough and wanted her to leave, but was shocked at what he truly did. He grabbed the handles to the doors and shut them. Locking them, he turned back towards her. He slowly walked back to her and she met him halfway. He caressed her in his muscular arms as they kissed. His pale face began to turn a peach color as he became aroused. He removed his armor until he was in nothing but his black loincloth.

Love was completely undressed and was waiting for him on his bed. He removed his loincloth and climbed on top of her. He slowly kissed her as he fondled her breasts. She moaned with pleasure as he penetrated her. He was the best she ever had.

"Oh, Death…"

He looked at her with pleasure and began to thank her as their love making came to an end, but he stopped when a loud knock came from the other side of his doors. They both were very quiet. He quickly, but as quietly as he could, put all his armor back on. He placed his helmet on his head and then helped Love get dressed. Once they were suitable, he walked over to the door, unlocked it, and opened it. He peered out into the corridor.

"Death, I was beginning to wonder if you were even in there," Life said.

"Life, what do you need? You have pulled me away from important business."

With fear in her voice, she said, "Death, I am truly sorry to bother you, but can I please talk to you? It's urgent."

He opened the door wider and allowed her to enter. As she did so, she saw Love standing over by the unmade bed. She sensed that she was nervous.

With attitude in her voice, Life looked at Death and said, "What is she doing here?"

"I asked her to come here. So don't go throwing your attitude at her," he replied, trying to cover up what they had just done.

With a bit of an irritated voice Life said, "I'm not. I was just wondering."

"Obviously you did, otherwise he wouldn't have called you out on it," Love replied.

Life glared at her, but Death quickly regained her attention. "What is it you needed to talk to me about?"

"I don't want to sound paranoid, but my oracle, Jennifer, is not responding to any of my attempts to contact her. I'm afraid something may have happened. That is why I came to you."

With anger rising in his voice Death yelled, "You think I killed her?!"

"No! Not at all. I was just going to ask you to contact your oracle since mine and yours are friends," she said with a plea in her voice.

"Fine, I guess I can contact mine to see if she knows anything."

He walked over to his dish of water and put his hand on the table to rest it on. Minutes went by, but there was no reply.

"Hmm, something is definitely not right. She never ignores me. I'll go visit Jade's village and you go to Jennifer's. Love, you stay here just in case my oracle tries to contact me while I'm gone."

"Yes, Master," Love replied as she bowed in respect.

Life and Death quickly left his chamber and ran down the hall to the main entrance. They passed by several new temple guards who seemed alarmed as they dashed by them. Temple servants fled towards the nearest chamber they stood by in fear that an attack was upon them.

"So what important business were you conducting? Why did you need Love's assistance instead of mine?" Life asked as they ran down the large stone steps towards the entrance of the temple.

"Life, I am not having this discussion with you." Death replied.

"Were you two—"

"Enough!"

Dashing out of the temple, Death transformed into the black dragon he had become once before. He flapped his large wings and lifted into the air.

Life yelled back at him and said, "Death, will you please tell me how you learned to do that?"

"Naravada helped me to clear my mind and think of becoming one. All you have to do is concentrate on becoming one and how you want to look as one, and then let yourself become that. I'm surprised you didn't know that since you taught yourself to transform into all of your other forms."

"Naravada, the former Titan of Nature, taught you?"

"Yes. He taught me just days before his untimely death."

Life thought back to the day that he gave her his immortality and power, and then faded into nothingness. It was truly one of the saddest days she had ever witnessed. She pulled her mind back onto the task at hand and focused on what Death had told her to do.

She closed her eyes and took in a deep breath. She thought of becoming a ferocious green dragon and, as she did so, her body began to bend and change into that of a dragon's. Within moments, she was as large as Death was, but her scaly skin was green. She also had no spikes on her tail or snout.

They both flew off in opposite directions. Death headed towards the west and Life headed towards the east. Death arrived at his oracle's village at midnight. To draw less attention to himself, he landed in a nearby field of wheat and transformed into an old farmer who wore tan rags. He slowly walked into the village with his walking staff.

Chapter 17 A New threat Arises

Death entered the village and noticed nothing out of the ordinary. The villagers were fine and no panic had arisen. As he walked down the stone paved paths of the village, he saw his oracle's hut far up the road on a hill close to the village's graveyard. As he approached the old hut, he stood outside for a brief moment wondering what it would be like to stand in the same room as his forsaken son. Grabbing the handle of the wooden door, he pulled it open.

As it swung open, it revealed the terrible truth that would mark the beginning of the end of the Titans once and for all. Lying before him in a pool of crimson blood was the Oracle of Death, Jade. He quickly walked up to her and knelt down beside her. He let his disguise fall away as he picked her up and laid her across his lap. He noticed that she had been stabbed but he also saw that her hands were faintly glowing with green auras of magic. He placed his hand to her wound but quickly pulled it away. He knew immediately that she had been stabbed by the Blessed Sword of Death. He knew there were only minutes left with her, but he had to find out who had done this to her.

In a quiet voice, he said, "Jade? Jade!" He shook her a little. "Jade! Can you hear me?"

Jade weakly opened her eyes and said, "M-master? Is that you? I don't have much time. The spell I am using is only slowing the effects of the Blessed Sword of Death."

"Jade, who did this to you?"

"Y-your son…ugh…" she said in pain.

Her hands stopped glowing and she fell limp as her body lost the last bit of life. He carefully placed her on the ground and walked out of the hut. He closed the door behind him and watched as a beautiful hawk flew down to his feet. Taking on her true form, Life stood before him.

"I'll be happy to tell you that my oracle was just in the village pub. I was worrying for nothing. What about your oracle?"

"Dead, she was killed by a monstrous beast, a revolting demigod!" Death said angrily.

With a confused look spreading across her face Life said, "That's…that's impossible. We killed the freed Gods at the fortress and the rest are still locked away within the Hourglass Dome. In order for a true demigod to be born, an immortal would have to mate with a mortal."

Looking away from her, he said, "Life…I, I haven't been completely honest with you. Years ago, I made love with a mortal. It was a moment of weakness."

Life's face turned red with anger as she said, "Death, how could you do this!? Do you realize you could have just single handedly doomed the remainder of the Titan Council?"

"I was being foolish. I told my oracle to kill him, but she refused. Now he is loose, and I fear that he may be headed to the temple to reap his revenge on me."

With squinted eyes, she said, "Then we need to head back and protect our home."

She began to walk away from him. He reached out to touch her, but she yanked away from him and said, "Don't touch me…"

Death sighed as they both took to the sky in their dragon forms and flew off. They headed towards the direction of the snowy mountains and grassy valleys of Rowmodea Isle.

Life and Death flew back to the temple to make sure nothing horrible was happening, but when they passed over the last few mountain peaks, they knew something bad was already taking place. Just as they flew into the valley, a massive explosion erupted, sending black smoke hurtling into the air. They looked towards the direction where the explosion had occurred and saw that one of the bridges that led into the temple from the valley grounds had collapsed. Death roared to warn Life that he had spotted Fire, Love, and Curse fighting water, earth, fire, and air elementals. Death knew that Phoenix had found one of the Gods' old spells that would grant him control over the elements. However, this spell didn't only give him control over them. It also twisted and tortured them so far into corruption that they would have no hope of rescue.

They dove from the sky and landed firmly on the ground. They took on their true forms and dashed by several of the enemy elementals that were attacking the new temple guards.

Yelling over all the loud noises of the battle Life said, "Fire, where did their leader run off to?"

"He turned into a bird consumed by molten flames and flew towards the Spire of Wisdom!" he said as he shot a bolt of fire out of his hand.

It flew by Life's head and ignited an earth elemental in molten lava. It ran away as its rocky flesh melted away, reducing it to a pile of burnt rubble.

Looking behind her to see the dead elemental Life said, "Thank you, Fire."

She quickly turned around to face Death, but noticed that he had walked off to talk to Love. She ran up to him just as Love was kissing him on the center of his helmet.

"Death, Fire has informed me that your son, Phoenix, is heading to the upper part of the Spire of Wisdom."

Turning to face her Death said, "Thank you, Life. I'll go and confront him. Do not come to the Spire of Wisdom until all these elementals are destroyed."

He ran away and, at the peak if his run, he leaped into the air transforming into his dragon form.

Watching Death disappear as he headed towards the Spire of Wisdom Life said, "He is a fool if he thinks he can do this alone. Love, I want you to assist the temple guards in destroying all of these elementals then gather Fire and Curse. Meet me atop the Spire of Wisdom after you are done."

Bowing in respect Love said, "Yes, Mistress. I will do as you command."

Life gave Love a small smile and said, "Oh, and by the way, congratulations."

Transforming into a hawk, she flew off to the Spire of Wisdom. Confused as to why Life told her that, Love slowly walked away to join Fire and Curse on the battlefield.

Death glided through the air, his wings slicing through it as he spiraled around the Spire of Wisdom. He assumed that his son would be waiting for his arrival. He landed on the flat platform of the spire and took on his true form. Phoenix hadn't realized that his Father had arrived until he was right behind him. He had been too focused on looking out at the horizon.

"Hello, Father. Do you like what I have become?" Phoenix asked as he turned to face his Father.

Death was almost shocked when he saw the face of Max, but the voice of Phoenix. However, he knew that Jade had used her witchcraft on him.

"I am not your Father, and you are a damned fool if you think that you will get away with what you have done here."

With a hint of sarcasm in his voice Phoenix said, "How did you like the little *gift* I left you in your pathetic excuse of an oracle's hut?"

"You're a monster, Phoenix. The Gods have been imprisoned for a reason! They couldn't control their powers, let alone the planet! Look at what their powers did to Max and, now, you. We could not stand by and watch them destroy what we had worked so hard to protect. Therefore, in the name of the Titans, I will put an end to you."

He grasped his sword tightly in his left hand and charged. Seeing that his Father was not joking about killing him, Phoenix grabbed the Blessed Sword of Death and ran towards him.

Life approached the spire and flew upwards against the wind. She knew Death was confronting Phoenix and she knew he would need her help. Once she finally reached the top, she landed on her feet as she took on her true form in midair. She knew she was disobeying Death, but she kept telling herself she would only help if he truly needed it.

Phoenix brought the sword upwards, causing his Father to lose his balance and fall onto his back. He dropped his sword, making him defenseless. Phoenix raised the blessed sword like a dagger into the air and knew that it would kill his Father no matter what. He brought it down, but his Father was not the soul the sword claimed.

Life had saw Phoenix about to kill Death and she knew, no matter the cost, she had to stop him. She could be replaced by one of her oracles, but Death's last oracle had been murdered. Without one to control Death, it would throw everything out of balance.

She dashed towards Death and threw herself across his lap screaming, "NO!!!"

The sword ripped into her stomach. She immediately lost all her strength in the arm that was holding her up across Death's lap and fell to the ground, limp.

It all had happened so fast that Death had not realized what had occurred until it was too late. He saw Life lying on the ground with the Blessed Sword of Death imbedded within her body. He laid her softly on the ground, grabbed his sword, and charged at his son. Before he could strike at him, Phoenix jumped off the edge of the spire. As he fell, he looked back at Death with a small smile, turned into a large bird, and flew off.

Once he was gone, Death ran back to Life and fell to his knees. He grabbed her and placed her across his lap. As he held her upper body in his arms, he said, "W-why would you do that, Life?"

With tear filled, weak eyes, Life looked at Death and said, "Y-you saved me f-from Max…"

"Why though? Why give your life for mine? I nearly destroyed the Titan Council with my foolish acts."

As tears streamed down her face, Life placed her shaking hand against his armored face and said, "Y-you are our leader…If you die… we all will slowly die out. W-we don't…stand a…chance without you." She paused for a moment. "I…" She slowly closed her eyes, and her skin turned cold as she died.

The valley turned cold and dark as rain began to pour from the sky. Thunder roared and rolled throughout the valley. Flashing across it, lightning lit up the sky. Feeling her life-force leave her body, Death grabbed the sword imbedded in her stomach and pulled it out.

"I should have wielded this sword instead of having War fashion me a new one so that this one could be hidden," he muttered as he stared at his reflection within the bloody Blessed Sword of Death.

Love, Curse, and Fire appeared on the platform minutes after Life's death. As they moved off the stairwell, the first thing they saw was Death holding Life in his arms and the bloody sword used to kill her lying next to them. Love slowly walked up to him and dropped down next to him.

With bitter hatred in his voice Death said, "He will pay for this…"

He slowly and gently placed Life on the ground and transformed into the black dragon.

"I'll be back soon. In the meantime, I want you three to move her body to her chamber and search for the Blessed Staff of Life. If you are able to find it, we will be able to bring her back. The Blessed Sword of Death may take life away, but the Blessed Staff of Life gives it. Find it and take it to the main chamber of the temple."

The three Titans watched Death fly away from the temple, and then they slowly surrounded the mangled body of the Titan of Life.

Love knelt down next to her and moved her lime green hair from her face.

"Do you think Death struck the killing blow?" she asked, the question painful.

Curse knelt down next to her and placed his ashy palm on her bare shoulder. "I doubt the killing blow was dealt by Death. In the short time that I have known Life, I discovered that she would lay down her life for Death, no matter the situation."

Love began to weep uncontrollably. She covered her face to conceal the tears, but the two other Titans already knew the sadness that had struck her heart. Fire knelt down on the other side of her and gently rubbed her back.

"Love, I didn't know you cared so strongly about Life. It's okay, though. We will bring her back," Fire said as he hugged her.

Chapter 18 The Search for Life

Jennifer was on her hands and knees tending to her garden of flowers. She pulled weeds that had sprouted next to the statue of Life when she noticed that there was a large crack across the middle of the statue. She stood up and wiped her hands on her apron. She got closer to examine the crack, but saw that smaller cracks were spreading across the surface of the statue. The statue grew weak from the damage it had received and fell to pieces under the weight of gravity. Jennifer stood in shock as she watched the pieces of her prized statue rest on the ground. She ran inside her hut to see what she could do to reconstruct the statue, but was stopped when she saw that her bowl of shimmering water was glowing more intensely. She swirled her finger in it and waited.

Within the bowl, a large black dragon appeared. She knew that this dragon was the Titan of Death, but she didn't know why he was contacting here. Death's voice came through after a few moments of flight.

"I have little time to talk, and it appears that you have little time as well. Listen carefully. I need you to come to the temple and aid the Titans of Love, Fire, and Curse in finding the Blessed Staff of Life. That is, if you ever want to see your mistress alive again."

The image of Death faded and Jennifer brought her right hand up across her mouth as she ran into her bedroom to prepare for a long journey to the temple of the Titans.

Back at the Titan Temple, the three Titans were still atop the Spire of Wisdom. They continued to stare at Life's motionless body.

As tears fell down her face Love said, "We can't leave her here. Let's move her to her chamber like Death asked us too."

They knelt down to pick her body up, but quickly backed away when small green cracks began to appear and spread across her body from the wound. As they watched in horror, green light began to seep out of the cracks along with small images of leaves. More cracks spread out from those cracks and began to do the same until her whole body was just a mass of green light. A bright green flash filled the air and blinded the three Titans. When their vision cleared, they saw Life's body had turned to a fine green glowing powder and blew away in the wind.

In shock Love said, "How will we bring her back without her body now?"

Looking at her with sad eyes Fire said, "I don't know but—"he began to say but was cut short by a small noise he heard down in the valley.

He walked to the edge of the platform and the other two Titans joined him. They saw a young woman probably in her mid-twenties to her early thirties walking into the main entrance of the temple.

"That is probably one of Life's oracles. We best get down there to greet her," Fire said.

The three of them made their way down the spiral staircase and headed to the main entrance. They opened a door at the end of the fifth hallway they entered and made their way into the throne room. From there, they walked through the doorway across the room and went down a large set of marble steps. At the bottom they were finally at the main entrance and walked up to the young women who had her back to the stairs. She realized that she was no longer alone and turned around to face her hosts.

"Masters, I am sorry to intrude. I know I didn't give any warning of my arrival, but I received a message from Death. He told me to come here immediately. I have been told to help you in your search for the Blessed Staff of Life. Unfortunately, searching here will get you nowhere. My mistress felt that it was unsafe to always have it near her.

When not in use, she would hide it far away from her. Only when in need of it would she summon it."

With a grim face Fire said, "It's nice to meet one of Life's entrusted oracles. We are pleased at your request to help us search, but since it is nowhere in the temple I don't know where we should begin to look. Would you happen to know?"

"We can't begin the search tonight. A horrible blizzard is headed this way and it is very dangerous to be out in one of those. We will have to wait until morning. Would it be possible to see my mistress's body?"

Tears began to stream down Love's face again. "Her body dissolved into green dust and blew away."

"We are going to wait until Death returns to ask him what we should do since her body is no more. In the meantime, we should probably search her room for any clues as to where she might have hid the staff," Curse replied.

Death flew across the snowy peaks of the Crystalrock Mountains in pursuit of Phoenix. Hours went by with no sign of him. He was about to give up and return to the temple when he saw a phoenix dive from the sky in front of him. It flew to the ground and took on the form of Max, and Death knew he had finally found his target. He dove out of the sky and landed on the ground. It shook and trembled as he landed and took on his true form. Grabbing his sword, he swung it quickly, but missed Phoenix as he ducked out of the way. He turned to face his Father and pulled out a new sword he had *found* in a faraway land. Death recognized the sword almost instantly. He went into a defensive stance and blocked the fatal blow Phoenix delivered.

The two-handed sword had a golden hilt and a large golden turning gear on it. Around the decorated blade swirled the ominous sands of time. The mysterious weapon had the ability to freeze time if the wielder knew how to use it correctly.

While the two swords were in contact with each other, Death looked at Phoenix and said, "Ah, the Time Maker's Sword. I'm curious. Do you know the power you hold?"

Obviously not wanting to listen to him, Phoenix broke the contact of the swords and charged at him again.

Several minutes of brutal fighting passed. Death used his great strength against his son as he swung his sword forward and knocked him out of his stance. He quickly brought up his foot and hit Phoenix on his chin causing him to fall backwards onto the snowy ground. He slowly walked up to his son and pointed the tip of his blade against his throat.

"You were never any son of mine. Do you have any last words?"

With an evil glare Phoenix shouted, "The Titan Council shall fall. A plot has been put into action far greater than any one of you could imagine! Max will usher the Lord of Darkness back into this world."

"The Lord of Darkness? That's impossible…Max is dead, and he is never coming back. I've seen to that personally."

Phoenix laughed. "You can't stop The Darkness. All you do only delays the inevitable."

Death quickly flicked the end of his sword across his son's throat, cutting it open as it went past. His crimson blood flowed steadily out of his throat, staining his armor and the snow all around him.

Death looked up into the sky as if he were in search for something and said, "I have avenged you, Life."

He took a few more moments and then looked back down at his dead son.

"You may have been in the body of Max, but that didn't make you any stronger or wiser. You were as much of a fool as he was. Enjoy your stay in the pits of Hell for all eternity."

He walked away from his son's body and was about to enter the Shadow Realms, but realized that he had little time. He couldn't afford to waste any of it on going into the Shadow Realms to place Phoenix's soul in Hell. He would have to wait for a while, but he didn't want some witch to find Max's body again and resurrect him a third time. He walked back up to his body and picked him up. He carried his limp body in his muscular armored arms to a nearby cliff. With incredible strength, he hurled the body over the edge and watched it smack on the rocks and branches until it hit the bottom. He began to turn away when a shimmer caught his eye. He looked on the ledge, right below the edge of the cliff, and saw a beautifully crafted staff lying on the ledge. It was made from an old tree that once grew in the very valley of the Titan Temple. At the top, it branched out and a fairly large emerald stone rested in the center of it. Wrapped around the shaft of the staff was a shear green ribbon. He stretched out his hand and concentrated on the weapon. The staff wobbled as an invisible hand grabbed it and lifted it towards Death.

Gripping it tightly, he looked closely at the design. He realized he was holding the Blessed Staff of Life. With adrenaline rushing through his veins, he morphed into his dragon form and placed the staff sideways in his mouth. He fiercely beat his large scaly wings. As his large body lifted off the ground, he turned in the air, flapped his wings, and allowed them to carry him back towards the temple.

Chapter 19 Life's Resurrection

As he carried the staff back to the temple, Death felt everlasting life course through every muscle of his body. He felt completely renewed. It was no wonder that Life always felt so great when she wielded this staff.

A blizzard was beginning when he passed over the last row of jagged mountains, and Death knew that it was even dangerous for a Titan to be trapped in a blizzard. The Titan of Winter had shown firsthand what would happen if one was ever caught in *her* snow storms. He reached the main entrance to the temple and took on his true form. As he walked inside and shut the doors behind him, he made his way up to Life's chambers. He opened her doors and walked inside, noticing that Love, Fire, Curse, and Jennifer were standing in the center of the room talking.

With a deep and commanding voice Death said, "Friends, you can stop your search for the Blessed Staff of Life, for I have found it."

The four of them had not realized that he had returned, but when they heard his voice they all turned towards him. He held the staff up into the air and allowed them to bask in its glory.

"What of Phoenix?" Love asked.

"We won't have to worry about him anymore because he is no longer living." He looked around the room for a moment. "Where did you put Life's body?"

In a sad and weak voice Love said, "Death, there's something I should tell you. Shortly after you departed, Life's body dissolved into green dust and blew away."

"What!? Without her body, we can't resurrect her. Life as we know it will begin to fall apart and die!"

The balcony doors to Life's chambers blew open from the forceful cold winds. As it came in through the threshold, green dust floated into the room as well.

The dust delicately swirled around in a circle on the stone floor as it began to morph into a body. The green dust began to glow emerald green as the last few specs of dust came together to form the deceased Titan of Life. While the others thought she had come back to life, Death knew the truth. He knew that this was only an image of her; a fragment of her very soul trying to communicate with them.

In a chilling voice the image of Life said, "Do not be afraid... This is what I look like in spirit form."

"Life, we found your staff but, without your body, how can we bring you back?" Death asked.

"The only way for me to live again is to have a mortal willingly give me their body, while whoever uses the staff says, 'Powers turn back the Time Maker's clock and undo Fate's decree.' It is the only way for my resurrection to be successful."

"Where could we possibly find a mortal willing enough to end their life so a Titan could take their place?"

Before Life could answer his question, Jennifer interrupted her and said, "I'll do it."

All of the Titans turned around and looked at her in shock.

Slowly approaching her Death said, "Are you absolutely sure you want to do this?"

"Yes, I want to do this for my mistress. I always swore that I would live and die for her."

"Very well then, please kindly follow me."

They walked through the cold halls of the temple until they came to a small room. It was completely bare inside except for a bed that rested in the middle of it. It had a large fluffy white pillow along with white sheets. As they filled into the room, Death walked up to the end of the bed and motioned Jennifer to lie down. Jennifer slowly walked up to the bed and sat down on the edge of it. She threw her legs up onto its soft surface and laid down.

"Now, Jennifer, I want you to know that you won't feel any pain. The only thing you will feel is fatigue," Death said.

"Is this how it feels to die?" she asked as tears filled her eyes.

"Sometimes but, remember, you won't feel a thing," he said, trying to comfort her.

Blinking her tears away Jennifer said, "I'm ready."

"You are such a great oracle. The best I ever had," Life said.

Death placed his left hand on Jennifer's chest and took in a deep breath. As he touched her, his hand began to glow black and she began to turn pale. After a few moments, she closed her eyes and drifted off into an eternal sleep of death.

In a sad voice the image of Life said, "She was the best oracle that ever served me, but we can't mourn her death right now. Death, you need to place the staff in her hands and say the spell now before it's too late."

He quickly placed the staff in Jennifer's right hand and prepared to say the spell.

"Powers turn back the Time Maker's clock and undo Fate's decree."

As he finished the spell, Life's image faded into thin air and the body of Jennifer remained motionless. The four Titans watched the body for several minutes, but nothing happened. They began to turn and leave as any hope of Life returning faded, but were stopped by a faint hum. They quickly turned around and saw that the staff was glowing emerald green and levitating in the air.

Jennifer's body floated into the air and met the staff. Her hand immediately grabbed the staff and she opened her eyes. A flash of light filled the room and, as it faded, Jennifer's body and the staff fell back onto the bed.

As the four Titans' eyes adjusted to the light, they saw Life standing before them and that Jennifer's body had vanished. Remembering her just like he did before she died, Death gave her a big hug.

With a little laughter in her voice Life said, "It sure is good to be back."

Later that night, Life took Death into the throne room and talked to him privately.

As soon as she knew that they were alone, she said, "We can't hide these weapons again, Death. It's too risky. We can't afford to take the risk that they might fall into mortal hands again. It would be the end of the world if someone evil got a hold of them."

"I agree. I love the sword War fashioned me all those years ago, so I am going to withdrawal the magic from the Blessed Sword of Death and place it inside my titanic great sword. It will become the new

Blessed Sword of Death."

He held both swords into the air and formed an X with them.

"Sword of my Father, you are no longer of any use to me. I hereby take the ancient powers trapped within you and place them inside my titanic great sword."

The Blessed Sword of Death created a swirling ray of black power on the outside of its surface. The ray twisted and twirled over the titanic great sword and faded into its blade. As the titanic great sword began to grow even stronger, Death let go of the previous Blessed Sword of Death and let it fall to the ground. The blade shattered into several large and small sharp pieces and turned rusty, while the hilt of the sword turned black.

"It is done. The powers are now safely by my side once again. This unsettles me greatly. Even though it will make me even more powerful and stronger, I now take an even greater step into becoming evil."

"I don't believe you could ever become corrupted, Death. You care too much for the balance. Besides you have—" She stopped, placing her fingers to her forehead, and closed her eyes with a frown. "I sense a great disturbance within the balance," she said.

"I sense it too. An uninvited guest approaches."

They both turned to the door that led into the throne room and saw a mortal they thought they would never see again. Shock filled both their bodies as they tried to comprehend how this was even possible.

With an evil chuckle in his voice Max said, "I had a little help breaking free from my prison." He slowly moved to his left and revealed Death's son. "You, of all people, should have learned that if killed, a God can repair their body if they were in another's. Phoenix was only half a God, and your precious little oracle placed him in my body. She told him if he were to die in this body I would come back and so would he. Don't you understand, he let you kill him? This is the end for the Titan Council."

"I killed you once and I'll do so again," Death yelled.

Death raised the new Blessed Sword of Death into the air and charged at Max. Before he got within striking range, Max did something unexpected. He brought up the Time Maker's Sword and used its powers to cause time to freeze. With time frozen, he was the only one that was able to move. He looked at Death, who was frozen in a running position, and Life, who was frozen holding her staff in front of her in a defensive stance. He saw the previous Blessed Sword of Death destroyed on the floor and knew that Death had taken its magical abilities and placed them within his sword. He ripped the new Blessed Sword of Death out of Death's armored hand and shoved it with great force into his chest. Pulling it out, he walked over to Life and repeated what he had done to Death.

Returning to Phoenix's side, Max unfroze time and watched the devastating effects take place. The powers of the Blessed Sword of Death took hold of the two Titans causing them to fall to the ground in excruciating pain.

"He…he used the T-time Maker's Sword…Ugh," Death said as he dropped his armored head onto the throne room floor.

As Life lay on the cold floor slowly dying, she grabbed her chest in pain, trying to stop the bleeding, and said, "N-not again…"

As she struggled to say those last few words, she laid her head on the ground and slowly slipped away into the darkness of death. As Phoenix watched the two most powerful Titans die, Max walked up to him and placed the Time Maker's Sword in his hands.

"Go through the temple and kill any remaining temple guards, servants, and Titans you may find," Max ordered.

As phoenix walked out of the room, Max walked over to Death's corpse and spit on it.

"You never knew how much I wanted to kill you and now that you are dead, I think I'll take my rightful place in your throne. After all, you won't need it anymore."

Chapter 20 Fall of the Titan Council

Phoenix walked through the halls of the temple in search of anyone that would get in Max's way. He opened door after door, and it seemed to him that each door led to either a room or another hallway. Each led him to another victim that fell shortly after their confrontation.

He walked into yet another hallway and began to walk down it when he was ambushed by the three Titans that were still alive. As they surrounded him, he began to panic and tried to find the nearest escape route. Thinking quickly, he froze time by using the powers of the Time Maker's Sword by stopping the turning gear at the end of its hilt. He took advantage of the moment, for he didn't know how long time would remain frozen. He stabbed Fire in the chest and slit Curse's throat. For Love, however, he went behind her and shoved the blade forcibly through her back. As he walked back in front of them, he watched as the gear on the sword began to turn again and all three of them fell over dead.

As Phoenix walked back into the throne room, he noticed that Max had taken a seat in Death's throne and was wielding Death's sword.

"So, I'm assuming that you are the new controller of Death?"

With an angry glare Max said, "The God version. I have waited a long time for this moment and now it has finally come. The Titans are finally no more and I am finally the one and only ruler of the world."

"What of the Gods still trapped in the Hourglass Dome?"

"They will be dealt with. Weak and pathetic creatures such as them deserve death."

The doors to the entrance of the temple blew open with another strong gust of wind. Through the doors, came a cloaked figure dressed in sand colored robes. With its face hidden beneath its hood, the figure slowly made its way up the stone steps towards the throne room. The figure stared at the ground before Max and Phoenix as if it were too shy to look into their eyes.

With an angry tone Max said, "What is the meaning of this? Why have you tainted the ground of the God of Death?"

Looking up at Max, the figure removed its hood and let it fall onto its back. It slowly walked out of the shadows and into the light where Max could get a better look at it. Max's eyes grew big as he looked upon the figure. He noticed that this strange person was a young woman, most likely in her mid-twenties.

With a small smile on her face the young woman said, "My name is Velyndral. Nice sword you have there."

Looking down at the sword in his hands, Phoenix looked at Max and said," Max, this must be the Titan of Time."

"She doesn't look like a Titan, but I don't like her so I order you to kill her," Max replied.

Showing Max respect, Phoenix bowed and quickly approached the young women. Raising the sword he held in his hands, he prepared to chop off her head. The young woman raised her right hand and caused the sword to rip itself out of Phoenix's hands and softly land in hers. She saw the stupidity in his eyes as he tried to stop running at her, but couldn't. She pointed the sword towards him and waited for him to take his own life. No matter how hard Phoenix tried to stop running, he couldn't. A sharp pain pierced his heart and he looked down to see that the blade was lodged halfway into his chest. Yanking the sword out of his body, Time watched him fall to the ground and bleed to death.

Time looked up from Phoenix's corpse and noticed that Max was still sitting in Death's throne, staring at her in awe.

"Stupid mortals…Always underestimating the powers of time." the young woman muttered.

"Who…Who are you?"

"My name is Velyndral, the Titan of Time, and I am here to reap what you have sown," Time calmly said.

"That's impossible. The temple library said that the Titan of Time disappeared thousands of years ago. The ancient tomes resting on those dusty shelves told of how she became one with her powers so that the fortress could be guarded. If you were to be the Titan of Time, then you would know everything about me."

With a sigh Time said, "You are Max Dawnalow, son of Edwin and Taylor Dawnalow. Edwin died at the age of sixty-five by your hand, Taylor died at the age of sixty-two, also by your hand. You had a sister whose name was Jessi and she died when she was eighteen years old. You had two twin brothers whose names were Jack and Luke. Jack died at the age of fifteen, and Luke is one of my faithful bodyguards. While Luke has become my head soldier within my city, you have managed to kill your Father in an act of betrayal and your Mother, sister, and one of your brothers by sacrificing them to the three Gods of Death, Fire, and Storms."

Max leaped out of Death's throne and dashed towards the nearest exit. Thinking he could get away, he ran towards the door that would lead him out of the throne room. Before he could get to the door, the Titan of Time froze time, walked over to him, and got in front of the door.

With an evil smile, the Titan of Time allowed time to start back up and said, "Where do you think you're going, pathetic God?"

Grabbing him by his neck, Time stared at him with coarse eyes. "I'm going to imprison you, Max. I will turn you to dust and place you in an hourglass."

"No, please. Don't do this. If you let me go, I'll forget that I ever saw you and allow you to leave here with your life."

With an evil laugh Time said, "That would be too easy. After I leave, you would send someone to hunt me down and do the dirty work for you. You're pathetic, Max."

She tightened her grip around his neck and brought the Time Maker's Sword up to his face. As she did so, small sand particles floated off of Max's face and into her blade. As the particles floated off of his face, he began to show signs of age.

His unkempt hair turned grey, his face began to show wrinkles around his eyes, and liver spots began to form on his hands. Minutes passed and Max continued to age. After almost ten minutes, his grey hair turned white, his face produced more wrinkles, and liver spots appeared on his forehead.

Feeling that he had been tortured enough, Time placed the sword back at her side and let go of his throat. After losing so much strength in his legs, Max fell to the ground in pain.

Looking down at him with evil eyes Time said, "You think that was the worst? That was only the beginning, Max. You should have learned your place. If you had, none of this would be happening to you."

She bent down, grabbed him again, and threw him against the wall. She gripped the Time Maker's Sword in her hands and raised it high into the air. She brought it close to his face and showed him his reflection.

As he looked at his reflection within the blade, he let out a scream of horror. Time took the sword back down to her side and placed it up against the wall. She reached into the pocket of her cloak with her free hand and pulled out an empty hourglass. She flipped the top open with her thumb and held it close to Max's face.

Acting like a vacuum, the small hourglass turned Max to sand and sucked him into its tiny lower compartment. As the grains fell through the top and entered the bottom, they formed together to recreate him. Once he was inside, his youthfulness returned to him. Time quickly flipped the lid to the hourglass closed. Sealing it tightly by pressing down on the top, she placed it back in her cloak pocket and picked up her sword. She walked to the center of the throne room and sadly stared down at the bodies of Life and Death. Her power over time was the only thing keeping them whole. If she hadn't placed an invisible cloak of her power to slow the effects of their decay, they would have already been gone.

Chapter 21 Return of the Fallen

Seeing the bodies of Life and Death on the ground, Time knew that it was not how they were meant to die. She held the Time Maker's Sword high into the air and stared blankly at it for a few moments. She closed her eyes and let go of her sword. Instead of falling like any other object would, it floated in the air in front of her. She reopened her eyes and stared at the sword once more. As it floated in the air, Time knew that if she allowed the Titans to remain dead, the world would soon fall apart without the guidance of the immortals.

In a soft voice Time said, "Powers change Fate's decree and heal those who have been ruthlessly murdered."

The sword began to radiate with yellow light and small particles of sand swirled around it. As the sand swirled around it, it fell out of the air and hit the ground with a clang. It glowed brighter and brighter until the sword looked like light itself. It furiously exploded into millions of pieces, sending shards of light in every direction. Light filled the entire room and began to creep through the rest of the temple as if it were alive.

When the lighting had reset to its natural state, Time saw all of the five Titans standing before her. She waved her hand, used her powers to reconstruct the Time Maker's Sword, and looked at each of the Titans.

In shock Life said, "Time, you're alive? When you left the Council, we assumed you died soon after."

With a small smile Time said, "I never lost my immortality, Life, but I did lose most of my titanic powers."

"How have you brought us back from the grave then?"

"After I left the Council, I went to the forgotten planes of Rowmodea where I could be in exile. Through the years, I have watched the Titans and mortals. I went to two futures that could take place. I went to one where Max had succeeded in destroying the Titans and I only saw pain and suffering. Then I went to the future to where the Titans were victorious. I saw peace and prosperity. Being the Titan of Time, I can control how events go."

"I suppose thanks are in order," Death said as he bowed.

Raising her hand Time said, "There are no thanks needed for what had to be done. Now, if you will excuse me, I shall return to my home. I also recommend that you get some rest. You're going to need it."

Later that night, Death stood and peered out his frosted window in his chamber as Life stood behind him with her arms on her hips.

"We can't go on like this, Death. The powers of the Gods are too powerful for us to keep locked up anymore. Mortals will begin looking for ways to tap in on their evil powers and use them against us. You know, more than any other Titan, that the mortals are actually quite intelligent."

"What do you propose we do then?"

"Put an end to it. Stop this madness at its source. Destroy what remains of the Fallen Gods. Their corruption is destroying the purity of the mortal race."

"There is only one way to destroy their evil powers once and for all," he said as he turned to face her. "Phoenix was not evil until he entered Max's body. We can bring him back and send him into the Hourglass Dome. From within that prison we can have all the magic surrounding him engulf the area and cause it to detonate, destroying him and everything else with it."

"Wouldn't that release the Gods?"

"No, in truth, the Gods are extremely weak from all this time trapped within the Hourglass Dome. It truly is the only thing that is keeping them alive. Time created it for that purpose. It was designed to imprison and keep the prisoners alive, but only just. It is a fate worse than death. Take that out and the rest will fall into place."

In a disagreeing tone Life said, "Are you sure this plan of yours will work? I don't want it backfiring in our faces."

"Of course it will. Now, go get Phoenix's body and bring him here."

Life left Death's chamber and headed back to the throne room to fetch Phoenix's body. An hour went by and Death was beginning to wonder if Life was ever going to return with his body. Just as he began to walk towards his chamber doors, they creaked on their hinges as they swung open. Life staggered into the room dragging Phoenix on the floor behind her.

Panting as she walked into the room, she said, "You have no idea how heavy he is…"

Death picked him up by his feet and helped her lift him onto his bed. He raised the palm of his hand up into the air and closed his eyes. A small blue ghostly orb appeared and began to slowly float above his armored palm. He opened his eyes, walked to the left side of the bed, and placed the ghostly blue orb on Phoenix's chest. Almost in an instant, the orb sank into his chest and gave Phoenix life once more.

As Phoenix gasped for air, Death looked at him and said, "You have been brought back from the dead to serve the Titans one last time. You will go into the Hourglass Dome located on the east side of the temple and blow it up."

Phoenix rose from the bed and looked into the cold eyes of his Father. Without a word, he left the chamber and made his way towards the Hourglass Dome.

"I hope your plan works, Death. I really do," Life said as she watched Phoenix leave.

Phoenix walked into the Hourglass Dome and looked around the glass structure. As he examined the room's architect, he noticed several small hourglasses with tiny humans inside them. The tiny prisons rested on glass shelves that stretched around the whole chamber. He also noticed a stone pedestal resting in the center of the room that held another hourglass on it.

As he approached the stone pedestal, he reached for the small object. Phoenix picked it up and looked through the crystal clear glass. He was shocked to see Max trapped inside its glass surface. To make sure he wasn't hallucinating, he blinked several times and looked back inside.

Still seeing Max, Phoenix said, "Master?"

Hearing a voice, Max looked up from burying his face in his knees and saw Phoenix holding his prison.

"Phoenix, smash the glass and release me from this forsaken prison!"

Without any thought, Phoenix raised his hand he held the small hourglass in and threw it as hard as possible towards the ground. As the small object hit the ground, the force of the impact was too much for it to take. Giving in to the pressure of gravity and the force applied to its fragile surface, the small hourglass shattered into hundreds of tiny pieces and scattered across the floor.

With his prison shattered, Max was able to break free from Time's enchantment and grew back to his normal height.

Looking to the ground in respect Phoenix said, "Master, the Titans have ordered me to destroy this place. They seem to think if they eliminate what remains of the Gods, they will never have to worry about future betrayals."

"Do what they command then. I was going to destroy them anyway. They are weak and self-centered. Where were the Gods in my hour of greatest need? I'll tell you where, DEAD! They went and got themselves slaughtered! They deserve to die!"

"Master, you should know that the Titans have ordered me to pull the magic within this area to this spot and use it to destroy this place. In doing so, we will not survive."

"Don't you worry about that. Being a sorcerer that was taught by a very powerful wizard has allowed me to learn things others could not. I learned how to teleport from place to place. I will be able to teleport us safely away from the blast."

Without any further objections, Phoenix bowed before his true master and allowed him to take care of the technicalities. Max used his powers to pull the magic contained within the Hourglass Dome to his location and allowed it to build in power so that it would grow unstable. He quickly grabbed Phoenix's arm and teleported a hundred yards outside of the Hourglass Dome. With a quaking boom, the Hourglass Dome exploded in a fiery rage, sending black smoke shaped like a large mushroom high into the sky and debris across the valley.

Chapter 22 A Tragic End

While Max and Phoenix stood up against the Crystalrock Mountains within the valley and watched what was left of the Hourglass Dome be consumed by black smoke and fire, Life strolled on the other side of the magical vale. She approached the tree that Regina had become and knelt down before it.

Placing her hand on the rugged bark, Life took in a deep breath and allowed her hand to radiate with emerald green power. As her magic sank into the beautiful evergreen, it slowly faded into a shimmering stream of green magic and floated towards Life's chambers. Settling in the center of her room, the tree reformed, becoming the final decoration that made her chamber complete.

Upon returning to her chamber, Life examined the beauty it expelled. "Regina…By moving you here, your safety is ensured."

"Nice tree…" came a deep, echoing voice.

"Death…" Life said as she turned to face him.

"It is done. The Hourglass Dome is in ruin. The remnants of the Fallen Gods is no more."

"Then…there truly is no going back from the events that have been set in motion. I wonder, though…Will we go away from this stronger?" Life said, and she transformed into a small bird and flew up to a branch of the tree.

Meanwhile, Max and Phoenix continued to watch the remains of the ancient prison of the Gods burn into nothingness. Max smiled with a nefarious grin as he brought his gaze towards Phoenix. "Phoenix, I want you to go back inside the temple. I have a little task for you within those sacred walls."

"That's suicide. The Titans think I was killed in the blast."

"Enough! Do as I command or I will kill you right here and now!"

With a sigh Phoenix asked, "What kind of task?"

"I want you to go back inside the temple and locate the Titan of Curses. He has been given a task since before he became a Titan. You will go and aid him in the murder of the Titan of Death."

"Yes, Master. He will fall in your name."

Phoenix slowly walked away from Max and walked through the quiet moonlit valley. He opened the doors to the temple and saw Curse walking up the main stone steps that would take him to the throne room and Death's chamber.

Practically yelling Phoenix said, "Curse, Max has sent me to aid you in killing Death."

Turning from his path Curse harshly whispered, "Keep your voice down, you moron. Do you want to blow my cover? Go on up, I have to grab something from my room first."

"Sorry, I'll meet you at Death's chamber."

As he reached the old wooden doors to Death's chamber, Phoenix stopped for a moment. Worry began to fill his mind.

Whispering to himself Phoenix said, *"What if this plan backfires and gets me killed? Or worse, what if after killing my Father, Curse uses one of his spells on me! No, no stop thinking that. You have been given an order and you must fulfill it."*

Grabbing the iron handles to the doors, Phoenix slowly opened them allowing them to creak on their hinges. Upon entering the room, he saw that Death was standing at his window looking out to the dark night sky of the valley.

"Hello, Father…"

Turning from his window, Death looked at his son with glowing, cold eyes.

With a slight hint of shock in his voice Death said, "Hello, Phoenix. What brings you here this late in the evening?"

"You aren't even the slightest bit curious as to how I survived the desolation of the Hourglass Dome?" Phoenix asked.

"I could only imagine how you escaped that fate. Alas, I know you haven't come here for a reunion."

"You're right. I have come to kill you, Father. I take orders from a higher power."

"That's interesting. If you are referring to Max, then you are unwise. He is no high power. He is just a foolish man who never knows when to give up."

"He's more of a man than you'll ever be!"

"Is that so? You may strike me down, but as soon as I'm out of the way, Max will toss you aside."

Phoenix was about to protest more, but noticed that his Father's attention was no longer on him. He quickly turned towards the doorway to see Curse. Curse stared at Phoenix for a moment then looked over to Death, who was now standing in front of his closed glass doors that led to his private balcony.

In a harsh voice Death said, "Curse, it seems that we have a traitor within our midst. You know as well as I what we must do with traitors."

Looking back at Phoenix and then back at Death, Curse seemed as though he was unable to decide what he should do. In an instant, however, he raised his right arm and stretched out his palm. He aimed at Death, who didn't seem shocked at all. Perhaps it was because he still wore his helmet, and with that on, it was difficult to see his emotions.

"So, the truth finally comes out. I felt a disturbance within the balance shortly after giving you your power, but I had assumed it was because you possessed powers in the art of demonology. I brushed the disturbance off when I shouldn't have. A mistake I will not make again," he said, looking over to his bed and glancing at the new Blessed Sword of Death.

"Oh Death, only now at the end do you truly understand what you are up against. My Master will remove the invisible cloak that you placed around the world and help the Aikanadenbaria reclaim his rightful rule on this forsaken planet. He will reshape this world in darkness!" Curse said in a demonic tone.

"The Aikanadenbaria is dead, destroyed many millenniums ago. As for removing the invisible cloak that the Titans placed around the planet, he will have to destroy everyone who participated in the ritual."

With evil eyes Curse yelled, "Melarnagas!"

A strange and forbidden dark magic shot like a coil out of his palm and hit Death upon his chest. The force of the impact knocked him backwards, sending him through the glass doorway. He landed halfway on the stone balcony outside his room while his lower torso remained inside.

Both Curse and Phoenix looked down at Death's body for a short time. He didn't move or breath and Curse knew that the spell he used had been successful.

"Phoenix, return to Max and tell him of our triumph over the Titans. I must stay here and act as though nothing has happened."

As they walked out of Death's room and began to head their separate ways, Phoenix said, "Curse, that was no spell a Titan has ever used. Nor is it a language that I can comprehend. What did you say?"

"I said obliterate in a demonic tongue. Now, off with you. I'm sure Life will know of this soon and you are supposed to be dead. You don't want to be caught by another Titan."

Phoenix bowed before him and made his way down the large stone steps to the entrance of the temple.

A horrific disturbance within the balance had Life startled. She had never felt a dishevelment of this magnitude before. She walked through the cold halls and up the stone stairs of the temple to visit Death and to ask if he had felt the similar disorientation. She trembled at just thinking of it. She had to know what it meant. As she reached his chambers, she walked inside to see the horror she hoped she would never see. Seeing her best friend and her secret love lying through his smashed glass doorway made her run up to him and fall to her knees.

Screaming in horror, she said, "Death, no...Please...come back."

She pulled him back inside and noticed a black mark on his breastplate. She quickly removed his helmet and looked at his snow white hair and white pale skin. She franticly looked for a pulse or any other sign of life, but couldn't find anything. She used all the strength she could muster to lift him and placed him on his soft bed. She placed the Blessed Sword of Death in his hands and stared at him with tears streaming down her face.

Sprinting down the hallway, Life made her way towards the throne room. She knew that all of the other Titans would be there watching over the mortals and discussing plans for the future. She burst through the doors and looked at everyone. They were in a small group all whispering. She saw another woman standing with the Titans. This woman had short, frosty white hair that didn't go past her neck, and she wore light blue robes that flowed onto the floor. On the gown were images of snowflakes along with frost around the bottom and sleeves of the garments. Life knew exactly who she was and seeing her caused tears of joy to stream down her face. She remembered that the last time she saw this woman was when Max had attacked the temple and almost destroyed the Titan Council.

She slowly approached the group of immortals and said, "W-winter...It is so good to see you."

All of the Titans turned towards her as Winter turned around and said, "Life, it's great to see you as well," she came forward and gave her a hug. "Wait, where's Death?"

Life closed her eyes grimly as more tears fell down her face. "Death...is dead. I found him in his room moments ago. Looking at his condition, he was killed by someone or something."

With wide eyes Love shouted, "What?! How could this be? What was the cause of his death?"

"I'm not sure what the cause was but whatever spell was used left a deadly black scorch mark on his breastplate. I can only assume that it killed him instantly. I came to find Curse because he is good with dark spells," turning her attention to him, she said, "Curse, do you think you can identify what spell was used and the effect?"

"Take me to his body, I can try."

Gathering around his bed, the other Titans watched eagerly as Curse used his powers to test what spell was used. He swiped his index finger across the mark and brought it up to his nose.

"Just by smelling it, I can tell that the spell that was used was demonic. This pains me because this makes me a potential suspect."

"But we all know it wasn't you. You would never do something like this," Love said.

He placed his hand on the mark and closed his eyes while taking a deep breath. A vision filled into his mind. He quickly pulled his hand away and stood up.

"What did you see?" Life urged.

"I saw some dark figure stretch his hand towards Death. He said something in a demonic tongue, but I will need time to translate it."

"Very well, but we need to resurrect him now before it's too late."

"We can't, not yet anyway. We can't risk bringing him back without knowing exactly what this spell does. What if we bring him back and it begins torching him? I will get right on translating the spell. In the meantime, move his body to the room we sacrificed Jennifer in."

The next morning, they entered the sacrificial chamber where Jennifer had given her life to the Titan of Life. Death's body rested on the bed in the center of the room and all of the Titans gathered around the bed. As Love, Fire, Curse, and Winter stood around the bed, Life walked up with the Blessed Staff of Life. She held the staff high into the air and prepared to do the resurrection spell, but was interrupted when she saw several small cracks appear all over Death's armor and face. The cracks released black smoke that evaporated almost immediately after rising into the air. As the smoke rose out of his body, the small cracks widened, causing the vapor to escape even quicker. His body disintegrated after all the black smoke had fled from his body, leaving everyone in the room in shock.

With a sad look on her face Love said, "What do we do now?"

"I don't know. I can't even sense his," Life began to say, but was interrupted as the door to the room opened with a whoosh and slammed against the stone wall.

Everyone turned their heads towards the doorway and saw a young woman who looked like she was in her early twenties standing in the threshold. She wore brown leather boots, tight brown leather pants, and a gold-trimmed white blazer over her white shirt. Around her neck was a silver chain with three turquoise stones. Her long brown hair was wavy and went down to the middle of her back.

As she approached the five Titans, Life recognized her as the Guardian of the Titans. The young woman bowed graciously before the five of them and then looked at Life with soft, loving eyes.

With shock in her voice Life said, "Sellithia? You're alive?"

"Yes, Mistress and I bring news. The dragon known as Nethemious is dead. His tyranny has finally come to an end. I also have to tell you something that you will find interesting. Before I left for my journey, Death gave me the ability to see what a Titan was doing or what was happening to a Titan at any time. I am well aware that Death is dead and I know how he died. I also know who his murderer is. It just so happens that he is standing in this very chamber."

Everyone looked around the room trying to figure out who the murderer was.

Laughing at the situation Sellithia said, "Oh this is just priceless. Give up the charade, foolish man. Go ahead and tell them how he died, Curse. Surly you can shed some light on the subject."

Realizing that his true identity had been revealed Curse said, "Yes, I killed Death under the orders of my true Master, Max. It truly is amazing that even the great and powerful Titan of Life couldn't see through this deception. Max and I had all this planned from the very beginning. There was only one flaw; one lose end we didn't think of."

In shock, everyone backed away from him, afraid of what he might do next.

He raised his hand, aimed his palm at Sellithia, and said, "My Master secretly raised that dragon from an egg. He trained it to be a weapon for the Titans. Death, of course, saw it as a monstrosity. Max was ordered to kill it but he had other plans. When Death sent you to go kill it, Max and I assumed that it would make you one of its meals. Instead, you managed to kill it. You have ruined my Master's plans for far too long, bitch, but I will take care of that."

He formed a ball of green fire in his hand and prepared to throw it at her, but before he could, Life stepped in front of her.

"We gave you all you could ever want, Herladrick, and yet you through your lot in with Max. You pledged an oath that you would use your powers for good and help keep the world in balance. How dare you betray us?" Life yelled as she transformed into a monstrous white tiger and leaped at him.

Knowing that he had just angered the last and strongest Titan, Curse threw the ball of green fire to the ground and created a large wall of green, demonic flames. Everyone stared at him through the green wall of corrupted fire as he began to teleport out of the room.

"None of you know what you are up against. You should have abandoned this world long ago! Don't you understand? This world is doomed. It was destined to burn along with everyone on it. It will be reduced to nothingness and from the ashes a new world order shall be born. The world's true master will come back and we will all be his eternal servants!" Curse said as he threw up his hand and teleported out of the room.

The fire died shortly after Curse fled the chamber and Life took on her true form. She, along with all the other Titans, sprinted out of the room and headed towards the throne room. As they entered the chamber, Life walked out onto the balcony and saw Herladrick running away towards the mountains.

Turning to face the others Life said, "Go and secure the rest of the temple and prepare for war. It's only a matter of time before Herladrick returns with Max and his army. As for you, Sellithia, I want you to come with me."

While the other Titans ran off to secure the rest of the temple, Life and Sellithia ran out of the main entrance to the temple and stood on the soft green grass of the valley. Life closed her eyes, threw her arms up into the air, and began to chant a spell that Sellithia couldn't comprehend.

Sellithia protected her while she cast her enchantment. She looked around the valley and saw large creatures that had rotting flesh and bone. They wore black tattered robes and one of their arms had been replaced with a metal scythe that had shadows circling around the blades.

In horror, she grabbed Life's arm and said, "What are those things?"

Slowly opening her eyes, Life looked towards the direction she was pointing in and said, "Shadowscythes, they are guardians of the Shadow Realms. It would appear that since Death is dead, they no longer are bound to the Shadow Realms."

"Why are they here though?" she asked as worry crept through every vein in her body.

"They have come to protect their Masters. The spell I was muttering was more of a prayer to Death so that he would watch over us. It seems that he wants the Shadowscythes to aid us in this fight," she said as they went back into the temple and waited for Max to make his first move.

Walking out onto the rectangular balcony overlooking the sacred valley, Life and Sellithia leaned up against the stone railing and stared out towards the mountains. They watched as the sun began to set behind their large jaggy peaks and knew that by sun fall someone would walk away the victor.

"Mistress, forgive me for disrupting the silence, but something has me disturbed."

Life looked over to her beautiful apprentice and placed her soft hand on Sellithia's. "What is it, my child?"

"When Death died…" she began as she looked into Life's emerald green eyes. She watched as Life's eyes closed and a grim expression spread across her face. "Curse told him that Max would usher the Aikanadenbaria back into this world. Who is that?"

"The Aikanadenbaria? He's ugh…nothing."

"No. I know that face. You're hiding something."

"Sellithia…The Aikanadenbaria was destroyed long ago. He was many things. In a way, he was our source of life."

"Why is there no mention of him in the temple library?"

"Death saw it best to purge all knowledge of him. He…He was terrible, Sellithia."

"And this invisible cloak that surrounds our planet. Will it hold even if the Titans fall?"

Life grasped Sellithia by her arms and stared into her eyes. "Sellithia, you need not worry about that. As long as the powers of the Titans remain, the protection around the planet shall not fall."

"Forgive the interruption, Life, but Love has reported movement through the mountain paths," Winter said as she walked out onto the balcony.

Turning to face her Life said, "Thank you, Winter." Looking back at Sellithia, she said, "Shall we prepare?"

"Yes, Mistress," Sellithia replied as she and Life followed Winter through the archway of the balcony.

Chapter 23 Fall of Peace

Gathering around Max and Curse, an army of an enormous size waited for the order to attack the temple and leave their deadly mark on the Titans. Looking around the valley, Max could see every defense they had put in place to slow him down. Shadowscythes slowly walked around the temple, several of the trees were waving their roots and branches around, and several men from the Nygensa Nation were even moving around the valley.

"Without Death, they don't stand a chance. His wisdom is what drove them for all these millenniums. Their defenses are weak and will easily crumble under the weight of my mighty fist! With the remainder of the loyalists who form up the Covenant, we will be victorious. Men... attack!"

As they charged across the valley, the Shadowscythes looked over to the sound of armor clashing together to see the army quickly approaching the temple. They screeched in unison and charged at the army of foolish mortals with their upraised scythed hands, ready to cleave their weapons into their skulls.

Max knew none of them would survive against creatures of that strength and knew he had to do something.

"Malnar setha fleus ta!" he said in a demonic tongue.

The Shadowscythes fell to their hands and knees, screeching in pain as the spell Max cast wrapped itself around their rotting minds. The spell bound them to his will and forced them to turn on their former allies within the sacred walls of the temple and release their deadly powers. They released shimmering black balls of corrupted energy and sent them sailing towards the temple. Each left a deadly mark on the temple as the corrupted energies seeped into the ancient stone walls and reduced them to rubble. One of the corrupted balls hit a small tower next to Love's chambers and caused it to collapse.

As the tower cracked, crumbled to the ground, and turned into a black mushy mud, Life ran up to it and grabbed some of the blackened, wretched sludge. She felt the dark magic coursing through the slushy muck as she held it in her soft hands and knew that this would decimate the entire temple if the Shadowscythes weren't stopped. She tightened her grip on the Blessed Staff of Life and raised it high into the air. The large emerald that rested in the center of the twisting branches of the staff blazed to life and shot a beam of emerald green power into the sky. A green sphere formed at the end of the beam and produced small lightning bolts of green auras that shot down to the valley below. Each bolt zipped across the sky and struck the Shadowscythes one by one.

Struggling to get free, the Shadowscythes thrashed about the battlefield, swinging their scythed hands back and forth taking out some of Max's men as they went. They continued to struggle against the small beams of lightning tethering them to the ground as it shocked them to death. Their high pitched screeches could be heard across the island as they exploded into shadows and faded away.

Though Max had suffered a great loss by losing the Shadowscythes, he and his men pushed forward and began to block exits so that the Titans couldn't escape again. What Max didn't realize was that none of the Titans planned on losing the war this time and to insure that they didn't, they used all the energy they could dwell on to defeat the mortals.

Hours of endless onslaught went by and Life could tell that Fate was on their side, for not one Titan had fallen but over hundreds of mortals had. The carnage spilt amongst the holy ground inspired the Titan Council to push forward through the darkness of despair.

"Push on champions of the light! Their numbers drop rapidly!" Life yelled over the clash of swords and armor.

The tides changed as those words left her lips. It was as though she had jinxed them because they all began to grow weak and they found themselves surrounded on all sides.

Producing a massive wave of flames, Fire kept his enemies at bay for only a few moments. While his attention was on the group of mortals, Max snuck up behind him and forcibly shoved his sword into his back. He fell to the ground as the air left him. He looked over to his assassin and saw Max.

As his life slowly slipped out of his grasps, he pointed a shaking finger at Max and said, "You will rue this day...I promise you that..."

He fell limp as he took his last breath. Orange cracks that flickered with small flames spread out across his body and began to consume him. The flickering flames turned his robes and body to ash as Max walked away as though murder had not just broke free.

Max climbed the large stone staircase within the grand temple and made his way towards the eastern wing of the temple knowing that the Titan of Love would be hiding in her room. He knew from the information that Herladrick had collected, that after she took on her role of love, she hated warfare. She believed in making love not war. She would avoid a fight as much as possible if she could. As he slowly walked through the eastern corridors, he could hear screaming from the valley. As he made his way towards a spiral staircase, he saw the room that Death had been taken to. He saw that Death's sword was still lying on the bed and knew he had to claim it as his own. He threw his sword to the ground, picked up the Blessed Sword of Death, and then proceeded to climb the spiral staircase to confront Love.

At the top, Love stood in front of her window within the chamber. The walls were pink, along with the bed sheets and curtains. There were love letters scattered all over the room and *toys* that Love used during her private times.

"Well, someone has been busy," Max said.

He walked further into the room and saw that she was staring out to the battlefield below. She slowly turned towards him, pulled two concealed daggers from her slutty robes, placed one in front of her chest, and pointed the other at Max. Looking at her made him feel strange. Strange enough that he wanted to spare her and procreate with her.

"You wouldn't kill a pregnant woman, would you?"

"Pregnant? Oh that is so precious. You aren't even a Titan for more than two days and you're already knocked up. Let me guess, the Father is Death, isn't it?"

Love seemed shocked, for how could he possibly have known.

"With you being the Titan of Love, it doesn't surprise me that you allowed Death to take you so quickly. How long did you wait?" he laughed evilly.

"I will not allow you to destroy what Life and Death have worked so hard on to achieve, even if it means losing two lives," she replied.

She charged at him with both daggers raised high into the air, but before she could plunge them into his body, he brought up his right knee and hit her stomach. She fell to the ground in agenizing pain as the air was knocked out of her. Max quickly tore the dagger from her left hand, shoved it deep into her side, and twisted it. He ripped it out and watched as her blood poured from the gaping hole.

"I have…failed you, Death. I'm…sorry," she said as tears fell down her face.

She slowly rested her head on the stone floor of her room and watched with weak eyes as her blood moved outwards and stained the stone tiles. With one final breath, she looked up at Max and died.

Max looked at her pale body for a few moments. As he turned to leave, he was stopped by a strange image that had appeared on her breast. An average sized, pink heart appeared on her chest. It had a crack down the center of it and other small cracks spread out from it across her sexy body. As the cracks spread across her body, they spread wider. Power the color of magenta began to flow from the cracks as her powers over love began to escape into the atmosphere. Her whole body faded away as the last of her power vanished into thin air leaving behind sparkling pink dust. As the dust particles settled over the pool of blood, Max turned towards the doorway to leave. He was stopped when he saw that the entrance was blocked by a shadowy figure.

"Hello, Max. I am the Guardian of the Titans. I know what you have done. It is time to step up and account for the atrocities you have committed," the shadowy figure said as it stepped into the light and revealed itself to be Sellithia.

She unsheathed two one handed swords that hung from her waist and charged at Max. He quickly grabbed the Blessed Sword of Death and violently swung at her, but was surprised at how agile she was. She dodged all of his attacks and this angered him. He brought up his knee and kicked her in the stomach. She quickly fell to the ground trying to catch her breath. Max took this opportunity to stab her, but with each deadly attempt to plunge the blade into her, he was stopped by Winter.

Winter had followed Sellithia and was now casting bolts of frost at the Blessed Sword of Death to knock it away each time Max brought it down. Max glared angrily at her and kicked Sellithia again as he ran past her towards Winter.

Winter ran down the hall and threw balls of frost at him, trying to get away, but he closed in on her. He threw the Blessed Sword of Death at her and struck her in the back. She fell to the ground and died instantly. Max quickly ran up to her, grabbed the sword, and then made his way towards Death's chamber.

Sellithia ran down the hall and saw that Winter had been killed. She saw Max running towards Death's chamber and knew she had to warn Life. She gave her respects to Winter as she ran past her and made her way towards the valley.

Max burst through the doors to Death's chamber, quickly shutting and locking them behind him. He waved his hand in front of him and summoned Phoenix.

As his sight returned to him Phoenix said, "Max, it would be wise to call off this attack before it is too late. Our numbers are dropping rapidly and though the Titans are also almost defeated, we will lose before the last one falls."

"Shut up, you buffoon! I will not call off this attack! The Titans are weak and will be extinct once and for all before the night has come to an end. Leave me! Go find Herladrick and have him report here!"

Phoenix bowed before him and teleported out of the room to find Herladrick. Max moved over to the shattered doorway of the balcony and stared out it in wait for his apprentice.

After an hour of waiting, Max opened the doors to the balcony and walked out on to it to get some fresh air. He could still hear fighting in the valley on the other side of the temple, but hadn't heard if Life had fallen yet.

With a bright flash, Herladrick teleported into the room and said, "You wished to see me?"

"Yes, I need to talk to you," Max said as Herladrick walked onto the balcony with him.

Max walked over to the doorway to the balcony causing Herladrick to turn away from the edge of the balcony.

"What is it that you need to tell me, my Master? You have pulled me away from the battle. Phoenix has fallen, and our numbers dwindle."

Max raised the Blessed Sword of Death and began to examine it. "This sword is not as strong as you said. No power should be able to force the blade away from its victim, but yet Winter was able to. She saved Sellithia by using her powers to force the sword away from Sellithia's body. If nothing is supposed to be able to challenge this blade, why is it that Winter was able to?" Max asked with wide eyes.

"You are not the sword's owner. Death created it himself. Only he could truly use it to its fullest. He was the only one that was able to make it resist power. Anyone else who uses it cannot do such a thing."

"So then, if one was tainted with his blood, the sword would recognize them as Death. You killed him, Herladrick, which means it will obey you."

Looking at Max with a stupid look spreading across his face Herladrick said, "Have you not been listening? I told you, he was the Titan of Death and the sword was created to best suit the wielder of death! It will only ever work best for him. He was the only one left alive that could control death."

He noticed that Max was ignoring him because all he would do is stare at him and smile.

With fear beginning to consume him Herladrick said, "Max, what are you…"

Max dove forward and shoved the Blessed Sword of Death deep into Herladrick. As he ripped it free, Herladrick gasped for breath as the power of the blade took hold of his soul. He grabbed Max's arm to support himself, but Max pulled his arm away and pushed him backwards. Curse stumbled and tripped as he bumped up against the railing of the balcony. He fell backwards off of the balcony and fell to his death. Max stared down at his body and looked at all the blood. He brought the sword up close to his face and moved his tongue across its metal surface licking the blood of his fallen apprentice. As he licked the blade one more time, he made his way out of the room and headed towards the eastern courtyard to confront Life.

The courtyard overlooked the valley between the temple and the Crystalrock Mountains. Standing at the edge of the wall, Life looked down at the valley as Max approached her with the Blessed Sword of Death raised high into the air. As he got closer to her, she turned around to face him. She grabbed the Blessed Staff of Life and pointed it at him.

With anger consuming every inch of her face, Life said, "We are going to finish this once and for all, Max…Just you…and me…"

She sprinted towards Max and raised the staff high into the air. As she got in range, she twirled her staff around her back and swung it forward like a bat. As it sliced through the air, it made a whooshing sound. Max blocked the staff just moments before it came into contact with his face with Death's sword. As the two weapons met, they made a horrific sound and used their very own powers to push each other away. Max ran towards Life again, but as he approached, he jumped high into the air and brought his sword down over his head. Life placed her staff in both her hands and placed it over her head to stop Max, but the sword's power was too powerful. The moment the sword and the staff made contact, the staff shattered and lost all its magical ability, except for its control over immortality. The sheer power of the impact threw both Life and Max to the ground.

Life slowly limped to her feet and saw that her staff was in hundreds of shards. She quickly regained her strength and did a flip in the air. As she passed over Max's head, she placed both her hands on his shoulders for support. She flipped around onto the ground behind him. She quickly grabbed his arm that held the sword and twisted it behind his back. In agenizing pain, he dropped the sword and struggled free from Life's grasps. As he backed away from her, Life began to realize how she could kill him once and for all. She knew from past experiences that since Max had been immortal, he still had small bits of immortal power coursing through his veins. With that, Max could cheat death if an immortal killed him. She quickly came up with a plan to kill him, but she knew it would mean taking her own life as well. She knew that Sellithia was down in the valley fighting what was left of Max's army and she knew that it had to be her that killed him. Though she wore the necklace that had all the Titans powers in it and it kept her immortal. Life knew that once she was gone, the last bit of the power contained within the necklace would be lost making Sellithia mortal once again.

Life transformed into a giant white tiger and dashed at Max. She head butted Max in the stomach which caused him to stumble backwards closer to the edge of the courtyard. She jumped into the air, clung to him, and sunk her claws deep into his flesh. He screamed in pain as they toppled over the edge of the courtyard. A few pieces of the Blessed Staff of Life fell with them as they came closer to the ground. With a massive thud, Life broke her neck on impact while Max landed on her back. He softened his fall just enough to survive, but he had broken nearly every bone in his body. He rose from the ground bloody and beaten and tried to run away, but fell to the ground. His left leg was broken and the bone was sticking out of his shin.

Sellithia slowly walked up to Max as he crawled away from her. She shoved one of her swords in his other leg so he couldn't crawl away.

Screaming in pain, Max looked behind him to see her kneeling beside him.

"Do you feel successful, Max? You finally completed your goal. But at what cost?"

Max looked at her with pain in his eyes and said, "I may…have lost my life…but I am…victorious. You have failed…"

As he finished, he coughed up blood and let it flow down his face.

With a bitter look on her face Sellithia said, "You may have killed the Titans, but you failed to kill their guardian. Your stupidity has caused you to lose this war. Since you failed to kill me and seeing that you are the last of your men, it looks like you lose."

She took her other sword and, with incredible strength, shoved it into his back.

With a gasp of shock and pain, Max looked at the two swords that were deep inside his body. He looked back up at Sellithia as she ripped the one in his back out of his body. He coughed up tons of blood, fell forwards, and died. Sellithia wanted to make sure he wasn't going to come back. She swung the sword down on his neck and separated his head from his body.

Now that he was dead, Sellithia could stop pretending that she wasn't weakened. She slowly limped over to Life's motionless body and picked up a shard of the shattered staff. The immortality that the Titans had given her was now beginning to fade since the last Titan was dead. She knew the only way to keep her immortality was to take the piece of the staff she held in her hand and keep it on her at all times. This would allow her not only to keep her immortality, but to continue to uphold the Titan banner.

She pulled the necklace around her neck off and removed the three turquoise stones. She took the silver chain and wrapped it tightly around the shard of the destroyed staff. She quickly placed it around her neck and felt the raw powers of the Titans return to her veins. She felt completely renewed. As her immortality retuned, she looked down at Life and saw that her tiger form had dissolved and Life's true form had been revealed.

Green cracks appeared all over her body and robes and grew wider. As they grew wider, Sellithia noticed small images of green leaves and green energy beginning to float out of her body and consume it. As her body turned completely green, a green beam erupted from her chest and began to lift her into the air. The power of the green beam was so intense that it caused a massive gust of wind to surround the area. It twisted and twirled around the temple, causing the whole structure to collapse with a loud thud. The green beam faded shortly after the temple collapsed and Sellithia saw that it had dissolved Life's body.

A whisper of Life's voice filled into Sellithia's head and said, "*Go child, go, and take from this a story to tell mortals.*"

Sellithia slowly walked away from the ruins of the temple and made her way to the beach. She saw a ship out at sea that Max had most definitely used to bring his army to Rowmodea and knew that the ship was her only way of getting off the island.

Chapter 24 Rise of The Aikanadenbaria

With a small smile on her face the young woman said, "And that's the story of the Great Titans and how they were destroyed by the greatest threat to our world."

In shock Thoi-Thagian said, "That...was an amazing story, madam. I wonder though, what happened to Sellithia?"

"Oh, she is out there somewhere, telling the story to others," she giggled.

The young woman rose from her chair, slipped on her long fur coat, and headed towards the door. She smiled at the bartender as he waved at her. As she opened the door, a young couple entered.

Thoi-Thagian rose from his chair as she took a step through the wooden doorway and yelled, "Excuse me, madam! You never told me your name."

Turning back to face him the young woman said, "My name is Sellithia."

She quickly turned back towards the door and walked outside into the snowy weather, leaving the young man in shock.

Moments later, after she had walked past two more buildings, Thoi-Thagian ran up to her and said, "You're Sellithia? Prove it."

She stopped walking and looked at him with soft eyes. "If I prove it, you have to promise me that you won't tell anyone about my true identity."

"I promise!" he said eagerly.

With a small sigh, Sellithia reached down her shirt and pulled out the shard of the staff that she had described in the story.

Shock filled his face as Thoi-Thagian said, "Wow...it really is you!"

With a small smile, she replied, "Yes, but you must keep this a secret. Even though Max is dead, there are those who would still attempt to bring forth The Darkness he attempted."

With an evil smile on his face, Thoi-Thagian twisted his wrist so that his palm faced upwards and produced a squirming ball of dark magic.

"There is no need to worry about Max or any of his men. There are far greater threats in this world than him. Just...like...me!"

Thoi-Thagian's eyes turned crimson red and his teeth became sharp points. Sellithia gasped in shock and brought up her left leg, kicking him in his chin and causing him to throw his hand backwards. The corrupted ball of energy fell towards the ground.

She quickly dashed away from him and ran into an alley. She slumped down behind a dumpster and quietly breathed while she waited for him to pass by. While she waited, she felt as though someone was behind her. She slowly began to turn to look who it was when a hand grabbed her mouth and pulled her backwards. She looked at the stranger with fear in her eyes, but realized that it was the Titan of Time.

In a quiet voice Sellithia said, "Velyndral? I thought you were dead. There were stories after stories of your death within the temple's library."

"No, and I see you need me now more than ever. It's time I took matters into my own hands," she replied as she grabbed Sellithia's arm and pulled her to her feet.

She pulled her alongside her as she walked out onto the street. As they walked to the center of the road, Sellithia noticed that Thoi-Thagian was standing in the center as well. He had his palm pointed at Time, and Sellithia wondered if Time knew who she was dealing with. She watched in horror, but squeezed her eyes shut when she saw him hurl the twisting orb of dark magic. After a few moments, she slowly opened her eyes to see if another spell was headed towards her. As she looked over towards Thoi-Thagian, she saw the corrupted energy source frozen in time directly in front of Velyndral's face. She looked down and saw that Time wasn't holding on to her anymore. She was using that hand to freeze time and her other hand to open a portal.

In a harsh voice Time yelled, "Go! Go through the portal! I'll be right behind you!"

Sellithia dashed through the threshold and was blinded by a bright light. She shielded her eyes and as the light set back to normal, she saw the Titan Temple completely intact. She looked behind her and saw Time, but noticed that the portal was gone.

With a confused look on her face Sellithia asked, "W-where are we?"

"I've taken you back to the time of the Titans. Everyone you knew back where you were, no longer exists. I have already informed the Titans that you are from the future and are here to be hidden. They are waiting for you in the throne room," Time said in annoyance.

Sellithia looked back at the temple then towards Time to ask another question, but realized that she was gone.

As she slowly walked towards the temple, Time's voice whispered in her head. *"You are still the Guardian of the Titans, Sellithia. Protect them just as they will protect you .When all is said and done, I will return you to your time that you currently live in if you would like. We have faced far worse threats than the betrayal of Max. We have even faced the end of the world, but with each other's help, we have survived. Now we face a far greater threat, a threat that will shake the very Fabric of Time. Thoi-Thagian has found our world again and now threatens to destroy everything we Titans have worked so hard on to create,"* Velyndral the Titan of Time whispered into the minds of all.

Chapter 25 The Reunion

Sellithia stood frozen in place as she stared at all of the Titans sitting in their thrones. She saw Death, Life, Winter, Storm, Fire, and even Shadow, but she didn't see the Titan of War. The throne of War sat empty. What she found interesting was that there was another throne in the place where Time's originally sat. This throne was constructed for a Titan of Nature.

Sellithia cleared her throat. "It is so good to see all of you. I have been so lonely without you presence."

Standing from his throne, Death stretched out his arms and said, "It's good to see you again, Sellithia. We are well aware that you are from a different time period of our reign. We have been informed by Velyndral, the Titan of Time, that there never was a Titan of Nature on the council when you were brought into the temple," He paused for a moment then moved his arm to the right towards a large ferocious tiger. "This is Naravada, the Titan of Nature."

"Why is he a tiger?" Sellithia asked in astonishment.

Quickly rising from her throne Life said, "He stays in the form of a tiger to keep his identity a secret. No one knows what he truly looks like."

Sellithia nodded in acceptance. "I see. I am, however, slightly confused. In the temple library there is no record of a Titan of Nature ever existing."

"When the Titan of War died due to the creation of the Frozen Wastes, Death knew that another empty seat amongst us could not stay a reality. Naravada, one of Life's oracles, was brought here and took on the role of the Titan of Nature. He was intended to fill the Titan of War's spot, but he politely refused the offer. Instead, he became the Titan of

Nature and took the throne that originally belonged to Time. Death took on the role of War so that it could remain a part of the responsibilities of the Titan Council," Winter coldly replied.

A loud noise from across the room filled the air as she finished her sentence. Everyone in the room turned their heads to the entrance of the chamber just as a small area of the floor gave away. Loud screeches could be heard from deep inside the hole just moments before several vile, black blobs of darkness began climbing from it. As they entered the chamber, they took on the form of a muscular, dark, demonic figure. In an instant, all the Titans leaped from their thrones and drew their weapons.

Death violently swung his titanic great sword at the relentless beasts. While he fought three in front of him, he raised his right arm and influenced his great and mysterious powers to levitate a beast across the room off the ground and crush its throat. To keep Death from being overrun, Life twirled the Blessed Staff of Life in the air above her head. She fiercely slammed it onto the ground and large, thorny green vines shot up from the stone floor and wrapped themselves around the bodies of several of the vile creatures. They stabbed and squeezed them to death as they drug them down to the darkness within the earth.

Storm and Fire did all in their power to repel the invaders while Nature ripped into them one by one with his large, sharp, talon-like claws. The beasts continued to pour from the rift even though Shadow was pouring his dark powers into it to try and prevent any further invaders from coming through.

For a while, it seemed as though the Titans would lose this fight as more and more black blobs poured from the dark breach. A bright flash came from the center of the room and Velyndral, the Titan of Time, materialized before them. Her golden armor shimmered with beautiful holy light as she raised her sword high into the air. She quickly brought it down, shoved it deep into the stone floor, and slowly stood back up. Rays of bright yellow power swirled around the sword and caused all of the beasts to freeze in mid place.

"Focus your powers on the perforation like Shadow! It is the only way to stop the invasion!" she screamed.

Death immediately turned around from the frozen beast he had been fighting and placed his sword back at his side. He slowly raised his left hand and pointed it at the opening. A massive beam of black power erupted from his armored palm and flew across the room into the dark hole.

Life took her focus from the frozen beasts. With a stern face, she forced a jet of green energy out of her soft white palm. Her power entered the hole and mixed vigorously with Death's and Shadow's.

Fire, Storm, and Winter ran up next to Life and Death and used their powers to flow into the chasm and mix with the other Titans. As Fire's and Storm's powers mixed, a hissing sound filled the room and a funnel of steam began to rise from the hole.

Time looked around the room and soon came to realize that every one of the Titans except Nature and herself were pouring their powers into the indention. Nature was not placing any of his powers in the hole because he was busy protecting Sellithia who was completely unarmed. She squinted at him, but quickly turned her focus back on the breach. She raised her right hand and allowed her powers to flow freely out of her palm. As her magnificent power combined with the other Titans' powers, a massive ball of holy light began to form and consume the entire rift. It grew brighter, stronger, and larger in size until it exploded sending a massive beam of yellow light hurtling towards the ceiling. The ceiling weakened from the blast and collapsed inwards onto the hole. This allowed the Titans to stop the invasion, but most of their precious throne room was in ruin from the ceiling collapsing inward on to the floor.

The dust settled on what remained of the throne room floor and Sellithia and the Titan Council gathered into a group.

In a horrified voice Sellithia asked, "What were those things?!"

"Those were spawns of the Aikanadenbaria. I believe that he goes by the name of Thoi-Thagian now," Time replied.

Shock filled every bone of Sellithia as Time said his name.

"He believes that if he can destroy us here in this time period it will make it that much easier for him to encase this world in darkness. His victory will be absolute if we do not take action," Time continued.

"What do you propose we do, Time?" Death asked in a commanding voice.

Answering his question sarcastically and with another question Time said, "Well, what do you think we should do, Death?! It's pretty damn obvious if you ask me. Sometimes I wonder if you have common sense."

"There is no need to be a bitch! You are the Titan of Time, one of the founders of the Titan Council, and you are supposed to be setting an example. You aren't acting like a leader, and you should be setting examples for the other Titans," he replied heatedly.

Rolling her eyes at him, she raised her hand and opened a portal to another time period. "This portal will lead us to the time that Sellithia is familiar with, the time when she was truly the Guardian of the Titans."

"Sorry to interrupt, Mistress, but wouldn't that cause a time paradox? I mean that seems very unwise to send us back to a time that I myself was the Guardian of the Titans and they were all still alive. Correct me if I'm wrong, but with us going forward in time and seeing our future selves, they would go insane by seeing us," Sellithia argued.

"Who are you to question my divine powers, you little—"

"Enough, Time! Sellithia, Time may be a bitch, but she is no fool. She very well knows the consequences that would take place if our future selves saw us. Which is why she is sending us back to the day after our demise and with you being your future self, you will have already moved on from the island. Your past self will have traveled far from our home to start her new life," Death replied.

"Thank you for the explanation, Death. However, there is one other thing all of you should know. As you pass through the portal, I will be using my powers to manipulate your minds into knowing everything you did before your untimely demises. As you come through the portal, you may also find that your armor and robes, along with your weapons, may have changed," Time replied.

The portal blinded them as they passed through it, but as they entered the new era, the truth was revealed to them. They saw what had become of their precious temple. The whole structure was in ruin, fallen to pieces, and smashed upon the ground. Hardly any walls still stood and all of the bridges that led from the mountains were blown to oblivion. Several of the towers were big piles of rubble, but a few had broken away from the structure and smashed into the temple. They noticed that the Spire of Wisdom had toppled over and smashed into a large portion of the temple.

"This is what happens in the future," Sellithia began.

Death slowly turned towards Sellithia and said, "It is still nerve-wracking that one of our very own was capable of doing something of this magnitude." It was then that Death noticed how his armor had changed. He also noticed that his sword had become the new Blessed Sword of Death.

As the Titans gathered around Death and examined their surroundings Death said, "My friends, we have been given the chance to live on after we were defeated by Max, the man of greater power than we once thought. However, we all know that Thoi-Thagian has found our world again and now threatens to destroy everything we hold dear. Everyone in the world is in grave danger and we must put this threat to rest once again. For now though, we must separate and go into hiding to make it harder for the hunter to find his prey."

A moment of silence fell upon the small group.

"Death, Life, and I must hide together and I know just the place for us, but where will the rest of you hide?" Time asked, breaking the silence.

In his raspy voice Shadow said, "I will hide in plain sight."

He stretched out his arms and allowed his shadowy cloak that surrounded him to fade away, leaving behind a man that looked like an unholy priest until he removed his hood and the armor on his shoulders.

"I will travel to the great city of Golmasik, the capital of the Nygensa Nation," he finished as he made himself look like a priest.

In her calm and peaceful voice Storm said, "I shall hide within the elements."

She walked away from the group and placed her right hand on the wall that was still partly standing. The earth shook violently, causing Storm to quickly pull her hand away from the wall. The temple collapsed even further as the ground shook and threw up dust. As the dust settled, Storm placed her arms back at her side and began to walk back towards the group.

The earth shook again, but much more violently than the first time. This quake caused the ground underneath Storm's feet to cave in, creating a large, endless, dark abyss. Hanging on to the ledge of the cliff for dear life, Storm struggled to pull herself up. Sellithia dashed up to her and grabbed her hands, but to no avail.

Though she continued to attempt to pull her up, she could feel Storm's grasp failing. It was if some invisible force was pulling her down. The Titans ran up to aid Sellithia, but as they approached, several spawns of Thoi-Thagian manifested out of the shadows from the ruins. Storm's grip was failing quickly and she knew that she was coming to her end. She blinked a few tears down her face and closed her eyes tightly. She released her grip from Sellithia's wrists and allowed herself to slip from her grasps. Sellithia watched as Storm fell into the deep, dark abyss as she listened to the echoing, horrified screams until they were suddenly silenced.

She couldn't stop staring down the crater, for she saw a strange small blue light. At first she thought it was her eyes playing tricks on her, but she noticed that it was growing larger. As it grew, she came to realize that it was a massive beam of lightning spiraling up towards her. She quickly stood up and moved away from the crater just as the beam of lightning shot up into the atmosphere with a loud roar and a cracking sound. Smaller bolts of lightning shot out from the larger beam and began electrocuting all of the spawns of Thoi-Thagian.

The Titans walked up to Sellithia who was lying in the fetal position. Her eyes were red and puffy, and they knew she was about ready to burst into tears.

"It's all my fault. It's all my fault that she is dead," Sellithia whispered to herself.

Death knelt down next to her and placed his armored hand on her shoulder. "Sellithia, there is nothing you could have done, if it's anyone's fault, its mine. I should have struck the killing blow to this atrocity when I had the chance long ago."

She began to break down in tears and placed her hands over her face so that she could prevent herself from being even more humiliated from crying.

Time hatefully looked at Sellithia and said, "Oh quit crying, you baby, and straighten up! You're the Guardian of the Titans!"

Death looked at her and shot her an evil glare from underneath his helmet. "This has affected her greatly. The least you could do is show some respect. You should learn to think about others and not just yourself. Maybe then, someone would actually like you!"

Time began to reply to Death's comment, but Life cut in and said, "Let us not forget what we were doing before this misfortunate event happened. I concur with Time on the matter of her, Death, and I hiding together."

Shadow bent down and stretched out his hand towards Sellithia to help her get to her feet. "I will take Sellithia to Golmasik and have her protect the King while I hide amongst the priests in the cathedral. If there is a threat against us, then there will undoubtedly be a threat against the King's life."

Fire looked around for a moment to see if anyone else was going to speak. "I will enter Hell's Domain and personally watch over the dark and twisted souls. If Thoi-Thagian is truly rising back to power, then he will want to free his followers."

Winter shed a few tears at the loss of her Mother and said, "With my Mother's untimely death, I have no one to help protect me. I will travel to the Arctic Wastelands of this world and hide within the very ice that I created."

Several of the Titans closed their eyes for a brief moment at the thought of her returning to the very place she created to prove just how powerful she was. A lot came true that day.

Nature sat on the ground and allowed his tail to move across the grass. His purring stopped and with his large yellow eyes, he looked upon the group of Titans and Sellithia. "War is coming to this world and I will have no part in it. With war comes carnage and I hate bloodshed. I hereby renounce my title as the Titan of Nature and give up my immortality along with my power over to Selineane the Titan of Life."

Life looked over to the large tiger in disbelief and said, "Nature, are you sure you want to go through with this. You know as well as I what will happen if you give up your immortality and power."

Without saying a word, he nodded his big furry head and stood back up on his four legs. Slowly walking up to him, Life knelt down next to him and held out her hand. Nature placed his large furry paw on top of her palm and took in a deep breath.

"I, Naravada, the Titan of Nature, hereby give my power and immortality over to Selineane the Titan of Life. She will now possess the powers of Life and Nature."

His paw and her hand ignited in bright green power as his was drained from his body and hers sucked it up. Nature's body began to transform as the powers left his body. His tail sank back into his rear end, his fur fell off, leaving behind a pink-skinned tiger, his ears lost their point and took on the shape of a human's, his long sharp claws retracted back into his paws as they themselves turned into hands. His long pointed teeth became flat and his head shrank in size as his transformation became complete. He had changed into a naked human being.

Life pulled her hand away as the glowing stopped and stood up. With his powers drained, Nature was now mortal and prone to the powers of death. Even Death himself could not stop what was to transcend upon Nature. Death knew it was only a matter of time before his powers would kill him. He removed his black cloak and placed it over Nature who was now lying on the ground moaning in pain.

Nature's body began to greatly age now that he was defenseless to the powers of Death and Time. His hair turned pale white, his skin wrinkled and turned pale from dryness, and his eyes glossed over causing him to go blind.

"Death…don't…fill this…role," Nature weakly cried as he took in his last breath and closed his eyes.

His lifeless body began to change color before everyone's eyes. His body turned to dust from such age and blew away. Death picked up his black cloak and placed it back on his back.

"We have all lost a great deal today. Serenity the Titan of Storms and Naravada the Titan of Nature have both been taken from us, but we can't afford to mourn over their deaths. We must remember them for who they were. Remember the deeds they have done," Life said as a tear trickled down her face.

Wiping tears from her face Winter said, "We should leave. We wouldn't want the Aikanadenbaria finding us."

They all nodded in agreement as Time waved her hand and opened several different portals. One led to a large city, another led to another city that no one but Time recognized, the next down the line was one that led to the Arctic Wastelands, and the last led to Hell.

Time looked at Shadow and pointed at the first portal. "This portal will take you and Sellithia to Golmasik."

Shadow and Sellithia said goodbye to the others as they entered the portal. Winter and Fire bowed in respect as they each entered their own portal. As the last ones, Time, Death, and Life each took in a deep breath and went into the portal one by one.

Chapter 26 Rebirth of the Aikanadenbaria

Sellithia and Shadow rubbed their eyes as their vision cleared. They stood outside the Gates of Golmasik and looked around to see if anyone had seen them teleport in.

"Sellithia, go on ahead to the palace. I'm going to make my way towards the cathedral and pretend to study alongside the priests," Shadow said as he nudged her forward.

She bowed in respect as she ran off to the palace in the middle of the city. Shadow began to walk into the city himself, but was stopped by a thief who had come up behind him. The thief held a jagged dagger to his throat and laughed evilly.

"Well, what is a priest doing out of the city at a time like this, hmm?" the thief asked sarcastically.

"I am simply here for refuge. My home was recently destroyed by scum such as yourself."

The thief pressed the dagger harder against Shadow's neck and bared his teeth. "You think I'm scum? I was much like you once. I sought redemption in the light and look how it has repaid me. Unfortunately for you, I don't feel like sparing anyone today. Say hello to that so-called God of yours, priest."

"It would be very unwise of you to try to kill me. I have very powerful friends and if they found out that you killed me, they would have your head."

"Please, God isn't real, priest. It's an illusion that was placed in your head."

"God is more real than you would lead yourself to believe," Shadow said as he quickly revealed his true identity and pushed the thief backwards with a shadowy explosion.

Terrified, the thief scooted away and said, "Wh-what are you?!"

In his raspy voice Shadow said, "I am the Titan of Shadows. I have created terrible creatures that your mind couldn't even begin to fathom. I should kill you right now, but it's not in my nature. I'll let you live this day, mortal, but know this, if you should ever fail to uphold honor as you did so today, I will personally kill you with no remorse and then deliver your soul to the Titan of Death. Now, off with you!"

The thief quickly got to his feet and ran away as fast as he could, never once looking back. As he disappeared into the distance, Shadow shed his true form and put on his priestly disguise. He peacefully walked into the city and acted as though nothing had just happened as he made his way towards the city cathedral.

Sellithia walked through the palace doors and made her way to the throne room. Blue banners with a silver trim hung on the walls with a symbol of a silver dragon roaring into the sky and she knew that this was the symbol of the Titans. Walking into the throne room, she knelt down before the aged King who was dressed in elegant tan and brown robes. She looked at the golden crown that rested atop his elderly head and saw her reflection in it.

"Your Majesty, I am Sellithia, one of the many loyal servants to the Titans and I am here to deliver you a message on their behalf."

The King nodded in agreement and leaned in closer to hear more clearly.

"Unfortunately, the Titans face extinction. An ancient evil that they believed to have vanished for eternity has found this world again. This evil has already gripped the lands of Rowmodea. The temple is in ruin and the valley it sat in has withered up and died. The effects are beginning to spread across the rest of the isle."

The King looked at her for a moment before speaking. "Young lady, what ancient evil would that be?"

"The Titans call it the Aikanadenbaria." Sellithia replied with a shutter in her voice.

The King struggled to his feet and slowly limped towards her. He placed his hand on her back as he nudged her alongside him. He took her into the library on the other side of the palace and shut the large wooden doors behind them.

They walked up to a table cluttered with books. The King pulled out a chair and motioned Sellithia to sit down. As she sat, he limped off deeper into the dark library. He returned moments later with a large leather bound book with fancy symbols on its cover. It had to weigh a lot because he struggled to hold it. He placed it on the table in front of her and opened it. Licking his fingers, he turned past a several pages. Skipping over the introduction of the book, he flipped to a passage titled "Birth of the Aikanadenbaria."

Survival of Fights

The King let out a long drawn out breath and said, "Here we go."

Sellithia looked at the book and began to read what it said:

Long ago, when Time was young, the Aikanadenbaria and his brother were created by a very powerful vacant planet. On this world there was water, forests, grassy plains, and mountains. After many years of living on this planet, the Aikanadenbaria and his brother began reshaping the world.

They created a large isle far out at sea in treacherous waters. These waters were so dangerous that if someone managed to cross them in one piece, they would be considered masters on the water.

As the planet began to flourish with life, the Aikanadenbaria's powers only grew in strength. He realized, however, that trying to rule the world on his own was too risky. He couldn't keep all the balance on his own and if he tried, he would risk becoming insane. He knew the risks of becoming insane and he didn't want to take the chance of himself becoming a demonic beast created only for desolation. He decided to create six creatures that would be his immortal champions. He named these immortals Gods. The Gods were given beautifully crafted armor and weapons designed by the powers of the Aikanadenbaria. As a final gift, they were also given extraordinary power.

For over ten thousand years, the Gods helped their creator keep the world in balance. Each time the Aikanadenbaria was successful in creating something new to take place on the planet, the Gods offered to watch over it for him, and each time he would reward them with gifts of magnificent power.

They were given a large temple with a sum of five-hundred rooms to live in. The temple was placed on the island that was surrounded by the treacherous waters. Another gift that they received was an entire race of people that looked a lot like the Gods except they were nowhere near as powerful as they were, nor did they live as long. The lives of the creatures that lived under the Gods were a mere blink in their eyes. The Gods observed that the mortals always died around the ages of seventy, eighty-one, ninety-three, and one hundred. They decided to call them humans, and they would become the Gods' loyal subjects.

More time passed, along with several generations of human lives. The Gods began to realize as the generations passed that their powers were growing stronger every day. One day when their creator came to visit them, they asked him to bless them each with a child. He agreed without any thought to what would happen and gave each God a child that possessed their power.

Each child had their parent's power, which made their numbers even stronger. However, there was a terrifying flaw with the creation of the infant immortal children. The flaw was that with the children being created as little infants that didn't know any better, they didn't know how to fully control their powers.

Every time the Aikanadenbaria would come to visit them, the children would unknowingly leach some of his power and place it inside themselves. With him falling to insanity, he began to create revolting illusions of himself and ordered them to attack the Gods and their children. These attacks forced the hands of the Gods and the Aikanadenbaria's brother. A full-scale war broke out, turning the very planet into a battlefield. The war lasted hundreds of years, and each day it took mortal souls with it. In the end, the Gods managed to drive the Aikanadenbaria from the planet.

The children, however, felt that one day he might return and come for them. They used their powers to create a shield around the planet that would turn it invisible from space. They did this in hope that he would be unable to find the planet again.

Sellithia shut the book and looked at the King with wide eyes. "So, in a way it was the Titans' fault for him becoming what he is today?"

"Well yes and no. You see, the Titan of Time used her powers to go back to that hiatus many times. With each shift, she was led to the conclusion that it was because of his foolish acts of over using his powers that caused him to go insane. She found that he was already on the brink of insanity when he created the children."

✵✵✵✵

Shadow walked up to the large stone steps of the cathedral. Slowly walking up them, he went inside the building and saw several priests practicing holy spells.

He walked up to one of them standing in the center of the room and said, "Hello, my name is Temhota and I would like to study the holy arts with you."

The priest looked at him for a few moments, not sure if he could be trusted. "Welcome Temhota, to the holy cathedral of Golmasik. You're welcome to stay as long as you would like. If you would follow me into my chambers, we will get you the necessary items you will need during your stay."

They walked away into a small room lit only by the sunlight. He expected to be handed several books on the holy light, but as he walked to the center of the room, the priest slammed the door shut and locked it.

"Fool! Do you have any idea what you could cause by coming here?! I know you are the Titan of Shadows. You shouldn't have come here, your power is all we priests fight against," the priest said as he raised his hand, sending a beam of holy light towards Shadow.

Shadow quickly raised his own hand and produced a beam of his shadowy power to match that of the holy beam. Pushing the link back and forth across the room, the two snarled at each other.

While Shadow and the priest fought up in the room, a portal opened deep within the catacombs of the cathedral. From it, a beast with black, charred skin, glowing red eyes, and torn ragged robes emerged. It raised its blackened hand as it glowed with dark power. It heard a noise coming from behind the door and raised its hand higher into the air. The door slowly opened as a city guard walked into the hallway.

Upon seeing the beast, the guard drew his sword and charged at it. Before he could get in striking range, the beast threw a ball of its dark, corrupt power at the guard throwing him backwards. It walked up to the guard and grabbed him by his neck, lifting him high off the ground. The guard looked into the glowing red eyes in fear and tried to get free.

Snapping the guard's neck, the beast looked at the body dementedly and used its dark powers to take on the guards form. The beast threw the guard's body up against the stone wall and walked up to the upper levels of the cathedral.

He walked over to the room that Shadow and the priest were fighting in and tried to open the door. It wouldn't budge. He slammed his body up against it, breaking the door off its hinges and slowly walked into the chamber.

In his deep, dark voice, the disguised beast said, "What is going on here?! Fighting is prohibited in this section of the city. You of all people should know that, priest."

The priest briefly looked at the guard as he said, "It's allowed in self-defense. You have over stayed your welcome, go back to your King!"

The disguised beast walked up behind him and shoved his sword deep into his back. He screamed in pain as he stopped attacking Shadow and fell to the ground dead.

"Thanks for your help. I will be sure to tell the King of your deeds today, soldier," Shadow said in exhaustion.

The beast walked up to Shadow and quickly grabbed him by his neck. Lifting him off the ground, the beast revealed its true self and bared his pointed teeth.

"Aikanadenbaria…Spare me…plea…" Shadow attempted to say, but was cut short by the Aikanadenbaria snapping his neck with a flick of his wrist.

"My name is Thoi-Thagian, and I am here to reclaim my powers!"

Thoi-Thagian opened his mouth extremely wide. As he did so, the powers of Shadow flowed from his face into Thoi-Thagian's mouth. Shadow's body shriveled up as the last bit of power left his body and entered Thoi-Thagian. Dropping the mummified corpse of the Titan of Shadows, Thoi-Thagian walked towards the window. Yelling could be heard as several priests ran into the room and began throwing balls of light at him. He yelled in pain as each ball of light went through him. He quickly smashed the window and vanished into the shadows as the sun set behind the trees.

The priests ran up to both bodies and examined them. They lifted the dead priest and took him to be cremated while the body of Shadow was taken deep into the catacombs.

The head priest looked at the others in the group and said, "I will inform the King of what has transpired here."

"What will you tell him, brother? That the priest broke the law and attacked the Titan of Shadows? That they were ruthlessly murdered by some unknown beast?" another priest asked.

"Yes, I will tell him that the priest engaged in fighting. Let's leave the beast out of this, at least for now."

"How will you explain their deaths?"

"I will tell the King that the priest was successful in killing Shadow, but it cost him his own life in return."

The group bowed before each other as they went their separate ways.

Back in the palace, Sellithia sat alone in the library that was illuminated with candlelight. She flipped through the pages of the book that the King had lent her and read passages from its yellow pages. She was shocked that this book had all the knowledge about the Gods and Titans. She flipped through the pages a little more and saw a passage called "The Creation of Winter."

A single tear is all it took. A tear filled with the doubts and sadness of the Titan of Storms. Storm stood in her room with her arms crossed over her chest as she stared out her window. No mortal or immortal knew why she was so depressed.

A tear filled in her eye and fell down her check. She took her index finger and brushed it across her face and moved it from her cheek to her finger.

She looked at the tear and said, "They ask why I am depressed, they ask why I have distanced myself. It's because Death banned the Titans from mating with mortals."

She held the tear in front of her face for a few moments while she used her other hand to open her window.

"Winds of the north and the elements of water hear my plea. Bless me with a daughter with extraordinary power."

The wind picked up and fiercely blew into the room destroying the place as it went. A pool of water appeared on the ground as well while the winds circled the room. The wind formed into a cyclone as it levitated over the water and sucked it up. The cold winds and water froze together as one and formed an ice sculpture of a frozen cyclone.

The frozen cyclone let off a cold mist that began to freeze and ice over the entire chamber. Storm slowly walked across the frozen ground careful not to slip and fall. She placed her hand on its frozen surface and allowed the heat from her palm to seep into it. The ice cracked and shattered sending tiny shards of ice flying across the room.

The mist that had formed on the ground around the sculpture began to move outwards revealing a pail skinned baby girl who was ice cold to the touch. To Storm's delight, she quickly grabbed a light blue blanket from her bed and wrapped the baby up in it. Cradling the sleeping infant in one arm and stroking her frosty white hair with the other, Storm smiled for the first time in almost a year.

Rocking the newborn back and forth in her arms as she stood on the balcony, Storm said, "Welcome to your new home, Nyads. Thank the elements for creating a daughter for me. You will do great things."

While Nyads slept in her arms, Storm came to the conclusion that with her doing this, a part of her power had been taken from her. The part that allowed her to control winter now resided within her daughter.

The doors to Storm's room burst open and slammed against the stone wall as Death stormed in. He saw the baby in her arms and what the room had transformed into.

In his echoing, deep voice, Death calmly but strictly said, "Storm, what have you done? You have gone behind my back and created a child when I strictly forbid it."

Storm was shocked that he wasn't yelling at her because he usually did when someone broke one of the rules. Perhaps it was because he didn't want to wake the sleeping baby.

"Death, please, I have longed for a child for so long. Can you blame me for that? Please overlook this rule just this one time. I'm begging you," she replied, shaking slightly.

In an unpleased voice Death replied, "Fine, but only this time. If you do something like this again, I will have no choice, but to dismiss you from the council. This 'thing' will be your responsibility. You will have to find a new room as well, seeing how it has permanently frozen over this room."

Death turned and left the room while Storm hugged her baby in her arms. The wind caught the doors, slammed them shut as more of the room produced pillars of ice and iced over furniture.

Sellithia looked up from the book and looked over to the closed doors of the library. She could hear shouting coming from the other side of the doors when they suddenly burst open and the King along with a priest walked in.

"Sellithia, I'm sorry to interrupt your reading, but I'm afraid I have some grave news. This priest has informed me that another priest had attacked the Titan of Shadows. Shadow lost his life due to some spell the priest used. The priest drained his powers and mummified his body, but it cost him his own life as well," the King grimly said.

Quickly standing up from the table Sellithia asked, "Where has his body been taken?!"

"His body has been moved to a crypt below the cathedral."

Sellithia quickly sprinted out of the library and ran towards the entrance of the palace.

"Poor girl, I wish I knew who truly was responsible," the King said.

"You know who the murderer is, but you won't live long enough to tell anyone," the priest replied.

The King turned around with a confused look on his face and said, "What did you just say? Are you threatening me?"

Without a reply, the priest pulled a concealed dagger from his sleeve and shoved it deep into the King's stomach. As he lay dying on the cold stone floor, the priest knelt down beside him and waved his hand across his own face. His image faded and Thoi-Thagian was revealed.

He leaned close to the King's face and said, "Stupid mortal, you will *not* intervene with immortal affairs." He chuckled evilly. "It's unfortunate that the true priest never made it here. He just had to accidently bump into me."

The King took one final, painful breath and died while Thoi-Thagian picked up his body, transformed himself into the King, and carried his corpse deeper into the library.

Chapter 27 Thoi-Thagian's Revenge

Thoi-Thagian walked down the streets of the city and deceived everyone he passed. Everyone that he passed bowed before him, not realizing that he wasn't the King of Golmasik.

He walked up to two guards that stood outside the entrance of the cathedral and said, "Follow me, I know who truly killed the Titan of Shadows."

He walked up the stone steps and entered the cathedral while the two guards followed him with their swords drawn. He slowly limped across the stone floor making his deception even more believable. They walked down a spiral staircase and entered the torch lit catacombs. At the end of the hallway they had entered, Thoi-Thagian turned towards the guards and briefly stared at them.

"Be ready to arrest the one I point out. I know she won't go down easily," he said as he placed his hand on the door and pushed it open.

The door swung open, revealing Sellithia kneeling down over the mummified corpse of Shadow and two priests on each side of her. She silently wept as the King made his entrance.

"Arrest that woman for treason against the Nygensa Nation and the Titan Council!" he yelled as he pointed his shaky finger at Sellithia.

The two guards rushed at Sellithia and grabbed her. She screamed and squirmed as she tried to break free from the guards, but their brute strength was too much for her. The two priests quickly backed up against the wall in fear.

They yanked her out of the small stone chamber and made their way up the spiral staircase while she screamed, "Let me go, I'm innocent!"

The guards took her to the prison on the southern side of the city and locked her away in a holding cell while they waited for her trial. The King looked at her through the iron bars and let out a long, drawn out sigh as he sat down in a chair across the corridor from her.

"I'm appalled at the atrocities you have committed, Sellithia. Why would you kill one of the Titans?" Thoi-Thagian said in his disguise as he tried to hold back his evil smile.

"I didn't kill him. You know damn well that I was in the library the whole time!" she screamed in outrage.

A bellowing laugh rumbled from deep within the King's throat as he said, "I know that, and you know that, but the citizens of the capital don't. I needed them to believe that you were the assailant."

"Why?!" she yelled as she pushed her face in between the bars of her cell and bared her teeth.

The King smiled as he waved his hand across his face, illuminating it with dark magic. Thoi-Thagian's illusion rippled and fell away as his true form came into reality.

Sellithia quickly backed away and slid down the wall. "Thoi-Thagian…What do you want from me?"

Walking up to her cage, he said, "I have plans far beyond anything you could imagine. My final act of revenge is slowly falling into place and you will be just one of the final pieces of the puzzle. Oh yes, I can already see her. The young eighteen-year-old, her long, curly, dark brown hair flowing down her back, and her long, elegant purple dress flowing behind her as she walks. She will be the final piece I need in completing my ultimate revenge."

"Who are you talking about?"

"Your granddaughter, of course. "He slowly reached forward as he stuck his hand through the cell bars and said, "My madness will consume all you know. You will start the twilight that will forever shadow this world, and your granddaughter will follow in your footsteps."

"I don't have a granddaughter, nor do I have a husband or child."

"Not yet, but you soon will," he replied as his hand began to glow with dark energy.

Sellithia feared that he was preparing to enslave her mind with his tainted dark magic. She squeezed her eyes closed and stiffened her body as she prepared for the possession.

The sound of bells tolling filled the air as the clocks ticked. Turning to midnight . Thoi-Thagian quickly pulled his arm back towards him and looked out the window within Sellithia's cell. The dark sky illuminated with a bright blue light that looked like all the stars had formed into one.

With an evil laugh Thoi-Thagian said, "Well, it would appear that it is Hallows' Eve. I think I'll make Death do my bidding first."

He quickly threw his hands up into the air and vanished in the blink of an eye leaving Sellithia alone. She slowly opened her eyes and stood back up. She looked out her barred window and saw the long string of blue lights shimmering across the sky. She looked around and saw that Thoi-Thagian had vanished and that there were no guards in sight. She decided to take this moment of opportunity to escape and knelt down. The guards may have taken her swords, but they forgot to check her boots. She reached down the side of her right leather boot and pulled out a concealed dagger. She took the fine point of the blade and placed it in the keyhole on the other side of her cell in an attempt to open it. The door made a clicking noise as the lock on the door unlatched. Pushing the door open, Sellithia quickly placed the dagger back inside her boot and walked up to the table across the hall. She grabbed her two swords, attached them to her sides, and quietly made her way out of the prison.

Once outside the prison, she stuck to the shadows so that no one would see her. For some reason though, the city was crawling with guards. They were ushering civilians towards the palace and Sellithia knew she had to see what all the commotion was about.

After an hour of evading the guards, Sellithia finally made it to the palace courtyard. Several guards surrounded the palace. To her surprise, the city guards were trying to control a crowd of civilians who were yelling and demanding answers. Through the crowd, she could see several priests and even a coroner standing near the doors to the palace as they prepared to bring someone out.

It was then that Sellithia understood. She realized that Thoi-Thagian carrying the disguise of the King meant that he had met his end. Two palace guards along with a priest came out of the palace holding a gurney with a human under a white sheet. She could hear the towns' people talking about the man under it.

A women that was holding a new born baby that was close to where she was hiding asked, "Who could have done such a thing?"

"I don't know, but whoever did this had no mercy," the woman's husband replied.

With the deceased King loaded up into the buggy, the rest of the palace guards came out of the palace and ushered people out of the courtyard as they evacuated it. The guards returned to the confines of the palace and locked themselves in once the courtyard was silent. Sellithia looked around to make sure no one else was around and that no guards were watching and slowly walked out from the shadows. She surveyed the courtyard in an attempt to find a way inside the palace. She came across a thick green vine that grew up the side of the tower closest to the balcony the King used to give speeches on and noticed that the window was open. She quickly proceeded to climb it before any guards came by and climbed through the window.

Knowing that everyone believed she was still locked away within the prison, Sellithia quietly snuck towards the library. Within the knowledge-filled chamber was the ancient novel she had been reading, and she had hoped that it would have an answer to her question about Thoi-Thagian's comment on making Death do his bidding first. She couldn't imagine that Death would willingly aid him.

She scanned the chamber for any patrols as she peeked through the doorway leading into the throne room. Making a mad dash for it, she sprinted through the room, but was spotted by a palace guard as soon as she passed by the throne.

"You there, stop!" the guard yelled.

The guard chased after her as she continued to make her way towards the library alerting more guards as she went. Reaching the library, Sellithia slammed the wooden doors shut and ran over to the table she had been sitting at earlier. She pushed it up against the doors and grabbed the book with fancy symbols on it. She flipped through the pages hurriedly as she looked for anything that talked about Death and Thoi-Thagian. She came across a long passage titled "Death's Fatal Flaw." Compelled to read it, she leaned in closer to the yellow pages and began to read.

With the fall of the evil Gods and the rise of the newly instated Titans, the Titan of Death sat in the throne room with all his other Titan friends.

"My friends, Hallows' Eve is upon us once again. We all know our responsibilities in the malevolent outbreak that is to come," Death said as he looked over to the Titan of Time.

Time used her outstanding powers to create a magnificent golden hourglass that glowed with bright yellow power. Everyone in the room looked over towards the hourglass and saw that a minute's worth of sand was left remaining in the top.

The last grain of sand fell from the top and into the lower chamber with the other grains of sand, and each Titan rose from their throne and followed Death out on to the large rectangular balcony.

The twilight sky illuminated with a chilling blue light as a massive portal opened up and allowed malevolent souls to flood the sky. They swept across the sky and began their search for a host to possess. Only so many could escape at a time, for the portal had to increase in size for more to come out. While all of the Titans but Death used their powers to keep the portal from opening any wider, Death raised both his armored hands high into the sky and began to produce a spell that would force all of the souls back into the portal. One soul, however, managed to evade his spell. It flew up to him and revealed itself to be his Father's oracle.

The old, hideous hag pointed at Death with her boney finger and said, "Mythdariz, the Titan of Death, you have tormented my eternal dreams every night since my murder. Now I am forever cursed to look like this because of what you did to me!"

"It was your foolish act of using mortal spells on an immortal that turned you into what you are. How everyone sees you is your own doing," Death replied, still casting the incantation.

The oracle snarled at him with her pointed teeth. "I shall have my revenge for what you have made me! From this day forward until the end of all things, I put a curse on you. Every year when Hallows' Eve begins, you will taste my torment. Weak and fragile, you will become powerless to everything around you. During this time, if you become possessed with any one of the deceitful souls that break free that night, the portal to Hell will remain open forever, allowing my fellow souls to wreak havoc across you precious world!"

The evil oracle raised her hand and shot a glowing red ball of evil power at him, expelling his power from his body. He fell backwards, unconscious, as she cackled evilly and retreated back into the portal.

The Titans took Death back to his chamber, where he would lay and rest for a full twenty-four hours.

Before leaving his chamber, Life said, "The souls will stop at nothing to try and get inside him. We must take all precautions in protecting him. I recommend that we place a protective barrier around him to keep them at bay."

The rest of the Titan Council nodded in agreement as they raised their hands and allowed their powers to circle around him to create a very powerful magical dome that would keep all other magic and souls away from him.

The Titans traveled down the halls of the temple in silence for a time.

Shadow looked over to Life and Time, who were walking next to him, and said, "The only thing that could ever possibly get through that shield would be the Aikanadenbaria."

"Lucky for us, he can't find the planet. It was a very wise choice of Death to have all of us use our powers to make the planet invisible from space," Life said as she turned towards him.

"Yes, but I sense a disturbance within the balance. The Aikanadenbaria already knows of Death's fatal flaw. He now tries even harder to find the planet," Time replied, not making eye contact with anyone.

Each Titan separated from the group and made their way towards their own chamber where they could all rest and restore the power they had spent that day.

Sellithia looked up from the book and noticed that the palace guards were still making a vain attempt to open the doors. She grabbed the book and backed away from the doors, hiding behind the bookcase closest to the entrance and waiting.

The guards burst through the doors and ran into the library with their swords drawn. Stopping at the first row of bookcases, the guards very cautiously looked around the large chamber.

The guard that had spotted Sellithia quietly said, "Search the area. I want no corner unchecked."

The palace guards dispersed and began to search every nook and cranny of the library. As the last guard moved away from the door, Sellithia took her chance and darted for the doors. Running down the halls, she could hear the guards coming after her at a fast pace. She ran up stone steps that led her to the top of a watch tower that over looked a large pond. She turned back around to leave, but saw her entrance was blocked by three guards.

The guard in the middle lowered his sword and reached forwards. "Young lady, let's not do anything rash. Give us the book and come quietly."

She raised the book as if she was going to give it to the guard, but as he leaned in to grab it, she brought it down on his head. The other guards jumped into action as he fell to the ground, but were unable to grab her. Sellithia turned around and dove over the edge of the tower with the book tightly pressed up against her chest. Coming closer and closer to the water, she used all her strength to throw the book far enough so that it would land on the sandy ground next to the water. Sellithia formed the swan dive just moments before she hit the water to prevent a harder impact.

Sellithia's head popped out of the water and she spewed water out of her mouth. Swimming to land, she crawled on to the sand and grabbed the book. She ran as quickly as she could away from the palace and ran into the forest to escape the guards that were still pursuing her.

Chapter 28 Death's Betrayal

Time and Life stood in a large stone room that was fit for a king or queen. The chamber they stood in was located in a city that Time herself had created. They watched over Death's motionless body as he slept in a large cozy bed. A shimmering dome of the entire Titan Council's powers swirled around his body to keep him safe.

"Shortly after I left the council, I used my powers in hope to become one with time, but instead, my powers had another idea. This city was created and a dome made out of pure holy light was formed around it. The dome protects me from any who would do harm. After the city was created, it was then that I decided to pick a handful of mortals to live with me. The mortals were so faithful they became my very own city guards," Time said without breaking eye contact with Death's body.

Slightly turning towards her, Life said, "How were you able to hide this from us for so long? I have passed over this valley several times and have never seen this city."

Breaking her eye contact with Death, Time stared into Life's emerald green eyes. "Being the controller of Time is a gift, but also a curse at the same time. A gift because I can see anything I desire, but a curse because, through the jumbled mess of puzzle pieces, I am powerless to stop those I care about from being taken from me. I foresee how everyone will die. You have no idea what it's like to be able to see one's fate and have no way to stop it. Using my powers, I produced a large, magical shield around the city to hide it from prying eyes. It didn't stop fate from taking the man I loved though."

"You lost someone you loved?"

"Yes. His name was Tentor. He was my consort."

"If you don't mind me asking, how did he…"

"He didn't die, if that is what you're getting at…He was taken from me."

"Taken?"

"Yes. He is lost in time. To this day I am constantly searching for him."

A knock came from the other side of the door. Time quickly crossed the room and cracked it open enough to stick her head out into the hallway. She saw one of her city guards standing with broad shoulders.

"I'm sorry for the interruption, Mistress, but the city has fallen under attack."

Time's face formed a frown as she said, "Under attack?"

The soldier nodded grimly. "Follow me."

Time and Life cautiously followed the soldier as they scanned all their surroundings. The soldier opened a door at the end of the stone hallway and allowed both Life and Time to enter. In the room there was a single golden throne. Long sand colored curtains hung on the large windows and flowed on to the floor. A large portrait of Time hung on the wall above the entrance to a circular balcony that allowed any who stood on it to see the entire city.

The three of them walked out onto the balcony and saw thousands of demented beasts using dark energy to pass through the city's shields unharmed.

"They are attempting to bring down the shield so that their host can enter the city. He is still too weak to do it on his own," the soldier said as he leaned in closer to Time.

Looking over to him with hatred in her eyes, Time said, "Join the others down below, Luke. Life and I will return to Death's side and protect him."

Luke bowed and ran off to join the fight.

SURVIVAL OF FIGHTS

As the fight pressed on, Thoi-Thagian materialized outside the shields and watched as the glistening golden dome surrounding the city shimmered with light as his darkness infected it. He raised his hand, placing it on the shield to try to pass through it, but the moment he touched it, his hand began to burn with searing pain. Quickly withdrawing his hand from it, he slowly backed away from the shield and closed his eyes. By his command, Thoi-Thagian created a thousand more spawns of himself and ordered them to enter the shield. Instead of them passing through it, they stayed in the shield itself allowing their impurity to weaken the shield. Each spawn moved around the shield until they had formed a ring.

The filthiness of the spawns' darkness caused the shield to crack in all directions and crumble to the ground like shards of glass. Thoi-Thagian let out a battle cry of victory, but it was short lived. Several city guards rushed at him and surrounded him on all sides. He quickly raised his hand and teleported out of the area as they approached.

His vision clearing, Thoi-Thagian realized that he had managed to teleport into the room that Death was sleeping in. He glared at the protective barrier surrounding him and smiled with his pointed toothy grin. He cautiously placed his hand on the shield afraid that it might burn him again. Upon his touch, the shield broke and left Death completely defenseless to his poisonous touch. Climbing on top of him, Thoi-Thagian glared evilly at the man who had caused him so much pain and suffering. He placed his blackened hand on Death's helmet, and he turned into a thick, dark vapor. The mist slipped through the armor of Death and slowly seeped into his pale skin, allowing Thoi-Thagian to take full control of him.

Thoi-Thagian walked in Death's body through the palace of Time and summoned more of his spawns to infest the rest of the palace. He turned down another hallway, but stopped suddenly when he saw both Life and Time.

Hesitating to draw her sword Time said, "Death? How are you awake? It hasn't been twenty-four hours yet."

Thoi-Thagian knew he couldn't speak because he knew his voice would come out instead of Death's. He had to act quickly if he wanted to destroy those who would oppose him. He slowly raised Death's left hand and shot a beam of unholy energy at Time. The beam threw her backwards against the stone wall, knocking her unconscious as she hit the ground.

Life looked from Time to Death a few times as she moved in front of her. Unable to finish his attack, Thoi-Thagian looked into Life's emerald green eyes. He bellowed with dark laughter at the sight of fear slowly working its way into her soul.

"Hello, Selineane, do you like what I am turning your precious world in to?"

In an unpleased voice Life replied, "Aikanadenbaria, you should be ashamed. You are trying to twist Death into a mindless abomination! In the name of Death, I will end you!"

With an evil laugh Thoi-Thagian said, "Selineane, you are weak and fragile. I am strong and everlasting. You will never stand a chance against me."

He raised Death's hand again and forced his unholy power out of his hand. It shot across the room towards Life, but she quickly reacted and raised her right hand. She forced a green beam of her power out of her hand and sent it towards the unholy beam coming at her. The two auras violently clashed together and mixed creating a half pure and half corrupted ball of energy in the center of the beams.

Time came to during the fight and quickly got to her feet. She walked up next to Life and raised her right arm to channel her extraordinary powers over time. As her powers zipped across the hallway, Thoi-Thagian saw her attack approaching from the corner of his eye. He raised Death's other hand and sent another beam of unholy energy towards her to stop her attack from reaching him.

Time looked over to Life and said, "Life, use your love for Death! Don't force your powers; let them flow with your emotions."

Life was shocked that Time knew about her secret love for Death, but listened to her and closed her eyes. She took in deep breaths and allowed herself to calm down. Her heart rate slowed and her breathing became shallow as she reached a state of enlightenment. Slowly opening her eyes, Life felt her powers surging through her as they pushed the dark unholy beam back towards Thoi-Thagian.

Time and Life allowed their powers to continue to push Thoi-Thagian's back until both their beams of power were at the armored palms of Death. Thoi-Thagian backed away as he cancelled his dark, unholy beam. While he was stunned, Life and Time rushed at him and quickly grabbed his arms.

"Life, your love for Death is the only thing that can cast Thoi-Thagian out of his body now."

Life removed Death's helmet while Time held him back and looked into his hate filled eyes.

"Life, hurry, if we don't do this now, Thoi-Thagian will take control over him, forever. We can't allow the demonic souls to break free," Time shouted as she felt the twenty-four hours coming to an end.

Life quickly placed her soft lips on his. Thoi-Thagian struggled for control, but Life pressed harder and made her kiss more passionate. Slowly pulling away, Life watched as Death fell to the ground limp. Thoi-Thagian materialized next to his body, but quickly opened a portal and ran through it to escape the wrath of Life and Time.

Time created her magnificent hourglass and watched as the last few grains of sand fell into the chamber below. As the last grain settled on top of the pile, Death opened his eyes and slowly sat up.

"He possessed me, didn't he?" Death asked.

Time helped him to his feet, handed him his helmet, and said, "Yes, and quite successfully too."

"Is the portal to Hell still open, then?" he replied, placing his helmet on his head.

"No, it closed a few moments ago," Life replied.

"But I was possessed. The curse is clear. If I get possessed during the time of Hallows' Eve, the portal would remain open forever, allowing the demented souls to break free and wreak havoc across the world."

"Yes, but the oracle said it had to be one of the souls that escaped from the portal. She didn't say that the Aikanadenbaria counted," Time replied reassuringly.

"You discovered a loophole," Life said in shock.

An explosion rang through the halls that startled all of them. The three of them quickly ran back to the throne room and walked out onto the balcony. They saw several spawns of Thoi-Thagian destroying building after building and overwhelming the city guards.

Time turned towards Death and grabbed his armored hand. "Death, please, open the Shadow Realms and have the Shadowscythes aid my men," she pleaded.

"If I open it, anyone that dies during this time will automatically end up in their final resting place. I would prefer them to go to the Shadow Realms first. I like to review their lives and determine if they actually deserve to go to Heaven or Hell."

Life placed her hand on Death's shoulder and said, "It will be okay, I promise. Open the Shadow Realms and have all the Shadowscythes aid Time's men."

Letting out a long drawn out sigh, Death waved his hand and said in a loud echoing voice, "Shadowscythes, come to your master's call and aid the warriors of Time!"

The earth began to shake as a massive portal opened up. The Shadowscythes slowly walked out of it and surveyed the area. When an enemy was spotted, they charged into action and began to destroy all in their path.

"Even with their help, this battle will last hours, if not days," Death said as he looked down to the battlefield.

Chapter 29 Sellithia's Downfall

Sellithia sat next to a river deep within the forest and read from the book she had stolen from the palace library. As she read passage after passage, she grew more fascinated with all the knowledge it had about the immortals and their lives. She turned the page and saw a passage with the title "Fall of Melagas." The name sounded so familiar, but she couldn't remember where she would have seen or even heard of the name. Curiously, she began to read the passage.

Thousands of years after the Gods and their children banished Thoi-Thagian from the planet, another war had broken out. This one was between mortal races far across the world. A once great and powerful nation that homed millions of people began to fall apart from within. It all began within the mortal nation's government. Many within the people didn't agree with the government's decisions and they wanted it to change.

After many years of constant bickering and fighting between the people of Melagas, the council of the city decided that it would be in everyone's best interest if Melagas split into two alliances. Both were allowed to stay within the city, but each alliance had its own government.

Once the decision was made everyone within the city was allowed to choose which alliance they wanted to join. After they had made their decision they were prohibited to speak, be around, or even help those in the opposing faction. The city was divided in half and each alliance was given their own section to live in. There were those that were always unhappy and thought that they had the shorter end of the deal. Each side began to fight again, for they thought that their section of the city was smaller than the other. They thought that those that had supported the original government were getting special treatment. Soon, they even had neighboring cities involved.

While all this was happening, the Gods and their children watched the mortals fight each other from the Pool of Images. All the fighting displeased the

Gods, but the one who was most outraged was Plentodeos, the God of Death. He knew action had to be taken if he wanted peace.

He rose from his throne and said, "Children of the Gods, I have grown tired of the mortals behavior. I want you all to go and destroy a city to set an example. You are to leave no survivors."

The children bowed in respect; though they knew what the God of Death was ordering them to do was wrong. They made their way up to the Spire of Wisdom where a ship would be waiting for them. Upon reaching the top, they saw that the Goddess of Life was already there waiting to give them their target. She hated how the God of Death made their children do all the dirty work so that they didn't get blamed. If anyone was to come and attack them, they would be coming after the children this way.

"Children, gather around please. I don't agree under any circumstances with what the God of Death is having you do tonight, but I do not have a say in the matter and even I must obey his wishes. There is always another way to set an example than to destroy a city and kill everyone inside it." She let out a sigh. "Your target will be Melagas. The God of Death believes if he destroys the source of the disturbance it will set a big enough example that no one will ever fight again." she motioned them towards the airship and said, "May the holy Father watch over you this night."

That night, they hovered over the beach and quietly snuck up to the city walls. They were quick on their feet and as silent as mice as they crept into the homes of all the sleeping mortals and quickly killed them. As the mortals died, the guards that were patrolling the empty streets saw one of the children run out of a home and into an alley. The guard managed to alert the rest of the guards before another one of the children came up behind him and stabbed him in the back.

With the city now aware of their hidden presence, the children no longer hid, but used their full powers to destroy the city and kill all who tried to flee. While those with swords ran around killing those that ran in the streets, Fire used his powers to set the homes and other buildings ablaze.

The Demigods showed no mercy in their assault. Not even the children were safe. Mythdariz, the son of the God of Death, entered a large house that was now consumed by fire. He saw a young woman underneath the table crying in fear while she choked on the black smoke. Mythdariz raised his sword high into the air to kill her, but saw a man come up behind him from the reflection of his sword. The man had a sword and was going to attempt to sneak up on him and kill him while his back was turned. He smirked and whirled around with uncanny speed and separated the man's head from his shoulders. Mythdariz looked at his bloody sword and back at the beheaded man.

"This isn't right. This isn't the only solution," he whispered.

He looked back at the cowering woman still under the table. He stretched his hand out to her, but she scooted away afraid that he might hurt her.

"It's alright, I will not hurt you."

The roof of the structure collapsed, blocking the entrance to the home.

"Take my hand! I will get us out of here!" Mythdariz shouted.

Reluctantly, the woman grabbed his armored hand and rose to her feet. They walked over to a window and Death used his sword to break the glass. He helped her out and then he climbed through. They ran from the house just as it collapsed inward on itself and stared at the burning debris. The other children ran up to him, gathered around, and watched as the wreckage burned.

"We should have never attacked them. This was a very unwise thing to do. We will take this woman back with us and hide her from the Gods. Something has corrupted their minds and we will need to be prepared for future events," Mythdariz said as they walked towards the airship.

As the ship flew away leaving the burning city glowing in the night, the children analyzed the sleeping mortal woman.

Mythdariz stood at the bow of the ship and stared out at the moonlit sky. Selineane, the daughter of the Goddess of Life, came up behind him and stood in silence for a brief moment.

"Out of the two million people that lived in the city, why choose her, Mythdariz?" Selineane asked.

"There is something about her. I can't explain it, but I felt odd when I looked upon her. There is something about her that will continue our legacy."

"That woman will have a horrific life after what has just transpired."

Turning to face her, Mythdariz said, "Not if we steal her memories. I found out that her name is Katarina. If we take her memories of her life and change her name, we can make her an immortal with our powers and fashion a fake life so that she doesn't think that she had no life until now."

"How do you expect to hide her from the Gods?"

"We can hide her in Time's room. She is never at the temple and the Gods never go down there."

"What will her new name be?"

Mythdariz looked away from her and up to the full moon.

Looking back at Selineane, Mythdariz said, "Her new birth begins tonight on a full moon. With a new life beginning, she should have part of your name. Let's call her Sellithia."

Selineane slightly nodded as she glanced over to the sleeping mortal woman and sighed.

Sellithia looked up from the book and said, "My whole life has been a lie…"

She stood up and began to walk away from the river as shock filled her mind, but was stopped by the sound of a twig snapping and a bush moving. She drew her sword with her free hand and readied herself for whatever might come out of the shrub. She moved closer to it, but quickly backed away as Thoi-Thagian came out from behind it.

"Well, if it isn't the person I was just looking for. I had received word that you escaped prison."

Compelled to attack him, Sellithia kept her sword pointed towards him and her feet firmly planted on the ground.

"Now is that any way to treat a friend?" he asked.

Thoi-Thagian raised his hands to show her that he was not there to harm her. "I mean you no harm, Sellithia. I'm only here to help you get your revenge on the Titans."

Sellithia slowly lowered her sword and fastened it back to her waist. It was at that moment that Thoi-Thagian realized what book she was holding.

"Ah, I see you have found the legendary *Book of Knowing*. Are you aware that Time created that book so that it could tell the stories of the past? Whenever something happens that involves the immortals, the book will magically write in the story so that all can read it."

Sellithia remained quiet and blankly stared at him as if she were frozen.

"We can become allies, you and I. If you help me regain all the powers that the Titans stole from me, I will spare you in the coming end. You can rule beside me when I reshape this world into perfection."

Thoi-Thagian stretched out his right hand and motioned her to give him the book. She reluctantly handed it over and bowed in respect. He turned to the back of the ledger and showed her a blank page. She stared at it as it began to reveal a passage before her very eyes.

"In short, the passage says all that has occurred in this spot today and how you just swore allegiance to me, "Thoi-Thagian said with an evil grin.

"What is your first wish, Master?" Sellithia shyly asked.

"You are to travel to the Arctic Wastelands far to the north of here. You are to find and kill the Titan of Winter. Now that her Mother is dead, she will be a fairly easy target. While you hunt her down, I will be searching through the elements to find her Mother's power," he concluded, raising his hand and opening a portal to the Arctic Wastelands.

"Master, I can't go there dressed like this. I'll freeze to death."

He rolled his glowing red eyes and said, "Wait here."

He threw his hands up into the air and vanished. Within a few minutes, he returned with a large white fur coat, white gloves, and white snow boots. She slipped on the coat and gloves then sat on the ground and took off her normal boots. As she slipped the snow boots on, she noticed that they had spikes on the bottom to help with walking on ice.

"The white will help camouflage you out in the snow-white mountains, "Thoi-Thagian said as she entered the portal.

The cold air within the Arctic Wastelands was unbearable even with the items Thoi-Thagian had given her. Sellithia's cheeks were rosy red from the harsh cold winds and she shivered with each breath she took. She looked around and saw mountains of glaciers surrounding her near and far. Her vision was impaired from the blizzard that threatened her. A thick layer of snow covered the icy ground.

Sellithia proceeded forward towards the large mountains of glaciers with ease. She was afraid that she might fall through a thin layer of ice and freeze to death. She lightly placed one foot in front of the other and pressed on it before placing her full weight on it as she moved forward. Upon reaching the first large glacier, she noticed that it had details of being a possible palace that had been incased in a block of ice. She walked around the perimeter of the glacier for some time until she stumbled upon a small tunnel opening. Getting on her hands and knees, Sellithia shimmied her way through the small hole to see where it led.

With each inch she took into the glacier, the air became colder and thinner. Sellithia felt like she was going to pass out from the lack of oxygen, but she pushed herself further. She came to the end of the tunnel and found herself in a large room sculpted completely out of the ice. A large ice statue of the Titan of Winter stood in the center of the room and a throne made of pure ice with the name *Winter* etched into the top of it set next to the statue. She removed her hood and slowly walked towards the statue, basking in its outstanding detail.

"Sellithia, is that you?" a chilling voice said from behind her.

Sellithia turned around and saw Winter standing in front of the tunnel. Her elegant light blue robes seemed to shimmer with power. She stared at Winter with cold hatred as she drew both her swords.

"You have something my Master wants back and I'm here to retrieve it for him."

Sellithia ran across the slippery floor towards Winter, but as she came close to plunging her swords into Winter's body, Winter moved sideways and tripped her. She slid across the frozen floor and hit the ice wall with an echoing thud.

"Are you mad?! You dare to raise your weapons against me?" Winter yelled.

She placed her hand in front of her and faced her palm towards the ground. The icy floor moved upwards underneath her hand and formed into an ice staff. Breaking it free from the ground, Winter gripped it tightly in her bare hands and readied herself for another attack.

Sellithia slowly rose to her feet in pain, but charged at Winter again. She sped towards her, but Winter pointed the staff at her and shot a ball of frost at her. It hit her on her face with incredible force knocking her backwards leaving a red mark on her face. She hit her head so hard that her vision blurred, and when she got to her feet she saw only a swirling blob of colors.

Her vision returned to her moments later, but she had no time to react. Winter had grabbed her by her neck and raised her off the ground. She slammed her staff on the frozen ground, causing the icy terrain to break and fall away beneath Sellithia.

"Any last words, you filthy traitor?" Winter asked.

"Goodbye," Sellithia replied.

She used her free hand to grab a dagger from behind her back and shoved it deep into Winter's stomach. Winter let out a painful cry and let go of Sellithia, who managed to grab the ledge of the jagged, icy cliff. It was slippery even with the gloves, but she managed to keep her grip long enough to throw herself back over the edge. She climbed to her feet and saw Winter lying on the ground bleeding while frozen tears fell down her face.

"You could have had so much more, Sellithia," Winter said as she took her last breath and died.

Sellithia stared at Winter's body for a while and watched as it turned into pure ice. She looked like she was now a sculpture as well.

A portal opened and Thoi-Thagian walked into the huge, iced-over chamber. "Well done, child."

He formed his hand into a fist and slammed it against the corpse of Winter. His hand broke through the ice and as he pulled it back out, he held a small frozen orb.

He placed it in his mouth and ate it as he said, "Now that I have the powers of Winter and Storm, you can now travel to your next target."

Sellithia knelt down on one knee and asked, "Who would that be, Master?"

"You are to travel to Hell and slay the Titan of Fire. But be warned. He is at his most powerful there and it will be much more difficult to kill him. If the opportunity arises, I would seek help from an ancient foe if I were you."

He turned to go back through the portal, but was stopped by the sound of Sellithia's voice.

"Aren't you going to open a portal for me?"

"Hell is under lockdown under the command of Fire himself. In order to gain access to that fiery inferno, you must kill yourself."

"Wouldn't the Shadowscythes hold me in the Shadow Realms until I receive my final judgment?"

With a small, evil chuckle, Thoi-Thagian replied, "No, my dear. The Shadow Realms is completely defenseless at the moment. All the Shadowscythes are in Time's city trying to stop my invasion. So if you kill yourself, you will go straight to your final judgment place."

Sellithia nodded, grabbed both her swords, and placed them back on her waist. She took the dagger she had used to kill Winter and placed the tip of the blade against her chest. She took in a deep breath, closed her eyes, and, with great force, shoved the blade of the dagger deep into her chest. She gasped in shock as the pain shot across her whole body. She lost feeling in her legs as she fell to the ground and watched herself bleed out just moments before everything went dark.

As she drifted into the hands of Death, she felt herself falling. She fell into the deep, dark abyss that led straight to Hell. As she fell deeper and deeper into the dark abyss, the darkness began to be consumed by flames. Her body slammed against hot lava rock as she reached the end. She raised her head slowly and looked around to see a world within her world made entirely out of black lava rock, molten fluid, and fire. She stood up, rubbed her shoulders, moved her arms to remove the stiffness, and removed her white coat and gloves as she limped towards a large stone archway in front of her. Carefully making her way towards the large stone archway, Sellithia glanced down at the twisting river of lava.

Walking through the archway, Sellithia could hear screams of agony. She continued to walk throughout the hollowed core of Hell and began to notice the black rocks were beginning to let off smoke and the ground above the river of lava was beginning to produce its own flames. She knew she was getting closer to the Titan of Fire, for everything was heating up even more than it already was.

The screams of agony grew louder, which caused Sellithia to look up. She noticed several people hanging from chains illuminated with a red glow. She slowly walked by as all the suffering people looked down at her.

"Sellithia, is that you? It's me, Max!" one of the humans called. He was hanging on the rugged wall in front of her.

Sellithia examined the man for a few moments, trying to picture Max out of the man she saw before her. She remembered the black unkempt hair, the dark eyes, pointed teeth, and even the bulky body. Though he had changed much, she could still see Max in the man he had become. His muscles had shrunk due to inactivity, his black hair was frayed, and his skin was charred. He was stripped of all his armor and left naked except for his tattered loincloth.

"What is the pet of the Titans doing here?" Max asked.

She stared at him for a moment. "I am…no longer their crutch. I have come to kill Fire under the orders of my new master, Thoi-Thagian."

Max smiled and said, "Help me get free and I will help you."

"What makes you think I would trust you?"

"My quarrel was never with you, Sellithia. You were merely an obstacle. If you let me out, I will assist you in defeating the Titan of Fire. You know you will need me. His power has increased tenfold within this wretched prison."

"How do I break the chains? They are searing hot and they were created by the Titan of Fire himself."

"You still don't know, do you?"

"Know what?"

"Your swords are not ordinary. They were created by all of the Titans' powers. They are almost as powerful as the Blessed Sword of Death and the Blessed Staff of Life."

Sellithia looked down at the swords in her hands for a few moments before looking back at the chains that held Max on the wall. With incredible strength and complete accuracy, she swung the swords at the chains, causing them to shatter on contact. Falling from the stone wall and hitting the ground with a thud, Max slowly rose to his feet. He took a step towards Sellithia but stumbled. She quickly grabbed him and helped him back to his feet.

Releasing his weak grip from her wrists Max said, "I must warn you that Fire will be extremely difficult to kill in his domain."

"Yes…I…will!" came a deep, dark voice from behind them.

Max quickly turned around to see the Titan of Fire standing in front of the archway that led to the next area where people were also being held.

"I would have expected something like this from Max, but you, Sellithia? No matter, the others will hear of your treachery soon enough."

Fire ran through the archway and created a wall of fire behind him.

Fire ran back to his palace made of lava rock, lava, and fire and quickly used his powers to contact Death and the others. He used the large fireplace that produced large flames to send his message. It heated the already hot chamber.

Back at Time's city, the battle pressed on, and neither Thoi-Thagian's spawns nor the Shadowscythes were winning. Death, Life, and Time stood in her throne room and watched the battle rage on. Their attention towards the battle was suddenly disrupted when the fireplace within the room ignited with large flames and a full image of the Titan of Fire appeared within.

The three of them walked over to the fireplace and stared into it in concern.

"Fire, what do you need?" Life asked.

"Sorry to bother you, my good friends, but it would appear that Sellithia has betrayed us. She is here, attempting to kill me," Fire replied.

"She is a fool! I will contact Shadow. I will have him come down there and aid you in killing her," Death said in outrage.

"There is something you should know." He paused for a moment. "Shadow and Winter are dead. I secretly heard her say that her new Master is none other than the infamous Thoi-Thagian. We must act before—" he began to say, but was cut off as he turned around.

"Fire, what's wrong?" Time asked.

"You will not destroy the Council!" the image of Fire said as it faded away and the fire within the fireplace died.

Fire stared at Sellithia and Max, who now were inside his palace.

"Death may be the controller of the damned, but he has given me some of his creations for my own use."

He raised his right hand and threw a ball of fire onto the ground in front of him. Within seconds, several beasts that looked just like Shadowscythes crawled out of the flames.

"I have used my powers to redesign the Shadowscythes. These are called Furyscythes and though they are much like the Shadowscythes, you will find that they are much deadlier than those stalking the Shadow Realms." He turned his attention to his minions. "Minions, seize them!"

The beasts with their flaming tattered robes let off a loud screeching cry and charged at both Sellithia and Max. Sellithia quickly handed Max one of her swords and charged at Fire's creations. Just as she got close to one, it whirled around with quick agility and sliced open her right cheek. She touched her wound, but groaned in pain. It burned to the touch. She looked at her fingers and saw blood. She looked over to Max who was dealing with two of the other beasts, but quickly looked back at the one who had wounded her. The Furyscythe's scythe came down towards her head causing her to dive out of the way. She twisted back around and plunged her sword deep into the demented thing's chest.

In doing so, Sellithia burned her hand. She yanked it back and pulled it close to her chest in pain. As she touched it, she could feel raw heat rolling off of it. She did her best to ignore her burning pain and ran over to Max to help him kill the final beast. The beast exploded in a fiery rage as Max turned to face Sellithia.

"Let me see your hand," he said, noticing the redness of her burned skin.

"It's fine, it doesn't hurt as much anymore," she replied, pulling away from him.

"No it's not, just look at it."

"Max, I'm fine. Really, I am."

Max placed his hand on her neck with his fingers slightly behind her head as he got lost in her beautiful brown eyes. They both slowly leaned in for a kiss. A ball of fire flew between their faces before they could lock lips and hit the stone wall next to them. Max removed his hand from Sellithia's neck and looked into the direction where the fireball had come from. They saw the Titan of Fire standing on the other side of the room, his hands consumed by fire.

"How sweet, two people who used to hate each other, in love," Fire said with a sarcastic laugh.

Fire raised both his hands and created a wall of fire in front of him.

The wall began to move forward as Fire yelled over the roaring flames, "You both shall be chard to ash!"

Max grabbed Sellithia's arm and said, "Call upon the Lord of Darkness and ask him for his aid!"

Sellithia squeezed her eyes shut and began to pray, "*Master, I ask for your aid. Show me what to do.*"

"*Throw your sword through the flames. It will disrupt Fire's concentration, giving you the opportunity to make the killing blow.*"

Sellithia raised the sword she had and looked at her reflection within the blade. Aiming it at Fire, she threw it with incredible force through the moving wall of flames and hit the stone wall right next to Fire's head.

The wall of fire died as Fire examined the sword that lay on the ground next to him.

"Foolish mortals, did you think that I would be defeated by a mere sword? You're in my realm now. You don't stand a chance against my power," he said as he began throwing fireballs at both of them. They barely dodged each that came towards them, but with each they dodged, the more outraged Fire became.

Death, Life, and Time hurried down the halls of the palace and entered a room with several different portals, each leading to a different time period."

"Time, what is all of this?" Life asked.

"I use these portals to travel across long since passed time periods," she replied.

"Why? What would you be looking for?" Death asked.

Time stared at him briefly before saying, "Nothing…I merely use them to reevaluate events."

"Are there any portals that could allow us entrance into Hell?" Death asked.

"Death, I am truly sorry, but the only way in or out of Hell right now is through Fire himself. Sellithia got there because she killed herself, but if we die we won't go there," Time replied.

"I've been able to open the portal to Hell before, though."

"Yes, but you were only able to through the Shadow Realms. Since you opened it to aid my city, it doesn't exist."

"Then I will send all the Shadowscythes back so that the Shadow Realms will exist once more."

"No! You can't! If you do that, my city will surely fall," Time pleaded.

Death let out a painful sigh. "Fine, I hope Fire will be able to handle this rebel."

Sellithia and Max dodged the fireballs one after another. Each ball of fire that shot by them pissed Fire off even more.

"Enough! I am done playing your childish games!"

He raised his arm at Sellithia and cast a spell in her direction. A rope of chains glowing with red power twisted towards her. As it flew across the room, Max ran towards her.

"Sellithia, watch out!" he yelled as he pushed her out of the way.

The chains tightly wrapped around his thin body and threw him up against the stone wall across the room. Blood splattered up and across the wall while smoke rose from the hot chains. Blood began to pour from his mouth as Sellithia ran up to him and place her hand on his face.

"Max, why?! Why would you throw your life away for mine?" Sellithia asked in shock.

"Because I…I love…you," he stuttered.

His head fell forward as he died from his wounds. The smell of charred flesh began to fill the stone chamber as his carcass slowly burned.

"Finally his wretchedness has come to its end. With his soul being destroyed, he has been removed from existence. Now, Sellithia. Shall we discuss terms for your surrender?"

Sellithia's face turned red with pure anger as she turned to face him. She ran towards him with her other sword gripped tightly in her hand. Realizing that she had no intention of surrendering, Fire threw more fireballs at her. She dodged each of them with ease as she approached him. She noticed that anger seemed to fuel her. She jumped forwards and plunged the sword in her left hand into the side of Fire's neck. She quickly ripped it out and watched him back up against the wall in shock. He slid down into a sitting position and stared back at her in pain as he took his last few shallow breaths before dying.

The ceiling of the palace cracked and tore away flying into a fiery cyclone that twisted upwards. Sellithia stared into it and was lost for a time, but quickly came back to reality as Thoi-Thagian teleported into the room.

He walked over to the body of the Titan of Fire and grabbed his neck. His black hand began to glow orange as he drained the powers of Fire. Fire's flaming hair faded leaving a mummified bald man as the last of his powers left his body. Thoi-Thagian let go of Fire's neck and walked back over to Sellithia in satisfaction.

"I believe it's high time I revealed my full form to you. What you see is a charred body with red eyes, but I am so much more."

He stepped backwards and raised his hand high into the air. Large tattered black wings sprouted from his back, his red eyes glowed even brighter than before, long, sharp, talon-like fingernails sprouted from his fingertips, his muscles grew in size, and large pointed horns sprouted from the top of his bald head. He bared his pointed teeth as he adjusted to the temporary pain of his transformation.

Slightly frightened Sellithia said, "You're…a demon…"

He nodded and said, "Soon I will be able to do things with my powers that the Titans could only ever imagine. I will be able to teach you how to understand the language of demonology, but for now we need to move. I don't know how much longer this place will stand."

"What of the other souls trapped here? Aren't some of them loyal to you?"

"Many of them are servants to me. However, they are no longer of use to me. You have proven to be my only asset."

"Where are you taking us?" Sellithia asked as Thoi-Thagian wrapped his fist tightly around her wrist.

"To the place where obtaining my powers will be marked as complete. Time and the other two remaining Titans will know defeat before our campaign has come to an end," he replied, laughing demonically.

Chapter 30 Time's Revenge

Death, Life, and Time stood out on the balcony and watched as the Shadowscythes dominated the battlefield.

"It's all a matter of time now. Soon my city will be saved and then the Shadow Realms will be in existence again," Time said trying to be reassuring.

"I will be able to enter Hell and lend my aid to Fire," Death replied.

The candlelit room became dark as all the flames snuffed out.

"No…" Death muttered.

Time grabbed his shoulder and said, "Death, look, the sun is coming up! He must still be alive!"

"He isn't. Years ago he told me if he were ever to die, he would use his powers not to save himself, but to make the sun live on," Death replied.

Life ran her fingernails against her upper neck as she scratched at her smooth skin, pressing a black thorn that she had secretly pulled from her robes into her flesh. In an instant, she placed her hand against her forehead and closed her eyes.

"Life, are you alright?" Death asked as he placed his hand on her upper back.

"I'm fine. Just a little light headed is all."

"Maybe you should lie down," Time suggested.

Life began to walk back inside when her vision blurred and she fell onto the stone floor. Before she lost consciousness, she could hear the muffled voices of Time and Death as they ran towards her. Death and Time knelt down beside her and tried to wake her up.

Placing two fingers on Life's neck Time said, "She is still alive, but I can't explain why she fainted. She seems completely fine."

She moved her hand up her neck and felt something sticking out of it. She grabbed the mysterious item and pulled it out to see that it was a small black thorn. She brought it up to her nose and sniffed it.

"Poison…causes the body to go into a deep sleep. However, this thorn is only found on the plant known as The Rose of Death."

"How did a thorn end up here?" Death asked as he grabbed the tiny black stub from her.

"I'm not sure…" Time began, but stopped as she examined Life's palm." Death, look at this," she said as she grabbed onto Life's wrist and pulled it upwards.

They examined the black smudges on her fingertips. "She did this to herself…But why?" Time concluded.

"The Rose of Death was formed from corruption that destroyed the land which later became known as the Dreadscar Valley. It's possible Life came across one of the flowers when she was searching for me. She may have planned on using it to subdue Max. Why she would use it on herself, though, is beyond me," Death replied.

"The rose of Death was once known as The Rose of Life, but the corruption changed it. The only way we can wake Life up is if we obtained a Rose of Life, but they have long since passed this realm of existence. I will have to travel back in time if we are to find one," Time replied.

"I will remain here and watch over Life while you go and obtain the herb," Death said as he picked Life up in both his arms and placed her on a cozy bed across the room.

Time nodded and waved her hand into the air. A portal opened to a time long since passed and Time felt sadness fill her. She brushed her emotions away and walked through the portal to find the precious Rose of Life.

Time went back four thousand years into the past and walked through a peaceful valley covered with thousands of flowers and other plants. Hills and mountains could be seen from miles around. All of which were covered in exotic vegetation. She looked up at the blue cloudy sky, but saw no hint of the corruption coming near. She assumed that it was many years yet until the day of the corruption, but she still ran through the valley. She gazed over all the different herbs, but could not find the Rose of Life. She was well aware that they were rare in number, but she knew they grew within the meadow she was in.

She looked for nearly an hour before she finally found the flower she was looking for. Isolated from the rest, the Rose of Life glowed with ominous power. She gently plucked the glowing green rose and smiled. Her smile faded though as the sky fell dark and a large meteor ignited with black flames fell from the sky. It smashed into the ground with a massive quake and shook the valley. The land began to wither away and die as the black rays of corruption seeped into and across the land. As it spread the corruption, it began to form into its own life forms. Any Rose of Life the corruption came in contact with changed into what would be known as the Rose of Death. The few Roses of Life that were around turned black and let off small streams of black poison.

Time quickly opened a portal that would take her back to the current time period and stepped through it just as the corruption came to the spot she was standing in. She saw Death kneeling beside Life who was still lying in her bed.

"Time, you're back, I was beginning to worry," Death said as he stood up.

Breathing heavily Time said, "I had to run from the corruption. I misjudged what day the corruption came."

"You do realize that you have been gone for three days, don't you?" Death asked as he approached her.

"Three days? That's impossible. I was only in the past for an hour. What have I missed?"

"Several of your brave soldiers have met their brutal end, including your head soldier, Luke. The Shadowscythes had to kill several of them because they had been possessed by Thoi-Thagian's spawns."

Though Time was saddened by this, she walked over to the bed and placed the rose in Life's hands. She looked as though they were preparing to bury her as the green power that shined around the flower began to seep into her soft body.

"She will need some rest," Time said as she placed her hand on Death's armored shoulder. "Would you follow me, please? I have a favor to ask of you."

Death followed her out into the hallway and shut the door behind him.

Time turned to face him and said, "Death, this is very hard for me to ask this of you, but I have seen every possible outcome of today. None of which show our survival. I saw one of us dying and another of us becoming mortal. Either way, the world is in grave danger. Unless…"

"Unless what?"

Hesitating, Time said, "Unless you kill all of the Shadowscythes…"

"What?!" Death said in an outraged voice.

"Death, please hear me out. They only obey you because your mind is superior to theirs. The moment the last Titan dies or even becomes mortal, they will run rampant across the world. They will kill everything in their path."

"Shadow created them to be nearly indestructible. It's not an easy task to kill them."

"There is only one way. My men can handle it from here. Order the Shadowscythes to return to the Shadow Realms, but once they are all within the desolate world and it is beginning to close, destroy it."

Death slowly walked back into the room and walked out onto the balcony. He looked down at all the Shadowscythes still fighting the remaining spawns of Thoi-Thagian. With the death of the last visible spawn, Death raised his hands into the air, but didn't say anything. He couldn't stop watching his minions just roaming around the city waiting for more enemies or their next order.

He took in a deep breath, used all the strength he could muster, and said, "Shadowscythes…return to…the Shadow Realms."

Obeying their Master, the Shadowscythes returned to the Shadow Realms, not realizing that this was their last moment alive. Death closed his eyes as the last one entered the Shadow Realms. He took in a deep breath and forced the Shadow Realms to explode from the inside out as the threshold closed. A loud bang filled the air and the sky turned dark for a brief moment. The dreams of betrayal roared in Death's head as the light returned to the world.

Time walked up behind him and placed her hand on his shoulder.

"You did well, Death. There was nothing else you could have done."

He walked away from her and said, "I want to be alone for a while."

He walked out of the room and slammed the door shut behind him.

***

Life quickly sat up and looked around the room. She saw Time standing out on the balcony. She looked as though she was taking in the smells the fresh, crisp morning air had to offer. She rose to her feet and walked out onto the balcony. She noticed that Time's eyes were closed as well and knew that she was meditating.

"Time?" Life softly muttered.

Time slowly opened her eyes, but without looking at Life she said, "You've awakened…Good."

"Where is Death?"

"He wanted to be alone for a while. He had to destroy the Shadowscythes along with the Shadow Realms."

"What?! Why?!"

She turned to face her and said, "I asked him to. I have foreseen the future and those beasts play a very dark and evil part in it, but that is of no importance. Life, we found the thorn from the Rose of Death. Why did you use it on yourself?"

Life looked over the edge of the balcony and remained in silence. She watched as the remainder of Time's guards disposed of their fallen brothers with dignity. A few of the guards focused on clearing rubble up from destroyed buildings. "It's my fault Sellithia betrayed us. I needed an escape."

"Sellithia's insubordination was her own choice. She could have refused Thoi-Thagian's offer."

"And die in the process?"

"At least she would have died a hero. A true enemy to The Darkness."

Thoi-Thagian and Sellithia teleported out of the hollowed core of Hell just as it collapsed in on itself and appeared on a hill just a mile away from Time's city.

"My spawns managed to bring down the shields and now it is time to kill your former Mistress, Life, but be careful, Death and Time are lurking within the city as well."

"Master, before I attack the city, I must know something. The Titans placed a shield around the world to hide it from you. How is it that you managed to find it even though the shield is still up?"

With a demonic chuckle Thoi-Thagian said, "When I fled the world, I saw the shield forming, but I was determined to get my revenge. I used what little power I had left and placed it within the shield. By doing so, the form you saw before this one is what was created. In putting my powers in the shield it allowed me to slightly see it though it was hiding the planet. In order for me to survive, I made my way to this planet's sister. No mortal life is possible there, but I managed to regenerate some of my power on that forsaken world."

"I always wondered how you did it," she replied.

A mile away, back in the city, Time and Life stood by the pool in the courtyard of Time's examining area. The water glistened from the light of the sun; behind them stood a tall tower that Time used to survey her city.

"Life, would you accompany me to the top of the tower?"

"Of course," Life replied.

They turned around and went through the doorway to the tower. It was a small room that could fit about five people on the ground floor. They climbed the stone steps to the top and Life saw a room just a bit bigger than the ground floor. There was a large stone table in the center of the room and windows around the walls of the room which allowed Time to stare out at the beautiful city.

"What is the stone table for?" Life asked.

"I place the Time Maker's Sword there."

She pulled the large sword from her side and held it over the table. Life watched as she let go of the handle. Expecting it to fall and make a loud noise, Life covered her ears, but was shocked at what happened. The sword remained in a vertical position and floated in the air. Time walked over to the sunlit window directly across from the table and stared out it.

"Time, I was wondering if you have any gardens in the city."

"I don't, but you are more than welcome to create one if you'd like."

"That would be wonderful, but I am still very weak from the Rose of Death. I think I'll walk around the city for a bit."

"I'll be here if you need me," Time replied as Life walked out of the room.

Life walked through the quiet streets of the city and was baffled at how Time had a whole city to herself. Every time she passed a soldier that was walking the street she was on they would respectfully bow to her. She walked onto another street, but didn't feel right. She felt a cold presence to the place. She slowly walked down it and watched all her surroundings. As she came close to the end of the street, an armored hand came out of the shadows and grabbed her. It pulled her off the street and up against the building. Life tried to scream, but found another hand on her mouth. She tensed up as she tried to break free from the strong grasps of the hands, but found it useless.

"Life, relax, it's me," came a voice that seemed very familiar.

She turned her head and saw Death. He let go of her and allowed her to relax.

"Death, what the hell are you doing?! You frightened me!"

"Keep your voice down. Look up ahead and you will see why I pulled you out of the street."

She peeked around the corner and saw Sellithia and Thoi-Thagian talking in the center of the two intersecting streets. She also noticed that Thoi-Thagian had taken on a new form. She looked back towards Death in shock and said, "He's almost fully regenerated."

Nodding his armored head Death said, "We must warn Time. We are the only two that are aware of their infiltration."

"One of us must stay and follow them. We can't afford for them to get away," Life replied. "I will stay, you run faster than me. Go and tell Time."

"How will we be able to find you, if you are following them?"

"I will use my extraordinary powers to leave a trail of flowers with each step I take."

Death nodded in agreement, peeked around the corner to make sure it was safe, and then sprinted back towards the center of the city.

Life closed her eyes and waved her hand in front of her. Her entire body glowed with beautiful green power for a brief moment.

Small flowers began to grow around her feet as she slowly walked back out onto the street. She turned to her right and saw Thoi-Thagian and Sellithia clear at the end of the street. They entered a large building and shut the doors behind them. Life sprinted down the stone-paved road after them in hope that she would stop more from being killed by the wrath of Thoi-Thagian.

Death ran towards a four way street as he approached Time's palace. He sprinted down the street without pausing, but as he reached the intersecting roads, Time walked out from the other. He didn't see her soon enough and ran into her. Hitting the ground, Time glared at him angrily.

"Could you watch where you're going?"

Death quickly got to his feet and helped her up. "Time, Thoi-Thagian and Sellithia have snuck into the city. Life is following them right now, but we need to go and help her just in case things get out of hand."

Time's face began to show fear as she said, "Death, Life is the next target!"

"What?! I wouldn't have ever left her alone if I had known that!"

"Take me to where you left her, hurry!"

They both ran back down the way Death had come in hope that it wasn't too late. They reached the spot Death had left her and noticed the trail of beautiful flowers of all colors leading towards the street that was connected to the one they stood on. They followed the trail of flowers down the road and noticed that it led to a large building at the end of it.

"Oh no," Time said in worry.

"What is it?"

"She went into the old barracks. It is very unstable. I stopped using it shortly after it was built because my powers weren't able to sustain it. We have been waiting for it to fall for some time now," she explained. "Death, I will go and get her. You go place the city on high alert. I have no doubt that Thoi-Thagian will try to run."

While Death quickly ran off to warn all the guards to be on the lookout, Life carefully walked through the empty building and listened to the creaking floor with each step she took. She looked over at the boarded up windows, but some light managed to squeeze through. There were holes in the floor and walls and it was really dusty. She walked over to a wooden staircase and saw a closed door at the top of them. She found this odd, for every other door was open. She slowly proceeded up them, each one creaking as she went. At the second to the last step the wood broke causing Life to fall. She caught herself on the not so sturdy railing. In the process of failing, she had twisted her ankle which made it hard to walk. She couldn't put much pressure on it, so she limped up the last step. The door creaked on its hinges as she opened it and limped inside the room. She could feel a very dark presence in the dusty air. She used her emerald green magic to summon forth the Blessed Staff of Life as she limped further into the eerie, dusty chamber.

The door slammed shut behind her causing her to quickly turn around. She saw Thoi-Thagian standing in front of it with his hand on it. He turned the little knob on the door locking it as he walked near her. She limped away towards the far end of the room.

"You think yourself so sneaky? I knew you were following us the whole time."

Sellithia emerged from the shadows with her swords drawn and stood beside her new Master.

"Sellithia, my child, go and fetch my powers for me," Thoi-Thagian ordered as he pointed his black, boney finger at Life.

Sellithia charged at Life with her swords pointed at her heart. Life knew she could not run on a bad ankle, so she began channeling a spell. Roots shot up from the wooden floor and attempted to wrap themselves around Sellithia's legs, but she was too quick. She tackled Life and threw her to the ground. She placed her left foot on Life's right arm and used her other hand to hold Life's other arm down. With her free hand, Sellithia placed the sword against Life's chest. Her eyes grew wide in fear as Sellithia readied herself.

"Any last words, Mistress?"

"Sellithia, you don't have to do this," Life said as she tried to free herself from Sellithia's grasp.

"But I do. For, you see, you lied to me. You stole my true identity and gave me a false alias. You took all I had and destroyed it."

"What we did was in your best interest. We wanted to give you a better life. That night…" Life began as the memory quickly flashed in her mind.

"And stealing my memories and lying about my true identity is how you were going to achieve that? No, you failed me, and for that you must pay," she said as she prepared to kill her former mistress.

"Do you really want to know the truth? That man had kidnapped you. You were the princess to Golmasik. The King that Thoi-Thagian killed was your Father."

"Did he know it was me?"

"No. We took his memories as well."

"Liar! You've taken everything from me! Now…You die." she screamed, tears running down her face.

Life took in a deep breath and said, "Even after my passing life will endure."

Thoi-Thagian anxiously stood by the locked door in wait for Life's powers, but was startled by something that slammed up against it. He slowly backed away into the shadows like a coward as the door gave away and broke off its hinges. Time ran into the room and scanned the area. She saw Sellithia on top of Life and knew she had to stop her. Every muscle in her powerful body tensed as she tried to come up with a proper tactic. Sellithia raised her sword into the air and Time knew she couldn't stand around waiting to devise a plan.

"No!" She screamed as she used the Time Maker's Sword to rip a hole in the Fabric of Time. A yellow vortex opened up and headed towards Sellithia. Time knew it was dangerous to rip a hole in the continuum, but Sellithia had to be stopped.

Time raised her hand and used her powers to push the vortex faster towards its prey. Unaware that Time was in the same room, Sellithia brought down her sword. Her hair began to blow around causing her to stop her attack. She looked towards the door and saw that Thoi-Thagian had left her and that Time had come to Life's rescue. She saw the vortex coming towards her, but she was determined to kill Life first. She quickly raised the sword again and quickly brought it down. As it came towards Life's chest, Sellithia's life flashed before her eyes as the vortex consumed her.

"Where did she go?" Life asked as she quickly sat up.

Time ran up to her and helped her to her feet. "I don't know… All I could think about was saving you."

As they made their way down the wooden steps of the rickety, old building, Life hugged Time and said, "Thank you. Without you, I would have perished back there."

"Life, I could never allow such a thing. Besides, what would Death think of me, allowing such a fate to fall upon our family?"

Life smiled again as they reached the bottom floor. Using Time as a crutch, she limped towards the entrance of the structure.

Chapter 31 Finding A Way Home

Sellithia's vision blurred, but she brought down her sword as quickly as possible. She continued to stab whatever was under her though she was blinded by the bright light of the vortex. Her vision cleared after a short time and she looked to see what she had killed. Disappointment and outrage filled her as she realized that she had been stabbing the damp, muddy ground. She stood up and wiped her blade against her leg.

Sellithia looked around as she walked through the tall, patchy grass. The sun was setting on the horizon behind her painting the sky orange, red, yellow, and pink. A small town rested behind a stone bridge that she approached. She walked alongside an asphalt road and watched cars zip by her. They sped under the bridge and towards the small town. After walking about a mile, she came upon a large green sign that said, MELINDAR, NEXT EXIT. A large white arrow was under the name, pointing towards the small town.

A silver Mustang pulled alongside the road as Sellithia began to walk again. The window rolled down revealing a young woman with curly black hair, white skin, and rosy red lips sitting on the other side of the vehicle.

The woman looked at Sellithia in worry and said, "Ma'am, are you alright? Do you need me to call someone for you, or can I give you a ride?"

Hesitant, Sellithia slowly walked up to the car and said, "Hi, my name is Sellithia and if you don't mind, I would like a ride to the small town over there."

"Hello, Sellithia. Get in, I'll take you into town," the young woman replied with a smile.

As Sellithia opened the door and sat down in the reclined seat, the young woman looked at her and said, "My name is Estevaliz, by the way."

Under normal circumstances, Sellithia would have been trying to figure out what time period she was in, but before she had returned to the time of the Titans, she had been in a time period with cars and advanced technology. The car ride was awkwardly quiet as they drove into town. As they pulled into the small town, Sellithia looked out her window and stared at all the different buildings. There was a liquor store, restaurants, and several hotels. She thought about asking Estevaliz if she could stop to get a drink, but she had already passed the building and she didn't want to make her go back.

As they approached the hotel to her right, the car turned left and pulled into a large parking lot cluttered with several other vehicles. A building called *Missy's Supplies*, with a logo that stated, *we stock you up so you don't have to!* rested at the back of the area.

"Sorry, Sellithia, but I need some school supplies and this is the best place in town to get them. Their service is superior, they have the lowest prices and they treat you like family," Estevaliz said as she parked the car up next to the building.

They got out of the car and walked into the store together. The moment Sellithia walked into the building, she knew people were silently judging her. To them she dressed weird. They all wore t-shirts and blue jeans, where as she wore a blazer with gold trim around its edges, a white silk shirt, and tight brown leather pants and boots. Though their whispers bothered her, she ignored them the best she could and continued to look around the store. There were school supplies, cooking appliances, auto supplies, home accessories, and even clothing. This store really was capable of stocking a person up with everything they would need.

Walking back up towards the front of the store, Sellithia jumped a little as the doors to the building flew open. Three cloaked figures walked in with their robes flowing across the floor. The one closest to her wore yellow hooded robes, the one in the middle wore black hooded robes, and the one furthest away from her wore hooded emerald green robes. With all three of them hooded, Sellithia couldn't see their faces, but she knew that it was Time, Death, and Life.

While she stared at them in shock, Time knew someone who did not belong was within her grasp. She slowly turned her head towards the exit and saw Sellithia staring at her. Her eyes widened with fear, but she knew she couldn't attack her here. If she were to draw the Time Maker's Sword and charge after her, it would give the Titans a bad name.

The three Titans walked towards the back of the store to investigate a disturbance between two couples when Time stopped both Life and Death and ushered them into an aisle with no customers.

"Friends, I have finally discovered what time period I sent Sellithia to," Time said.

"Excellent, now we can go and destroy her just like we did to her Dark Master," Death replied.

Time looked to the ground and said, "It's this time. I saw her by the mortal woman known as Estevaliz."

Death's face hardened with anger as he said, "We must find her before she finds the Librarian!"

"You two go, I'll take care of the disturbance here," Life said as she walked back into the main aisle and headed towards the back.

Sellithia and Estevaliz drove down the road and came to a stoplight. Sellithia began to think about the book she had given to Thoi-Thagian. Seeing how he was nowhere to be found and that Time, Death, and Life were still alive, she assumed that he had been defeated, which made her come to the conclusion that the book would now be in the Titans' possession.

She adjusted in her seat and asked, "You wouldn't happen to know if there is a library nearby, would you?"

"As a matter of fact, I do. It is at the old High School. About twenty years ago the Titans decided that it would be best if they taught all of the mortals. They closed all the schools and began training all the mortals themselves. They assumed it would save them from anymore betrayals. It wasn't long after that, that it was turned into a library."

"Would you mind taking me there?"

The light turned green and Estevaliz began to drive down the road. "No can do, unfortunately. It's a private library, and only friends of the sacred librarian can enter."

"I am a friend of the librarian. She and I go way back," Sellithia lied.

"Really, what's her name?"

"You don't know?"

"No, no one does. She never comes out of there. Some of the town believes that she is a myth that the Titans created so that no one would go in there."

"Oh, well maybe I shouldn't tell you her name. If no one knows her, then she probably only tells people she can trust."

Though Estevaliz knew Sellithia was lying about something, she turned down one of the more busy roads and headed towards the old High School. She pulled alongside the brick building and unlocked the door so that Sellithia could get out.

"Thank you for the ride," Sellithia said as she got out of the car and slammed the door shut.

There were bookcases, chairs, and tables all over the place. Sellithia walked across the blue carpeted floor and stared at all the different knowledge filled novels. Staring down at an open book, she saw movement from the corner of her eye. She quickly looked up and over towards the movement to find a young woman holding a book in her arms. She wore a short blue dress and her dirty blonde hair was pulled up into a bun.

"Can I help you find something, dear?" the woman asked as she pulled a pencil from her hair.

Sellithia cleared her throat and said, "Yes, I am looking for any information you have on the woman known as Sellithia."

The woman looked at her in shock. "I haven't had anyone ask about that woman in years," she motioned Sellithia forwards. "Follow me, please."

The Librarian went through two white doors and into a small hallway. She walked up to another pair of doors and pulled a key from her pocket. Placing the key inside the keyhole, she turned it and unlocked the pair of wooden doors. She pushed them open and walked inside.

"This entire room has everything you would want to know about yourself, Sellithia."

Her eyes grew big in shock as the Librarian said her name.

"Yes Sellithia, I am well aware of who you are. I have dedicated my whole life in research of your life. I never thought that I would live long enough to see you in person. I used to write stories about you when I was just a little girl. One day when my parents were preparing dinner the Titans came to our house and showed my parents my short stories. They were fascinated to how accurate it was to your actual life. It was then that they took me from my parents and granted me the title of Librarian."

Sellithia looked around the room in awe. All the knowledge contained within the books was all about her.

With a small smile the Librarian said, "You are more than welcome to"—

The sound of the front doors slamming shut startled her.

In a quiet, but startled voice the Librarian said, "Hide!"

Sellithia dashed behind the bookcase directly in front of her and quietly breathed. She watched the Librarian pretend to be busy at work from a slot where a book was missing. She watched as Death and Time walked through the doorway.

"Nekota, we are searching for the woman you know as Sellithia. Have you seen her?" Death asked.

"Sellithia? Here in Melindar?" Nekota said with a bit of a chuckle as she tried to hide her worry.

"We know it sounds unrealistic, but unfortunately it is true," Time replied.

"What do you want me to do if I find her?"

"Contact us. We will take action from there," Time ordered.

Nekota bowed in respect as they turned to leave. Once they were gone, Sellithia came out from behind the bookcase and walked up to her.

"Nekota, please, tell me what has become of the Aikanadenbaria."

With a small sigh, Nekota went behind her desk and opened a small hidden compartment from underneath the drawer. She pulled out the very same leather book that the King of Golmasik had once owned. She walked back over to Sellithia and placed it in her hands. Turning towards the back of the book, Sellithia found a passage titled "Fall of the Aikanadenbaria."

Though Life had been saved, the continuous threat of the Aikanadenbaria continued to grow stronger. Time helped Life to her feet and ran out of the building. As they came out onto the street, Death ran up to them with three guards following closely behind him.

"Time, Life, where is Thoi-Thagian and Sellithia?" Death asked.

Looking to the ground Time said, "I sent her to a different time period, but I don't know what one. I was too focused on saving Life to really think of an era."

Death tightened his grip on his sword and was about to begin ranting, but Thoi-Thagian emerged from the shadows like a venomous snake and snuck up behind the guard to his left. He grabbed the guard's neck and snapped it like a twig. He picked up the dead man's sword and violently swung it to his right. The tip of the sword sliced open the next soldier's throat causing him to bleed to death. He quickly brought the sword down as if he were going to stab himself, but moved it in between his arm and side, shoving it deep into the third soldier's stomach. Ripping the sword free, he glared at the three Titans in pure hatred. They all had their sacred weapons drawn and pointed at his demented, black body as they circled him.

With an evil cackle Thoi-Thagian said, "You may have banished my successor, but that won't stop me from reclaiming what is rightfully mine. Your quest to restore balance to the universe is futile. In the end I will be the one to succeed and your precious planet will be forever cloaked in my dark shadow."

"Your insanity has overcome you, Thoi-Thagian. We will release you from your curse," Life replied as the three of them charged at him.

Thoi-Thagian brought the sword he had stolen down to block Death's fatal blow, but the sword shattered on contact. He tried to flee, but Life cast a spell to root him to the ground. Time cut his tattered wings from his back while Death delivered the killing blow. He shoved the Blessed Sword of Death through his chest and watched as its dark power took hold of what was left of Thoi-Thagian's dark and twisted soul.

Sellithia turned the page to continue reading, but was startled to see that the page was blank. The book turned to sand and lost its form. The grains of sand flowed through her open fingers and settled on the ground.

In shock, Nekota grabbed Sellithia by her arm and pulled her out of the room. "This is not good. They know you have been reading from the book. By turning it to a pile of sand they will surely be on their way here. We need to get you out of here."

She pulled her alongside her down a long corridor. She burst through a closed door at the end and pulled Sellithia inside. They quickly walked down a set of concrete steps and into the pit of the room.

"This was once the High Schools' gym, but it has long since been remodeled so that it could be used as a science lab," Nekota said as she run up towards a large structure resting in the center of the room.

There were more tables in this room. Each was cluttered with beakers and books. Nekota pressed a few buttons on a computer that sat nearby, pulled a lever down that was attached to a large circular structure, watched as it hummed to life and produced an image of an ancient city.

"Assuming that my calculations are correct, this should be Time's city. I've been tinkering for many years now in an attempt to get this thing to work. I figured if I could make it work then I could go back in time and meet you. However, since fate has brought us together this machine will be used to help get you home. Does this place look familiar to you?"

"That's it!"

"Are you absolutely sure? Once through you will not be able to return."

"I would recognize those brick paved roads and buildings anywhere. That, and the tower in the center, gives it away."

"Very well, the portal will close behind you. It was nice to meet you, Sellithia. In sending you back, I hope you make the right choices," Nekota replied, giving Sellithia a quick smile.

Sellithia took in a deep breath and walked through the shimmering portal. As she passed through the threshold the machine lost connection and powered down.

Nekota sighed and turned to leave the room, but bumped into an armored man. With uncanny speed, Death grabbed Nekota by her neck and lifted her off the ground. Fear consumed the whole of her body as she grabbed Death's armored hand and tried to break free.

Tightening his grip around her throat, Death said, "You dare to betray the Titans, Nekota?"

"Please don't kill me, please. I was only trying to help."

"I…am not…my Father! Therefore, I shall allow you to live, but your freedom will come at a price. From this day forward you will be—"

Nekota fell to the ground and looked around in shock. She saw that Death had mysteriously vanished and that everything was starting to disappear. The building tore away from its foundation and was sucked into a yellow vortex that was consuming the entire town. She realized that by sending Sellithia back in time, it was erasing this timeline from existence; now this time was uncertain.

Everything went black and then back to light as Sellithia awoke on the floor of the barracks. She stood up and walked down the creaky wooden steps. She exited the building and saw Death, Life, and Time circling Thoi-Thagian. She sprinted at them, dove in front of Death, and used herself as a shield.

"Ah, Sellithia, as always you appear at the worst of times," Death said keeping his sword high in the air.

"Move aside and allow us to kill him. Then we can discuss your punishment," Life replied, taking a step forward.

Sellithia refused to move and Thoi-Thagian took this distraction as a time to escape. He used his dark powers to summon up three large spawns of himself to hold the Titans down while he got to his feet and took Sellithia by the hand.

They ran down the streets of the city and Thoi-Thagian summoned dozens more of his demented army to begin another attack.

He pulled Sellithia into a dark alley and said, "I realize now that trying to destroy Life first was a very unwise decision. In order to prevent you from getting sent to yet another time period, you must first kill Time and then focus on Life," He paused for a moment as he looked around to see if the Titans were approaching yet. "Go to the central tower and confront Time. She will undoubtedly be headed in that direction. She will try to act like a general and command her forces from there instead of joining the battle."

Sellithia bowed in respect and ran off to destroy the Titan of Time. While she ran more malevolent spawns of Thoi-Thagian materialized out of the shadows and began flooding the streets. Time's city and the holy powers within the sacred walls would surely be destroyed by sunset.

Chapter 32 The Truth Revealed

Time gazed down at the city from the central tower and watched as a battle created by the malevolent Thoi-Thagian razed her city to a pile of rubble. Chaos spread across the city like a hurricane, destroying more and more of her beloved home. An explosion ran through the air as it reduced her castle to rubble and the ground surrounding it gave away. The forces of Thoi-Thagian were dominating the battlefield and Time knew if she didn't act soon, her city would be lost. She grabbed the Time Maker's Sword from the table and began to leave, but stopped when she saw a dark figure blocking the doorway.

Sellithia had her swords drawn and smiled evilly. She realized that Time had not expected an attack.

Glaring angrily at her Time said, "My powers wane…I am unable to see events unfold before they take place…"

"Your powers are failing you because Thoi-Thagian's power is stronger than yours!"

Time swung the Time Maker's Sword at Sellithia's head, but she had blocked the attack with her own two swords. She used all her might to force Time into a defensive stance. She backed her up towards the window she had been previously looking out of and dove towards her. They smashed through the window and fell towards the ground. Shards of glass sailed by Time's face and cut open her rosy cheeks.

She managed to break free from Sellithia's grasp and used her divine powers to slow her fall while Sellithia plummeted towards the stone ground. As she floated to the ground, she saw a dark and mysterious force take hold of Sellithia and gently place her on the ground. She landed shortly after Sellithia and looked at her with pure hatred. They both breathed heavily as each waited for the other to make their move.

Time raised her sword and went into a defensive stance as Sellithia charged with her two swords. Forcing time back into the tower, she eagerly jabbed her swords at her. She continued to back away from Sellithia, but tripped and fell backwards. She quickly sat back up to see Sellithia pointing her weapons at her. Any sudden move she would make would cost her life. Sellithia wanted to make Time suffer before she brutally murdered her. She brought up her foot and kicked her in her jaw. She fell backwards and spit up blood. Sellithia kicked her again and again along her sides until she knew her ribs were shattered. She grabbed Time by her neck and brought her face close to her own. She placed the tip of her sword on Time's chest and smiled with satisfaction.

With beads of sweat dripping down her face, and in a breathless attempt to speak, Time said, "What are you waiting for? Ha…I knew you couldn't go through with it…Even now…At the peak of your triumph…You break down."

Sellithia snarled as sweat dripped down her face and tightened her grip on the sword still pushing against Time's breastplate.

"You could have been the one immortal to live forever…With our powers…Oh, wait, no you wouldn't."

"What do you mean?" Sellithia asked.

"Thoi-Thagian never told you did he?"

"Tell me what?!"

"Once he has all of our powers, including the ones within the shard around your neck, he will toss you aside like the piece of trash you are…He will kill you once he is done with you."

"No, that's not true, you're lying!" Sellithia yelled as she pushed the sword harder against Time's breastplate. The blade slightly went through Time's armor as Sellithia pushed harder against it.

Time took a painful breath. "Open your damn eyes you dumb bitch! The evidence that he has just been using you is to clear to pass! Why do you think he sent you to get all the powers? He could have done it himself, but he had hoped you would die in the process so that he would have to hunt down one less immortal. The only reason he cared when you were banished was because you still wore the necklace."

Sellithia screamed in fury and shoved the sword through the breastplate, deep into Time's chest. She twisted it and yanked it out as hard as she could. Time cried in agony as the blade that pierced her immortal heart was torn from her body. Tears trickled down her face and ran into the cuts on her cheeks. The tears stung as they seeped into the wounds. As she watched the life leave Time's body, she heard her say a prayer.

"May the Fabric of Time live on and never fall to corruption…" she said as she took in her final, painful breath and died.

The shadows grew dark within the room as Death materialized and slowly lurked within their darkness. He watched Sellithia with blood boiling anger as she looked down at her cold, dead victim.

He quietly walked out from the shadows and said, "Are you happy now, Sellithia? Do you feel pleased with what you have done to the Titan Council? You just killed one of the founders of the Titans."

Slowly turning around to face him, Sellithia replied, "I do this because you stole these powers from Thoi-Thagian. Your futile rule has finally come to an end."

Death walked up closer to her. "Allow me to show you what this world will come to if you kill Life and me…" he said as he placed his armored hand on her forehead and pushed it backwards.

Sellithia squeezed her eyes shut as her head began to burn with searing pain. She screamed in pain as her life flashed before her very eyes. Everything went dark as the pain intensified. Suddenly, however, the pain vanished as though it was never there. She slowly opened her eyes, but squinted as they adjusted to the light. She saw that she stood within a room reduced to rubble. There were chunks of stone scattered all around the area. She examined the ruins as she took a few steps forward. She heard a crunching noise on her last step and quickly moved her foot backwards to see a rusted, broken sword with crusted blood on it.

Sellithia looked around and noticed that Death was nowhere to be seen. Her mind jumped to the conclusion that she had succeeded in killing Death and Life and that this was what was left of Time's city. The sky turned red, the shadows that painted the ground came to life, and formed together to create Death himself. As he materialized before her, Sellithia's face changed from relief to shock.

"Do you like the future you helped create?" Death asked as he finished materializing.

"This is the destiny you create for the world if you continue down the path you are on. This future of yours ends soon, however, because Thoi-Thagian only keeps you around for a year after our deaths."

A loud noise filled the air forcing Sellithia to turn her head. She saw an extremely large demon flying towards the ruins. This demon was the largest she had ever seen; it was even bigger than Thoi-Thagian.

With a long, drawn out sigh Death said, "Unfortunately, that demon was almost defeated, but you had to show up and attack Life and I. With you doing that it gave that demon the opening it so desperately needed to win. He killed Life and me and took our powers." He paused for a moment. "If you are still oblivious to what I am saying then let me inform you that that demon flying towards you now is Thoi-Thagian himself."

Sellithia looked away from Death and back to Thoi-Thagian only to notice that he was almost to the ruins. She turned back to face Death to see that he had vanished and that she was alone again.

"*What happened to you, Master?*" Sellithia wondered.

The demon landed behind her with a loud thud. She hesitated to look, for she was afraid of what it would do. She slowly turned around trembling in fear to see the muscular demon with sharp talons raised in the air. He brought his mighty arm down and struck her head, causing her to fall to the ground and black out. Her head was filled with the searing pain again, but as her vision returned, she saw that she was standing in the fully constructed tower with Death standing in front of her.

"That is what will come to pass if you continue down the path you are on," Death said.

Sellithia looked to the ground. "I don't believe you, I need more proof that you are right. How am I supposed to know if you manipulated my mind to see that?"

Death used his great powers to bring forth the book that had turned to a pile of sand within the library. He opened the front cover and handed it over to her. Glancing down at the page, Sellithia noticed that it was titled, "The Light, and Darkness."

Deep within the darkness of space there was a cluster of three planets and a very bright star. The first planet was too close to the star to sustain life. The second planet was surrounded by a dark swirling mass known as The Darkness. The Darkness had claimed this planet as its own and had hoped to create revolting creatures to help it in its never-ending quest to destroy the light. The third planet, however, had a special trait to it. It was not to close to the star, nor was it surrounded by The Darkness. This planet was also covered in water and had good fertile land, but above those two elements it was full of a beautiful magic known as The Light.

One day, the elements began raging a war on each other and it was causing the world to tear apart. In order for it to protect itself from dying the world used every drop of magic it had to create two beings of great and wondrous power. As the earth crumbled away, the magic escaped from within the core of the planet and fused together to create two immortals that had peach colored skin, black hair, and shining golden armor. They immediately calmed the elements and then celebrated their new life.

The following night, one brother looked at the other and said, "Brother, it will be our eternal duty to protect this world and keep the balance. We should fashion ourselves names so that when this world flourishes with life all will know our names. I shall be known as the Aikanadenbaria. What will your name be?"

"We do not need names to be known and do you really think it wise to have more life forms on the planet? The world chose to create the two of us, not more."

"Well I figured that we could use some help protecting this world. I think we should create others that will fall under us," The Aikanadenbaria replied.

"I do not wish to have a name. As for creating others under us, I fear that it could result into something bad. If you wish to create beings under us go ahead, but I shall have no part in it," the other brother said as he stood and walked off leaving the Aikanadenbaria alone next to the campfire.

From that night forward, the two brothers parted each other's sides to keep balance on the other parts of the large world. They never would see each other except for rare occasions. Ignoring his Brother's advice, the Aikanadenbaria used his powers to create six other immortals. He looked at each of the naked immortals and knew he would have to give them armor. He wanted to equip them with armor that would suit their very own power, but he realized that he hadn't given them any yet. He began to give each of them a power and created armor to suit that trait. Powers he gave them to freely wield were: Death, Shadows, Fire, Wars, and Storms, but as he approached the last one, he noticed that it looked different from all the other muscular ones. This one had larger breasts and a smoother face, and its hips were wider. He decided there would be a gender role that would come into play. This immortal would not be male, but female. He gave her power to control Life and smiled as each now stood before him fully equipped with freshly created robes and armor along with weapons of great power.

"The six of you are to watch over this world and protect it from The Darkness. I have given each of you power, but use it wisely, for they are limited."

The six of them bowed graciously as the Aikanadenbaria used his powers to construct a large temple out of the mountains. What was left of them was placed around the temple to protect it. The ring of mountains would later be known as the Crystalrock Mountains because of their strange ability to quickly form crystals.

Years passed by and the immortals continued to help shape the world to perfection. As the years passed the immortals gave themselves titles. They were now known as the Gods. As the planet came closer and closer to being finished, the Gods went to their creator and asked him to gift them with children of their own. Their master politely obliged and used his powers to create small infants that had their parent's power. For the God of Death, he was given a small baby boy with black hair. The Goddess of Life was blessed with a baby girl that had lime green hair. The Gods of Fire and Shadows were also given baby boys, but they didn't have any hair yet. The God of War was given a boy as well, but the God of Storms received a baby girl instead of a child the same gender as he was.

The small babies giggled and squirmed in their parents' arms. They waved their arms in the air and their hands began to glow with yellow power. A small beam of yellow power came from each hand and connected with each other to form one big beam. The beam shot to the ground and created a loud crash that sounded like thunder. The beam exploded with a blinding flash. As all the immortals' vision cleared they saw a very beautiful young woman with long golden curly hair and golden armor on her feet, thighs, arms, and chest.

The Aikanadenbaria slowly approached the young woman and attempted to touch her hair, but she had great reflexes. She quickly grabbed his arm and tightly squeezed it.

"You will not fondle me like you have with the others. I have watched this planet form into what it is now for eons," the woman sternly said.

"What powers do you possess young one?" he asked in curiosity.

"Isn't it obvious? I control time."

The Aikanadenbaria scratched his hairy chin and said, "Very interesting."

Twenty-one years later the little babies were now young adults and just as everything seemed to be going great it all went spiraling down a very dark road. Relations between the Aikanadenbaria, the Gods, and their children were changing. On their twenty-first year of life, the children were given the title name of Demigods which ranked them directly under their parents. Though they were fully immortal their parents gave them the title of Demigods because they didn't want them to share in their rank. The following day turned from a great celebration to something regrettable.

The Gods and Demigods sat at the long rectangular wooden table within the temple's dining room for a great feast. There was food to keep them full for weeks. The table had dishes of all kinds of fruits, vegetables, and even many different types of meat.

As they sat and ate, Mythdariz turned to his Father who sat in the seat next to him and asked, "Father, why are we having such a great feast today? Our day of birth was yesterday."

His Father finished the food he had in his mouth and said, "We are being visited by both our maker and his brother today."

All of the children looked up from their dishes in excitement as the doors to the large room slowly opened. The Aikanadenbaria and his brother slowly walked into the room as everyone stood from their seats to welcome them into their home.

As the two brothers entered the room all those who stood around the table knew that something was terribly wrong, for the Aikanadenbaria didn't look like himself. He was extremely pale, his black hair was a tangled mess, and he was also losing parts of his hair as he had bald spots all over his head. He had purple bags of exhaustion under his eyelids and his eyes looked dry and irritated. As the Aikanadenbaria's brother helped him into the room, he looked at everyone still standing around the table.

"Please be seated. My Brother just isn't feeling very well today."

"Today, yesterday, this has been progressing for over twenty-one years," the Aikanadenbaria weakly replied.

The two brothers took their seats at the table and began to eat, but Mythdariz soon came to realize that the Aikanadenbaria was staring at him like he was a meal.

"Master, is everything alright?" Mythdariz asked.

"Shut up you pathetic maggot!" the Aikanadenbaria shouted.

The God of Death immediately stood up from his chair and said, "You will not talk to my son like that!"

Rising from his seat, the Aikanadenbaria prepared to yell back towards him, but was stopped by his brother.

"I can see we have overstayed our welcome. We will just be going," he said as he grabbed his brother by his arm.

They began to leave, but the Aikanadenbaria broke free from his grasp and grabbed his sword. He jumped up onto the table as everyone backed away in fear. The God of Death drew his sword which happened to be the very weapon that Mythdariz would wield many years later. Outraged at the Aikanadenbaria's behavior, Mythdariz's Father climbed on top of the table and charged at him. Their swords clashed violently together while the others cheered the God of Death on.

Shouting over all the yelling, the Aikanadenbaria's brother said, "Enough fighting!"

He used his powers of pure light to create a small sphere between the two of them and threw them in different directions. The Aikanadenbaria looked at his brother in fury as he stormed out of the room. The God of Death rose to his feet and placed his sword back at his side.

"I call for a council meeting! All Gods, Demigods and you are to report to the throne room immediately," he said as he pointed at the other brother.

The Gods sat in their thrones with their children standing next to them in the candlelit room. The other brother stood in front of the Pool of Images and explained to the best of his knowledge what had just occurred within the dining room.

"Again I apologize for my Brother's actions, but what has transpired here today is what I have feared for many years," he paused for a moment to see if anyone had any questions. "When my Brother created the Demigods, he didn't know that they would unknowingly steal some of his power so that they could thrive."

The God of Death looked at him in curiosity as he asked, "Are you saying that it is our children's fault for this occurring?"

"Not at all, but you see my Brother wasn't rational when he cast that spell. Drunk on power, he assumed that he was powerful enough that he didn't need to concentrate on the spell. Now, he has begun his dark decent into insanity and will stop at nothing until he has regained every ounce of the powers that the Demigods have taken from him. He believes that they have stolen this from him, but they have not. It is their birthright to feed off of him. Otherwise they would have never been able to survive."

"What do you propose we do about this incident?" the Goddess of Life asked.

The brother sighed in disappointment. "The only way to prevent any further damage to the balance would be to," he paused for what seemed like forever. "Kill him. It will not be easy. If he lives past our attempt to end him then he will destroy this planet and with it the very foundation of The Light."

While they discussed their plot to destroy the Aikanadenbaria, they didn't realize that he had been listening to them the whole time from the other side of the closed throne room doors. Hearing that they were planning to execute him angered him to the point of tossing around in turmoil. The little sanity he had left in his mind snapped like a twig causing him to begin a dark and insidious transformation. He pushed open the doors to the throne room and glared at all of the immortals who conspired against him.

"So, you wish to kill me? It will be the last mistake you make."

Everyone within the chamber looked at him as the transformation began to become visible. All his hair fell out and his armor fell off leaving him naked in all areas except for the cloth pants that he wore. His skin turned black as night and his fingernails became sharp talons. He fell to his hands and knees as horns sprouted from his head. His eyes turned crimson red and began to glow while his teeth turned yellow and formed into sharp points. While his muscles grew broader, two large, black wings shot from his back and draped onto the floor. Fear consumed everyone as they drew their weapons and prepared for him to stand up and attack.

The Aikanadenbaria's brother slowly approached him and said, "Brother? Please…You know the man you truly are…Don't let The Darkness consume you now."

He slowly rose to his feet. In a demonic tone, he said, "I am your brother no longer. Forevermore, I will be an affront to The Light. Forevermore, I will be known as, Thoi-Thagian!"

Sellithia looked up from the book in shock. "He…betrayed you? He told me that it was you that betrayed him and it was because of your acts of deception that made him what he is."

"No, Sellithia, he fell to insanity and tried to destroy The Light. We did what had to be done," Death replied.

"To this day, I remember what happened to the Gods, but what happened to Thoi-Thagian's brother?"

"He was badly injured during the final fight and had to retreat into the clouds. He hasn't been seen since. He created a glorious city that floats on the clouds known as Heaven."

Sellithia fell to her knees, looked to the ground, and said, "I have committed heinous crimes against the Titan Council. I ask now for forgiveness and I will do anything to get back on the side of The Light."

"Your sins are great and you have taken the lives of many Titans. That what you have committed will have to be paid, but you can start on your path of redemption by helping us kill Thoi-Thagian once and for all."

Chapter 33 Battle of Light and Darkness

As Death and Sellithia ran through the ruins of Time's city, Life confronted Thoi-Thagian. They stood in the plains just outside the ruins of the city with their weapons drawn. She charged at him with a stern face and her staff gripped tightly in both hands. Just as she got in range of him, he moved out of the way and, with uncanny speed, brought up his knee and hit her stomach. She fell to the ground and he kicked her staff away from her. The sky grew dark as the clouds blotted out the sun. Thunder roared throughout the plains and lightning cracked across the sky. As a storm of evil approached the wind intensified, bending the uncut grass backwards. Life's hair blew around in a tangled mess.

Thoi-Thagian smiled evilly and said, "Finally the light goes out."

He raised his sword high into the air and watched as Life's eyes grew big in fear. He brought the sword down to plunge it into her chest, but was knocked off his feet by Death. Death rolled to his feet and grabbed his own sword as Thoi-Thagian crawled away and rose to his feet.

Outraged at Death's interference, Thoi-Thagian angrily yelled, "Do you really believe that you can stop what I have wrought? This world along with all on it deserves to drown in darkness!"

He saw Sellithia helping Life to her feet. "Sellithia…You're helping them now? They betrayed me!"

Finding the courage within her Sellithia yelled, "No, Thoi-Thagian, you betrayed them! Even if you manage to kill us, The Light will never die! Don't you understand? The Light will always win!"

Thoi-Thagian roared in anger and flew up into the air. "You cannot stop me! I…am…God!"

The sky shook and roared in rage as Thoi-Thagian announced his supposed title. The sound was startling even to him. They all looked up to the cloudy sky to see it split apart and reveal Heaven. The city behind the golden gates was magnificent, but what everyone was in awe about was the man who was standing just outside the glowing threshold. He had long, flowing white hair and a golden crown atop his head. He had smooth white skin, large and soft white wings, and white flowing robes that shimmered like diamonds. As the golden light hit him, the man took flight and landed on the ground next to Death, Life, and Sellithia.

Landing on the ground in shock Thoi-Thagian said, "What are you doing here?"

A tear fell from the white-robed man's face. "Brother, I am here because your darkness has been unchecked for far too long. The tyranny of your fear ends here."

He raised his hand and formed a ball of pure holy light. He threw the ball of light towards his brother's chest. Thoi-Thagian screamed in pain as the ball of light passed through him. He fell to the ground clearly weakened. He slowly rose back to his feet and used his dark energy to chain his brother to the ground.

"Have you any last words, Brother?"

"Brother, what is about to transpire you will regret and your punishment will be death." He turned to Life and Death. "It will be up to Sellithia's line to keep this world safe now."

Thoi-Thagian raised his sword, ready to behead his brother, but as he swung, his brother turned into holy light and exploded. This threw Thoi-Thagian backwards and blinded everyone in the area. As the light returned to its natural setting, Death realized that only pure power could destroy Thoi-Thagian. He knew that the opposite of light was darkness and light always consumed darkness. It had to be Sellithia who killed him. This would be the strongest purity she could muster.

Striking down her dark master would show The Light the purist part of her soul.

"Sellithia, you have asked for forgiveness and by doing so your soul has begun its journey to purity. Strike down your dark master and you will muster enough pure energy to cleanse your soul," Death said.

"I am weak compared to him," she replied.

"Remember back to when you killed that dragon that threatened our world. You had to be right with the Titans in your heart for our powers to aid you. Now you must be right with The Light for it to aid you. Remember, Sellithia, the Titans will always be with you as long as you are right with them," he said as he pointed towards the shard around her neck.

She turned to face Thoi-Thagian when Death stopped her and handed her his sword.

"My sword will help you."

Taking a hold of the new Blessed Sword of Death, she walked towards Thoi-Thagian. Death looked over at Life who was glaring angrily at him.

"Don't look at me like that. It was foolish of you to face him alone. You're lucky I arrived when I did."

"I'm not mad that you saved me, Death. I'm mad because you just gave that traitor one of the most powerful weapons in existence."

Death removed his helmet and looked into Life's green eyes. He saw the reflection of his blue eyes within hers.

"It's always been her. She has always been the barrier between both The Light and The Darkness. She is the only one who can destroy him now, but we have to help break the barrier," Life continued to stare into his eyes. "Her necklace is the key. It carries a small bit of each of the Titans' powers; just enough to keep her immortal. If it were to be destroyed the unharnessed energies would cause a blast so large it would rip Thoi-Thagian apart."

Life broke eye contact and looked to the ground. A few moments later, she looked back at Death and said, "Wouldn't it kill her and us in the process?"

For the first time in thousands of years, Death's face showed sadness. "Life, the blast needed to destroy him will take every ounce of our power and immortality. We must place all our powers within Sellithia's necklace. Only then will it overload and explode. It is the only way. While the last of our immortality will save us from the blast it will kill Sellithia, yes."

Sellithia and Thoi-Thagian clashed their blades with brute force. Thoi-Thagian swung his sword and locked it with Sellithia's. He pulled her closer to him and glared evilly into her eyes.

"You have betrayed the Titans, your allies and worse you have betrayed me! No one will have to stomach your betrayals anymore!"

He broke the connection of the swords and pushed her backwards. He raised his free hand and unleashed the powers of the Titans that he had stolen. Dark shadows that were as cold as icy circled around her while a cage of lightning formed over the circling shadows. As a finishing act, Thoi-Thagian formed a large ring of fire around the cage to make sure Sellithia couldn't escape.

With her trapped, Thoi-Thagian turned towards Life and Death who were now holding hands, meditating, and floating in the air. Their powers elegantly danced around them as they rose higher and higher into the air. Moving closer to make his kill, Thoi-Thagian took one step after another until he stepped on a twig. It snapped with a loud crack that echoed across the plains. Thoi-Thagian saw both Life and Death immediately open their eyes, but he was shocked at what he saw. Instead of seeing their normal eyes, he saw that they were glowing green and blue.

In unison, Death and Life yelled, "The tyranny of fear ends here!"

As they spoke, their voices sounded as though they had over a thousand voices spewing out of their mouths.

In an echoing voice, they said, "By order of the two leading members of the Titan Council, we hereby grant our forgiveness to the one known as Sellithia and release her from her imprisonment within The Darkness!"

As the command left their lips the powers that held Sellithia diminished. They faded away and flew into her necklace as she rose to her feet, and she charged at Thoi-Thagian once again. Their swords clashed again, but this time they sent dark and light sparks in all directions. While they fought, Death and Life influenced their powers to combine with one another so that they could become even stronger. They raised their hands as their powers entered their veins, and allowed them to drain out and enter Sellithia's necklace. Thoi-Thagian noticed the power transfer, but he didn't realize what the true plot was.

He looked at the two Titans and bared his pointed yellow teeth. "Store your pathetic powers in that fragile necklace if you must, but in the end they will be mine!"

The necklace began to illuminate with red energy as the last bit of their powers flowed within its prison. Life and Death fell face first onto the ground as the last of their powers left their bodies. Thoi-Thagian smiled and pushed Sellithia away to go and kill the two Titans while they were unconscious, but stopped and quickly turned back to Sellithia when she let out a blood curdling scream. The necklace not only had turned red, but also became hot and was now burning her. He laughed at her as she screamed in pain and walked up to her. He ripped the necklace from her neck and watched her fall to the ground and sigh in relief. She rubbed the burn mark on her chest in hope that it would help in soothing the burning sensation.

Thoi-Thagian placed the necklace in the palm of his black hand and tapped it with his sharp, talon-like fingernail.

He looked at Sellithia and smiled. "Now all I need is the powers of Time."

He closed his eyes and used his free hand to withdrawal the golden power of Time out of the ruins of the city. As the powers entered the necklace, the burning stopped, but it remained red. He ripped the chain from the shard and threw it to the ground.

He held the shard in-between his thumb and index finger and said, "With my regained powers, I will reshape this world in darkness!"

He placed the wooden shard in his mouth and clamped down on it. A crunching noise could be heard from within his mouth. He let out a deep, demonic laugh as he raised his sword into the air. He readied to kill Sellithia, but she did not react in the way he had hoped she would. All she would do was smile at him.

"Why do you smile? You have just lost and your precious light shall be no more!"

Without saying a word, Sellithia pointed at his stomach. He looked down to see that a small portion of his lower abdomen, no bigger than the shard he had just consumed, was now glowing with red energy. He ran his finger across it in curiosity, but then howled in agony as pain that burned uncontrollably erupted from the glowing spot.

Thoi-Thagian flew to the sky and began clawing at his stomach, ripping it open, spilling his black, tainted blood. He tried to rip the shard from his body, but it was too late. The shard had dissolved in his strong stomach acid and the energy from it was now building. He let out one last, horrifying cry before he exploded into nothingness. The blast formed a large shield of light and broke through the sound barrier. As the lighting returned to its normal setting and the dust settled, a large crater was revealed where Thoi-Thagian had been.

Life and Death slowly looked up from the ground as the last bit of their immortality faded. Death helped her to her feet and then limped to the edge of the massive crater. It was two hundred feet deep, but they tried their best to find Sellithia as they searched through the debris. As they scanned the area, Life nudged Death to get his attention. She pointed over by the wall of the destroyed city. He slowly turned his head and saw Sellithia's mangled body lying underneath some of the rubble of the wall.

Death placed her in his muscular arms and carried her to the cities' graveyard.

"Death, how is it that her body survived the blast? Shouldn't it have been disintegrated?" Life asked.

"She was right with us and The Light in her heart before the explosion occurred. Her body was seen as pure when it passed through her, so it spared her, but as for the actual blast when it threw her up against the wall, I fear that is when it killed her."

They entered the graveyard and slowly approached a large stone crypt. Both Life and Death knew that this tomb was meant for the head soldier of Time, but since his body was destroyed in the battle of Time's city, they felt it was only fitting that Sellithia, the Guardian of the Titans, received this tomb as her final resting place.

They placed her on the stone table in the center of the room and placed a soft blue pillow under her head. Life placed Sellithia's hands on her chest and noticed the burn mark.

"Death, look at this…"

Looking at the burn mark then back at her, he said, "The necklace must have burned her while we were placing all that power in the necklace."

Life leaned in and kissed her forehead. "Thank you for all that you have done for us. Rest in peace my brave apprentice."

They walked outside and sealed the crypt behind them. As they took their leave, they saw a dark robed, hooded man with a walking staff approaching them. Under normal circumstances, they wouldn't have found this odd, but they could see through this man, for he was transparent.

The man stopped in front of them and said, "Mythdariz, Selineane, it is so good to see you again. It's me, Naravada."

"Naravada, what are you doing here?" Life asked with confusion spreading across her face.

He smiled bravely. "You guys did it. You defeated The Darkness. Though it will always find a way to return and threaten this world, you have destroyed its master and that is why I am here. After I renounced my title as the Titan of Nature and died, I awoke outside the gates of Heaven. I can still see the golden gates. Their shine was magnificent. When I tried to enter, however, the angels refused to let me in. I asked them if I had done something wrong, but they told me I hadn't."

"Then why were you denied entrance?" Death asked.

"They told me that they had other plans for me. Their leader, God, came before me and told me that he needed me to watch over the world of the living and the dead for all eternity. They made me the Spirit Walker. That is why I look transparent. I can see the living and the dead at the same time. By making me the Spirit Walker, I have gained an equal amount of the entire Titan Councils' powers. After several days of walking the earth watching over the dead and the living, I realized that I would need some help to cover the whole world. I have been searching for you two so that I could ask you to become Spirit Walkers with me."

A loud noise came from the sky which made Life and Death look up and Naravada turn around. They saw three angels with golden armor descend from Heaven and float just inches off the ground.

"Spirit Walker!" the Angels shouted in unison. "They are not to become what you have been gifted! We have other plans for them. We have decided that they will join their powers."

The three angels turned towards Death. "Mythdariz, the previous Titan of Death, you are to combine with your powers and become half of the Circle of Life for all eternity."

They raised their hands and shot a beam of holy power at him. The power didn't hurt him, nor did it have any affect except raise him off the ground and make him evaporate into thin air.

They turned to Life and said, "Selineane, the previous Titan of Life, you are to combine with your powers and become the other half of the Circle of Life for all eternity."

Then, like Death, they shot a beam of holy power at her. It lifted her off the ground and she evaporated into thin air. The angels looked back at Naravada once Life was gone and smiled warmly at him.

"Remember, Naravada, it will be your eternal duty to protect this world along with all in it. Most importantly you must be willing to destroy those that would threaten the Circle of Life. If it were ever to be destroyed life as we know it would be forever changed. We trust that you won't fail us, so we are turning our gaze from you forever. Good luck and may The Light live on for eternity," the Angel in the middle said as they flew to the sky and entered Heaven.

Naravada watched as the gates closed on him never allowing him to enter. He began to walk away from the crypt when he looked to the ground and noticed a silver chain. He picked it up and looked at the broken end. He knew that whatever this chain had held had been broken off and was somewhere else. He began to stand back up when he noticed that his transparency was gone. He looked around, but could no longer see the dead. Confused, he began to take a step forward, but fell to the ground in excruciating pain. He looked at the silver chain and saw that it had turned black as night and had faded into his flesh. His hazel eyes turned red and his dark robes turned coal black. He slowly rose to his feet and took in a deep breath. He examined his hands as though he had never seen them before as he turned back around and headed towards the crypt.

He walked inside and up to the stone table that Sellithia's body was resting on. He stared at her for a few moments and noticed the burn mark on her chest. He touched it and used his powers to heal the mark. He moved his index finger from her chest to her forehead and closed his eyes. His finger briefly ignited with green power as he made contact with her forehead. As he retracted his finger, Sellithia's eyes shot open and she slowly sat up. She looked around the room dazed and confused. She noticed him smiling at her and she wondered why.

"Come with me," he said as he grabbed her hand and ushered her outside. They looked up into the golden cloudy sky as Naravada said, "What do you see?"

"I see peace and serenity. The Darkness has been destroyed. But where are Life and Death?"

"The Heavenly Father saw it best that they joined their powers to create the object known as the Circle of Life."

"Why did you bring me back from the dead?" she asked.

With a small chuckle Naravada said, "You will help me protect the Circle of Life until such a time comes that I can do it on my own. Then…you will be…tossed aside…"

As those words left his lips, Thoi-Thagian took full control over his mind. Sellithia knew nothing of the demonic parasite that infested his mind. As Naravada walked away from the ruins of Time's city, Sellithia blindly followed him, unaware of the threat The Darkness possessed. It would be only a matter of time before it would reveal its evil plan and destroy everything those who protected The Light held dear.

With the wisdom of the Titan Council destroyed, the gaze of those within Heaven turned from Naravada and the unsteady scale The Light teetered on, the world slowly began to grow dark as The Darkness was allowed to walk freely, undefeated.

"Now all will know the true power of The Darkness and how it is the only salvation for them. The world will be my domain, and you, Spirit Walker, you will be the physical vessel that I will administrate my reign through," Thoi-Thagian said in the clouded mind of Naravada.